beneath
the glitter

beneath
the glitter

elle & blair fowler

St. Martin's Griffin
New York

BENEATH THE GLITTER. Copyright © 2012 by Elle and Blair Fowler. All rights reserved. Printed in the United States of America. For information, address St. Martin's Press, 175 Fifth Avenue, New York, N.Y 10010.

www.stmartins.com

ISBN 978-1-250-00618-9 (hardcover)
ISBN 978-1-250-01633-1 (e-book)

First Edition: September 2012

10 9 8 7 6 5 4 3 2 1

To our lovely readers,

We're so thrilled to bring you *Beneath the Glitter,* our very first novel. There is nothing we love more than curling up with a good book and a cup of cocoa and letting our imaginations run wild. Writing our own book really has been a dream come true!

This is the story of Sophia and Ava London, two sisters who create online makeup videos and wind up moving to LA (sound familiar?). We based the London sisters on ourselves, but everything else that happens in the book and all the other characters are completely made up. In other words, the story is very loosely based on ourselves and our lives, but please don't think this is an exact retelling of our story!

We worked really hard to put this book together with the help of our publisher and our writing partner, and we hope you have just as much fun reading it as we did dreaming it up.

Get ready to get lost in the world of Sophia and Ava London!

xoxo
Elle and Blair

For our YouTube supporters,
who give us more love than we could
have ever dreamed.
And for our parents and youngest sister,
our favorite people in the whole world.

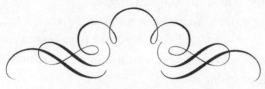

prologue

once upon a crime...

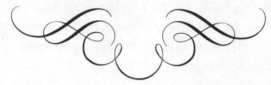

The Malibu Colony, 6 P.M.

The two girls on the beach in their flowing gowns could have been mistaken for water nymphs, if water nymphs wore gold-edged togas. They stood barefoot side by side, one blond, one brunette, hair fluttering around their faces with their toes curled into the cooling sand.

From behind them a breeze carried the sound of what people were already calling one of the top ten parties of the season—everything wonderful about LA seemed to be spread out before them on the balcony of Ronald Ralston's beachfront palace. In front of them the last rays of the sun painted the wind-sculpted surface of the Pacific Ocean orange and blue and pink.

Sophia and Ava London couldn't help it, they were feeling giddy, and not because of the sugar high from the sixteen different desserts being served, all of which they'd sampled. It was as though everything they'd gone through in the past five months, everything they'd worked for and everything they'd very nearly lost, had brought them to this moment.

Moving to LA had been a different adventure than they'd expected but after tonight it looked like it was turning out great. Their agents, and their potential sponsors, could not have been happier. Everything was—

A commotion behind them caused both of them to turn back to the party where a ribbon of police officers was moving through their guests like a snake through tall grass. They paused to talk to someone, and then, as the London sisters watched, a finger pointed them out and the police began moving toward them.

"Sophia and Ava London?" the plainclothes officer asked, as though there was anyone else on the beach.

They nodded.

"You're under arrest. Please come with me."

As the two sisters, still in their togas, were led across the patio and back through the house, the Prada- and Cavalli-clad guests' eyes were riveted on them, every face a mask of shock and horror.

Or almost every face. If anyone had been standing close enough to the striking woman at the edge of the crowd they might have heard her murmur to herself, "London bitches going down," or seen her take a sip of merlot to hide her smile.

But no one was close enough, she was sure of that. No one ever knew what she was really up to.

That was the key about LA, the number one thing that new-comers would never understand: in the town that practically invented make-believe, nothing—and no one—was ever what it seemed.

1

sisterdarity

Five Months Earlier . . .

It was the kind of day that was made for kissing, Sophia London thought, and immediately wished she hadn't.

Still, there was no denying it. Blue sky, puffy clouds, rich buttery light that gave everything it touched a slight golden sheen, turning skin luminous and the grass that bordered Beverly Boulevard a rich green. Behind her, her younger sister Ava tried to coax her puppy, Popcorn, away from a particularly delectable fire hydrant. It was warm with a hint of breeze, just enough to make you want to nestle against someone's neck and get them laughing as your hair tickled their nose . . .

Stop it, Sophia told her brain.

And no checking messages, she ordered her hand, already on its way to the pocket of her bright coral blazer.

Sophia caught her hand sneaking back toward the pocket and

rerouted it to check the bow at the neck of her lacy cream blouse. There wasn't a message; there wouldn't be a message. There *shouldn't* be a message.

So why did she care so much? Her life was pretty much perfect—*ideal,* she corrected herself, just the way it was. Sure it was a lot of work, but it was still amazing, a dream. What else could you call waking up every morning in Los Angeles, a place where the weather was almost always fantastic and you could find yourself in line at the supermarket next to someone you'd been watching on TV the night before? Living in Hollywood with Ava, seeing where they could take the London Calling brand, every day a new adventure—she had everything she needed.

And yet there were days, days like this one when everyone around her seemed to be living in a romantic comedy movie montage, strolling arm in arm and feeding each other strawberries from a farm stand and talking about what movie to see and smiling up into each other's eyes and giggling for no reason and running to catch lights and exchanging quick, intense kisses . . .

Days like this Sophia felt a little lonely. As she toyed with the ends of her blond hair she thought that it didn't help that today was—*would have been,* she corrected herself—her third anniversary with Clay Cutter, the football player with the boyish smile she'd dated from the summer after her freshman year of college until three months earlier. She could still picture him standing there in his tuxedo, his face all gorgeous and intense in the light of the full moon, could still smell the slight perfume from the red rose boutonniere she'd pinned to his lapel, could hear the sounds of music and laughter from the Valentine's Day formal behind them, could feel the fingers of cold creeping over her as he said—

"Do you think I should shave my head?"

The sound of Ava's voice next to her jolted Sophia out of the memory, but it took her a moment to register what she'd heard.

Ava and Popcorn shot by her so she had to rush to catch up with them. "Did you just ask if you should shave your head?"

Ava nodded, her dark brown ponytail bobbing up and down. "I was trying to see if you were listening." Popcorn zigzagged across the pavement in front of them, rushing from side to side to sniff at everything. "Do you have any idea what I've been talking about for the last five minutes?"

"Of course," Sophia said, pretending to be hurt by the accusation.

Ava moved her eyes from Popcorn to her sister. "Really? Pinkie swear?"

Sophia sighed and her shoulders sagged. "Well. No."

Ava stopped walking, much to the dismay of Popcorn who began popping up and down at the end of his leash like he was trying to live up to his name. Crossing her arms over her chest, she said, "Are you finally going to tell me what's wrong?"

Sometimes Sophia wished that Ava didn't know her as well as she did. It was like being scrutinized in a slightly-too-effective magnifying mirror.

"It's Clay, isn't it?" Ava said, her eyes filled with sympathy.

"Yeah, I guess I'm still feeling a little bruised." Sophia let out a deep breath she didn't realize she'd been holding. Just saying it out loud made her feel a little better. Acknowledging how one minute she'd been a princess in a fairy tale heading into the Happily Ever After sunset with her Prince Charming and the next she'd been frozen on the steps of her sorority house, staring into the empty space where he'd stood, back at square Once Upon a Time and wanting to be anywhere but there.

"Alright, I know just what you need." Ava nodded positively, pulling out her phone. "I'm staging a sistervention."

And that—as well as some string pulling by their connected-to-everyone-and-their-housekeeper neighbor Lily van Alden—was how half an hour later Sophia found herself seated at the coveted corner table on the patio at Toast with Ava, Popcorn, Lily, MM (no one knew what the initials stood for but when asked he said, "It's pronounced *mmmm mmmmm* like the Campbell's Soup ads, because I'm that good"), MM's new boyfriend Sven, and a massive cinnamon roll.

"No pausing!" Ava ordered. "And no sharing! You have to eat the whole thing right away for the cure to work."

"Cinnamon rolls are not medicine," Sophia said, hastily taking the pastry back from MM.

"Wow, remind me to get Ava a prison guard uniform next time I'm shopping with you two," MM whispered to Sophia.

She and Ava had met MM one day when they were having coffee at a Starbucks between appointments, before they'd even moved to LA. They'd already had three meetings that morning and were so exhausted they weren't even talking. Then out of nowhere this guy about Sophia's age had come up to them, said, "You two are adorable. Is that jacket vintage or vintage *nouveau*? I'm a stylist and have a client who would die for it." They spent the next hour chatting and made a shopping date for the next day. That's when they discovered he was not just a stylist but on his way to becoming *the* go-to stylist for young Hollywood after making a splash with what the blogs called his "boho-mod" look. As fashionistas themselves, he was a good person to know. But it was clear from day one that he was more than just a professional contact—he was an instant BFF.

Now he was eyeing Ava with a combination of surprise and fear. "I wouldn't have thought Little London had it in her. She's scary when she's like this."

Sophia nodded. "You think this is frightening, you should see her on her third cup of—"

"No talking!" Ava said sternly. "And you"—she looked hard at MM—"stop distracting her or I'll sick the guard dog on you."

She held Popcorn up and made growling noises, but his menacing appearance was reduced by the way he started licking her face all over.

"I am unsure," Sven said to MM with a concerned frown. "Which one is it who we should be scared of?"

Sophia nearly choked on the coffee she was sipping, and everyone else cracked up too except Sven, who continued to look confused.

Which was pretty much his standard expression—whether because he didn't understand English well or because, as Lily thought, all the cells that should have gone to his brain went instead to making him godlike in his handsomeness, was unclear.

He and the super-outgoing MM were opposites not just socially but physically as well. MM was barely five and a half feet tall with cinnamon-colored skin, dark curly hair, and a wiry, lean physique, while Sven, a foot taller and blond, with the chiseled proportions of a bodybuilder, looked like he could hoist MM with one bicep. MM was always cleverly dressed with every detail attended to like the way the penny in his just-the-right-amount-beat-up loafers was tarnished the same color as the band on his coconut-husk fedora; Sven, on the other hand, wore only warm-up suits with the names of Eastern European countries on the back. And yet, somehow their relationship seemed to be working.

How, a tiny voice inside Sophia's head asked. How come they could do it and she couldn't?

Glancing across the table and seeing Ava's eyes on her, she quickly pushed the thought into a corner of her mind, stopped shredding the napkin she'd been destroying in her lap, tucked a stray strand of blond hair behind her ear, and broadened her smile. She really appreciated what Ava was trying to do and she wanted her to know that her sistervention had been a success.

She whispered, "Thank you," and was rewarded with a big grin from Ava. They spent the next twenty minutes being entertained by Lily, who launched into a guided tour of the plastic surgery on display at the tables around them.

Although Lily's thick, wavy blond hair, olive skin, light green eyes, and perfectly symmetrical features were natural, she'd been raised around so much plastic surgery that she was an expert and she prided herself on her ability to recognize different doctors' work. Or, as she called them, "market enhancements."

It was one of the legacies of growing up in LA as the great-granddaughter, granddaughter, daughter, and niece of movie stars. Despite having the looks and the storied van Alden name, she'd chosen not to follow in her ancestors' footsteps. When Ava, who had a secret fantasy about being in movies, asked her why, Lily said, "I want to watch movies, not live them. Like a normal person. That way I get all of the perks without the stint in rehab."

Lily's version of "normal" wasn't exactly, well, normal though. Like the way Sophia and Ava had met her when she'd knocked on the door of their apartment the day after they'd moved in, introduced herself as their neighbor, and asked if they had any lace doilies she could borrow because she had to go to a black-tie dinner that night and she had nothing to wear. They'd lent her a dress instead, which she'd worn backward and somehow landed on four Best Dressed of the Week lists, and they'd been friends ever since.

Now Lily was excitedly zooming in on a woman three tables away who was a prime example of the latest in nose jobs—"You see how the curve of her nose plays off the curve of her chin? That is true artistry!"—when Sophia's pocket started to buzz.

Sophia jumped. She'd been so distracted she'd forgotten to think about checking it but now her heart began to race. *It won't be him*, she told herself sternly.

Still her fingers were shaking with excitement as she reached into her pocket to pull it out and turned the screen toward her.

It wasn't him. *You knew it wouldn't be,* she reminded herself. And yet—

"Anyone exciting?" Lily asked.

Sophia swallowed hard and kept her eyes down, blinking back the tears that were burning at the corners. "Just my date from the other night," she said.

Lily lost interest in the nose and directed her green eyes to Sophia. "Wasn't that the doctor who started talking to you in line at Starbucks?" she asked, excited now. "The one who seemed nice? Spinner?"

"Skinner," Sophia corrected. "He was nice and smart. And he made me laugh, a lot. And he likes me."

"But . . ." Ava prompted.

"But." Sophia flashed them a gorgeous smile. "He collects spiders."

Ava goggled at her. "You just made that up!"

"No," Sophia said brightly. "He claims they are the only ecological pet."

"This is a fact," Sven confirmed, nodding vigorously. "The spiders they are very good pets."

For a moment everyone just stared at Sven. MM patted him on the thigh, said, "Thanks for that, sweetie," and returning to Sophia asked, "So, how long did you last?"

Sophia's fingers picked at the edge of her napkin. "I made it through the main course but left before dessert." She looked at Ava. "I'm afraid you had an emergency."

"Always glad to help," Ava said. "Was it something gross?"

Sophia shook her head. "You locked yourself out of the house. In your pajamas."

"Nice detail. I like that better than the time I was lost in the Valley." Ava sighed.

"How come you never use me?" Lily wanted to know. "I'm dying to be locked in a Tijuana jail."

"That can be arranged," MM said. He ignored Lily sticking her tongue out at him and went back to Sophia. "Is that a new record? Making it through the main course is longer than your last date, right?"

"Yes." Sophia sighed, shredding another inch of her napkin. She had no problem getting dates, it was just getting *through* them could be a challenge. "I left that one before the food even came."

Lily leaned her chin on the palm of her hand and assumed a look of intense concentration. "Was he the agent who brought the fake bug so you could get your entrée free, or the screenwriter who interrogated the waitress about whether the pine nuts were harvested during the day or by moonlight and if she could ask the chef precisely where the striped bass was caught because he didn't eat fish from certain latitudes? Or was he the one who talked about himself like he wasn't there and in all caps?"

"BLAIN KNIGHT!" Ava yelled happily, then lowering her voice two octaves, "BLAIN KNIGHT! would like a double cappuccino!"

Sophia dumped a handful of shredded napkin snow onto the table. "None of those. It was that real estate developer who tried to convince me to go see his therapist because she'd really helped him and he could finally admit to his mother it was him that stole her lace underwear when he was twelve, not his sister."

"I can't believe you left that one so early," Lily said, meaning it. "Just think what else he could have shared. But I like the spider one best. He reminds me of the Buddhist guy who refused to exterminate his cockroach-infested apartment because the roaches might have been his reincarnated ancestors."

"Gross!" Ava and Sophia said in unison.

"Yeah, I totally *bugged* out," Lily said, grinning at MM's groan. "But that's why I decided to do a boytox."

"A what?" Sophia asked.

Lily's eyes got huge. She turned and grabbed Sophia's wrists and said, "You should do it with me. It will totally help with your dating block."

"I don't have a dating block." Sophia tried to gently pull away. "It's just that I think I attract weird men. Seriously . . . who else here can say they have gone on dates with such strange guys? All of whom were perfect on paper and very good looking.

Lily kept hold of her wrists. "Uh, Spider-Man, BLAIN KNIGHT!, and lace underwear guy sound like a dating block to me. Something is out of balance about the romantic energy you're sending out, so you're attracting the wrong kind of person. I learned all about it in my 'use your energy to save the world' seminar."

Ava's dark ponytail slid over her shoulder as she tilted her head to one side and said, "But what *is* a boytox?"

Lily addressed the whole table. "A boytox is like a cleanse, but for your personal life. I read about it in a magazine." On her left MM began folding his napkin into a noose. Lily ignored him and went on. "It's a way to clear out stagnant dating energy. Like after you end a relationship. A lot of times after a breakup people distract themselves by taking 'manex,' which means having flings or going on dates with lots of different people. But that just leads to more negative energy. The way to heal is to stop going on dates entirely—do a total boytox. If someone asks you out, you automatically say no. It takes away the pressure of thinking you should be dating."

Sophia frowned. "I'm not sure that sounds fun."

Lily shook her head emphatically, sending a wave of thick golden hair swinging back and forth. "It's the complete opposite of that. I know someone who knows someone who did it and said it's the *best* way to meet men. It's like they can smell your unavailability. So while you're *avoiding* bad dates, you're meeting tons of guys and then when you're done with your boytox, you can choose the ones you connect with. Think of it like being at a fat-free buffet, all the choice and none of the downside."

Sometimes I go to buffets just to look at the food, but then I don't eat any of it. Is it like that?" MM asked.

Lily ignored him and stayed focused on her sales pitch. "If not for yourself, do it for me. In fact, let's all do it together in a spirit of sisterdarity."

"I don't know . . ." Sophia said. She looked at Ava. "What do you think?"

Ava toyed with her fork for a minute, looking torn, then spent a little too much time straightening the napkin in her lap. But when she finally looked back up she gave a smile and said, "Sure. So, how long does a boytox last?"

LonDOs

Cinnamon rolls

Lacy blouses

Bright blazers

A nail polish collection the size of a nail salon

LonDON'Ts

Being forced to eat an entire large cinnamon roll yourself. Rude.

Boys who collect spiders

People who talk about themselves in all caps

Puppies who don't act menacing when you need them to

Ava after more than one cup of coffee

Sophia before one cup of coffee

2

haute dog!

Watching Popcorn bounce down the sidewalk happily, stopping every now and then to sniff a sprinkler or a crack in the pavement, Ava wished she felt the same kind of freedom.

As soon as she'd heard Lily invoke the word "sisterdarity," Ava had known she was in trouble. After all, she wanted to support Sophia. But she was still a growing girl, and she wasn't sure a boytox was a good idea for her—

"Heads up!" a voice yelled, and the next minute a volleyball came bouncing along the lawn toward her and stopped at her feet. She picked it up and was going to toss it back when a cute guy with dark curly hair wearing a grin and no shirt jogged over and took it from her. "Thanks," he said, and gave her a wink before heading back to the game.

No, Ava thought, watching the way the muscles in his shoulders moved when he tossed the ball to his friends, not a good idea *at all.* What good was living in LA, land of endless hunky men, if you didn't get to kiss at least a few of them? Not dozens but maybe three. Or five.

A boytox really didn't fit into her plans. But if Sophia needed the moral support, how could she refuse?

And Ava knew full well how hard the breakup with Clay had been on her sister. Sophia had always been a hopeless romantic. When it came to love, she fell deep and she fell hard, and that's exactly what had happened with Clay. And that's exactly why the swift and brutal breakup had been so difficult for her. Sophia's heart had been wide open, which just made it all the more painful when Clay decided to crush it.

Ava looked down at Popcorn. "I guess we're going to be doing a boytox. Are you okay with being the only man in my life for—*ouch!*" She yelped the last word as Popcorn nearly yanked her hand off straining against his leash. "Where are you trying to go, little man?" she asked him, rubbing her hand, but he was apparently in no mood to talk. Instead he took off diagonally across the lawn, bounding over a blanket where two girls were sunbathing and narrowly missing being hit by a little boy furiously pedaling a Big Wheel.

Running behind Popcorn, Ava saw he was heading toward an area of the park where a cluster of booths had been set up. Someone pressed a flyer into her hand as she sped by and, looking down, Ava read, "Paradise Lost? SAVE PET PARADISE, a NO-KILL SHELTER! Fund-raiser today!" Looking up she saw that they were approaching an arch with a picture of a dog and a cat on it and she just had time to read the words NOW ENTERING PET PARADISE before Popcorn whipped her past it and into the middle of a knot of people, people with dogs, and people selling products for people with dogs.

One thing that Ava and Popcorn had in common was that while they were outgoing with their friends they were totally shy around strangers, so rather than plunge into the thick of things,

Popcorn led Ava toward the edge of the crowd. Ignoring the other dogs he buried his nose in the grass, moving slowly now as he drank in what Ava imagined was probably the doggie equivalent of Chanel No. 5. And if it wasn't, Ava saw that they were passing a booth that sold "artisanal scents for your dog" including one called "Grampa's Old Boot" and another called "Red Fire Hydrant."

Next to the Elite Pawfumes booth Ava discovered Dogalates™—"Pilates for your pet!"—followed by the Dog Lover's Book Club, and then a booth decked out in leopard skin for Dressed to Thrill, "Couture Formalwear for Pets of Any Size from Kitten to Clydesdale."

Ava was trying to figure out where a pet would need formalwear and had just seen the answer in the Doggie I Do Chapel of Holy Muttrimony ("the #1 choice for dog weddings since 2009!") when Popcorn started tugging hard against his leash. Glancing along its length she saw he'd gotten himself tangled around someone's legs.

Ava dropped the Planning for Muttrimony brochure she'd been looking at and rushed over. "I'm so sorry," she said, falling on her knees and trying to liberate the guy's legs from the tangle of Popcorn's leash. "He must be really keyed up by all the other dogs," she went on, holding Popcorn's collar with one hand while pulling the leash free with her other. "I mean he's not usually so—"

"Bondage oriented?" the guy supplied with a warm chuckle.

"Yeah." Ava glanced up to give him a grateful smile—

—and froze.

She was staring into the blue-eyed-dimpled-smile-shaggy-blond-bangs-falling-over-the-forehead face of Liam Carlson. THE SAME LIAM CARLSON WHOSE POSTER SHE'D HAD HANGING OVER HER BED BETWEEN THE AGES OF TWELVE AND FIFTEEN AND WHO SHE'D

SAID GOOD NIGHT TO EVERY NIGHT ONLY ALL
GROWN UP AND EVEN CUTER NOW IF THAT WERE
POSSIBLE.

Somewhere over the sound of her mind screaming she realized
that he was laughing and saying something which, when she managed to hear it, turned out to be, "I'm glad you liked my poster."

The only thing that kept Ava from blushing any more deeply
was that she was already blushing as much as she possibly could.
"Did I say that out loud? Oh my goodness I'm mortified. First my
dog attacks you and then I scream that. You must think I'm a
moron. I think I'm a moron. Although maybe people do this to
you all the time. Do they? Am I babbling? I am, aren't I?" she
asked as she gathered Popcorn into her arms and stood up.

Liam nodded. "A little. I like it." And then he smiled again.

Ava lost the ability to form sentences. LIAM CARLSON
WAS STANDING THERE IN A LIGHT BLUE THIN
CASHMERE SWEATER SMILING AT HER AND TALK-
ING TO HER. HIS SWEATER FIT HIM REALLY WELL.
HAD SHE REMEMBERED TO PUT ON LIP GLOSS?
WHY HADNT SHE WASHED HER HAIR THAT
MORNING? HE WAS SO CUTE, HIS EYES—

"Hello?" he said.

"Oh, sorry. I just—when you smile it kind of makes it hard
for me to focus. You have the nicest eyelashes." Then her eyes got
huge. "I said that out loud too, didn't I?"

"You did." He started to smile again then stopped himself.
"Sorry. Is it better if I frown?" he asked, frowning.

"Um, no, not really," Ava admitted. "Oh my god and I've been
babbling and I totally forgot to apologize for Popcorn, that's my
dog. I hope he didn't hurt you or anything."

"Naw," Liam said, reaching toward Popcorn who eyed him a
little skeptically but finally let him scratch his head. "No damage. Besides, I love dogs."

LIAM CARLSON'S FINGERS ARE ON MY DOG! LIAM CARLSON IS TOUCHING MY—"Do you have one?" Ava asked, forcing her mind back to the conversation.

Liam shook his head a bit wistfully. "Not yet. But I've been thinking about getting one. For a long time I wasn't settled enough to have a plant, let alone a pet. Now, finally, I think I could. Having a dog has been"—Liam gazed into the distance—"well, one of my dreams."

There was a quality in his tone that conveyed loneliness and bravery, long nights spent alone in unfamiliar hotel rooms with neon lights clicking on and off through the thin curtains. . . .

Ava told herself that was ridiculous, that movie stars didn't stay in hotels with thin curtains and neon lights outside and that the chances of him being lonely were, well, none. And yet even knowing all that, there was something in the way he was looking at her that made her think of a lost little boy who needed comforting.

"I could help you," she volunteered, speaking before she'd realized what she was saying. "If you are serious about getting a dog now. I mean, I did a lot of research before I adopted Popcorn. Or you could come and spend the day with me. I mean with him. Like a trial run."

What was she saying? Had she just invited Liam Carlson to *DOG SIT*? Next she'd be admitting that she knew he was an Aquarius, liked sushi and old Bruce Springsteen songs, and his favorite color was "the color of my girlfriend's eyes." She saw him laugh and clapped a hand over her mouth. She'd said that out loud too. Great. Why was there no iPhone app for "Make the ground open up and swallow me alive," she wondered desperately.

For the fourth time in as many minutes, Liam Carlson found himself doing something he'd pretty much stopped doing: he laughed. Sure he'd been photographed laughing and he'd grinned at the right places in other people's stories but he hadn't laughed, not for real, since . . .

Well it had been a few months. But it felt like a lifetime. And now here he was, standing at this ridiculous PR event his publicist Tana had ordered him to attend, actually having a nicer time with this girl than he'd had in any VIP room in a long time. It didn't hurt that she was really cute, but it wasn't just that. There was something about her, she seemed sweet and untouched—

God, always with the clichés when you're hungover on vodka, a voice in his head said, and it was true, although usually the clichés ran to "man, I've never felt this bad before" and "I'm never drinking again." But this was different, because with this girl, they didn't seem like clichés. It was in the way she looked right at him, not trying to be coy, and in the tentative smile that played around her full lips which any other girl in Hollywood would have used for a come-hither pout. She wasn't posing. She was just—adorable.

The lips started to move and he realized she was saying something, asking him what he was doing there.

"Damage control," was how Tana had described it when she'd stalked into his bedroom the previous day at the ungodly early hour of 12:45 and pulled the sheets off of him.

"Remember me?" she'd said, her Louboutin heels clicking against the gray stone floor his designer had convinced him would make his bedroom feel like "a soothing Zen sanctuary." Apparently the designer had never heard what a $1700 stiletto sounded like when tapped by an angry publicist against a stone floor. "The woman you pay a lot of money to keep you off the cover of *People* looking like this?" She held up a photo of him being carried out of a nightclub between two bouncers.

Glancing from it, to the T-shirt he'd still been wearing in bed, he had frowned. "Hey, that was last night."

"Yes," Tana said in her sweetest voice. Which was bad. She

only sounded sweet when she was angry. "Let me read you a few snippets: 'Bystanders say that Carlson was "so out of it he was pawing everyone in sight." At least one female server at the club said she was considering pressing charges for assault with a deadly weapon.'"

"That's ridiculous," he told her, starting to sit up but stopping halfway when his head protested. "I wouldn't do that. You know it. Besides, I've never had a weapon. What did she say I assaulted her with?"

"Your breath probably, if it was anything like it is now. It doesn't matter because I'm having the story killed."

"But?" Liam said. He'd learned early on that there was always a but.

"But they're going to have the exclusive on Liam Carlson's fresh start. You had your little 'getting wrecked at nightclubs in the wake of a bad breakup' fun, now it's time to grow up. I don't care what you do in your personal life but your image is mine and you have one chance to save it."

Both his mind and his reflexes were working a little slowly so she nearly hit him with the *LA Times* when she tossed it on the bed. He rolled away from it, wincing at the pain in his head. "What do you want me to do with that?"

"Find a county fair. Kiss babies. Starting tomorrow I don't care what you do as long as it involves either animals or babies. Baby animals would be even better. You don't have to like it, just look like you do."

Which was how he'd ended up at the Pet Paradise or whatever it was the next day, as part of his image reboot. Show up, have a few dozen pictures taken, and head for the nearest bar.

But now, looking at this girl, he felt something spark inside of him. Something strange and unfamiliar. Maybe this didn't have to be just an image reboot. Watching her laughing and fending off licks from her puppy while she tried to discipline him, he thought she looked like someone who would understand that just because he'd been bad once didn't mean *he* was bad. Someone who would help him, not punish him. Someone who would support his making a fresh start. A real one. Someone who would care about him, not just how he looked in pictures. Maybe this time *could* be different.

And now we've gotten to the penance part of the hangover, the voice-over in his head said. *Let's see how fresh your start is when cocktail time rolls around.*

"Shut up," Liam said.

"What?" the girl asked. Both she and the dog were staring at him, looking a little shocked.

Oh crap, he must have said that out loud. "Nothing," he stammered. "I was just—I mean I was—well—would you like to go out sometime?"

The girl glanced behind her, then put her hand to her chest and said, "Me? Are you talking to me?"

"Yes," Liam said, laughing (again!). This girl was good for him. "And I'm not just talking. I'm asking for your number."

The words took a moment to filter into Ava's brain. Liam Carlson was asking for her number. LIAM CARLSON WAS ASKING FOR HER NUMBER! Be cool, no big deal, act like LIAM CARLSON!! famous people NUMBER!! ask you out MINE!!! every day—

"Oh man, I should have realized," he said. "Of course you have a boyfriend. That was—"

"No, oh no, I'm totally single," Ava rushed to assure him one second before remembering that you weren't supposed to announce you were single because it frightened guys off. The word "boytox" drifted through her mind, but as Liam raised one eyebrow the way she'd seen him do in half a dozen movies, boytox became a distant memory. "My number. Sure. Okay," she said, studying one of Popcorn's ears and trying to sound nonchalant as though movie stars WHOSE NAME SHE'D ONCE WRITTEN ALL OVER HER NOTEBOOK IN SHARPIE were always asking her for her number. Had she said that out loud? A quick glance at him told her she hadn't. "But I don't have anything to write with."

Liam looked around, crooked his finger at a woman in black with a massive bag standing impatiently next to the Spots Miracle Eyewash booth. "This is Tana, she's my publicist," he said when the woman joined them. "Tana, meet—I'm sorry, I didn't get your name."

"Ava," Ava said, putting out her hand.

"Ava," Liam repeated, making it sound like it was covered in caramel. "That's a nice name."

Tana smiled at Ava and then, speaking through the smile in a tense voice said, "Liam, we're here to work to support the shelter and the adorable animals, not socialize, remember?"

"I was just telling Ava about how I'm thinking of getting a puppy." He was talking to Tana but his eyes held Ava's the whole time. "Do you have a pen? I need to get her number. Ava says she'll let me spend the day with her puppy Popcorn." Eyes still on Ava's, he reached out to scratch Popcorn's head again, and their fingers brushed.

Ava's heart stopped and her mind went completely blank and she lost feeling in her entire body.

Then suddenly it all came flooding back and Tana was holding a pen toward Ava and saying to Liam, "Great, hon. Now if we could—"

Ava put Popcorn down to scribble her number on the flyer she'd been handed when they walked in.

When she handed it to Liam he said, "I'll text you tonight." Then he'd taken two steps backward, still looking at her with his goofy heart-melting smile, given a little wave, and turned and disappeared after Tana into the crowd.

Ava was still staring after him when she became aware of something whipping at her ankles and, looking down, she saw that it was the end of Popcorn's leash.

Everything seemed to go in slow motion then. Her mind registered that she must have dropped the leash as the end of it moved just beyond her grasp. She saw Popcorn, a tawny ball of fluff on a direct course for the curb and the five lanes of traffic on Third Street beyond it. She heard a desperate voice—her voice—yelling "Popcorn!" and started after him. She saw the guy in the PET PARADISE VOLUNTEER T-shirt leap—literally jump, like he was in an action film—and catch Popcorn in midair just before he ran into the street.

By the time Ava reached the guy he was on his feet, the side of his shorts and his shirt one long grass stain. "Oh my god, thank you so much," she said. "I don't know what happened. The leash must have slipped—are you okay? Are you hurt?" Noticing how Popcorn was licking the stranger's face with wild zeal, Ava laughed. "Wow, Popcorn—that's his name—the dog's name, I mean—he totally seems to like you—he doesn't usually lick strangers—oh my god, your clothes—if you tell me where I'll pay to have them clea—"

The guy turned Popcorn around, shoved him into Ava's arms, growled, "Next time take better care of your dog," and walked away.

Ava stared after him for a few moments, feeling a little shell-shocked by his rudeness, before managing to call weakly, "You bet."

Under her breath she said, "Rude," then turned her attention to Popcorn. "What were you thinking running off like that? Bad boy," she started to say, but stopped herself. She wasn't really mad at him, or even at the (meanie!) Pet Paradise guy, she knew. She was upset with herself. She never should have let go of his leash like that. She didn't know what she'd do if something had happened to him.

But nothing had, she pointed out to herself. He was fine. "You are fine, aren't you?" she asked him, and the way he licked her face reminded her of what they'd learned in obedience school, that a dog's long-term memory was about two minutes. "Do you even remember your brush with death?" she asked him, and he licked, her some more.

She glanced around to see if she could get one last glimpse of Liam but all she caught was the top of his head surrounded by people near the main stage. Which was disappointing but it also meant that he hadn't seen that mean guy yelling at her.

She arrived at Toast just in time for dessert. "No thanks," she said when Lily offered her some of her Tarte Tatin and one by one every fork at the table clattered onto the plate.

"Did Little London just refuse dessert?" MM asked Lily in a stage whisper.

"Are you okay?" Sophia asked, her concern somewhere between joking and genuine.

"I'm in love," Ava sighed.

MM picked up his fork. "Oh, is that all? What is this, the hundredth time this year? You fall in love as easily as you fall asleep."

"Which I saw you do the other day next to a fifty-percent-off sale rack," Lily added.

"Ha ha. But this time it's different," Ava said. "This time it's Liam Carlson."

"Of course it—" Lily started to say, then stopped. "Liam Carlson? The actor?"

MM's boyfriend Sven said, "But he dates Whitney Frost, no? The one who is famous for making porno sex with the vegetables?"

"It wasn't porno, it was an indie film," MM corrected him. "And they broke up a month ago."

Lily said, "I went to high school with her. Or with parts of her—she's had so many enhancements there's almost none of the original equipment left."

Sophia, ever the big sister, had a different question. "Isn't Liam Carlson a lot older than you are, Ava?"

"He's only two years older than I am," Ava said.

MM frowned. "Are you sure? I could have sworn—"

"Fine," Ava huffed. "He's three years, eight months, and seventeen days older than me. That's hardly too old."

"Wow." MM leaned back like he was impressed. "Someone was Wiki-ing while walking."

"I didn't have to look it up on Wikipedia, I knew when his birthday was already. I've been in love with him since I was twelve," Ava said proudly. "You see, it's destiny. We were *meant* to be together."

As they all put in money to pay the bill, Lily sighed. "I guess while Sophia and I are doing our boytox, you'll be running a manathon."

Ava hesitated, holding Sophia's gaze. "Are you okay with that? I really want to be supportive . . ."

Sophia waved her away. "Don't worry about me. It's you I'm a little concerned about. From what I've read, Liam Carlson doesn't sound like the safest choice in boyfriend material. Besides, I don't need boytox company. Apparently, it's all about getting your inner energy cleared out, which sounds like it's all on me."

"Well you can't believe everything you read," said Ava. "And anyway, all I did was give him my number. It's not like I accepted his marriage proposal. And in the meantime, just because I won't be boytoxing with you doesn't mean I can't help you with another essential step on the path to wellness."

"And what's that?" asked Sophia.

"The doctor says that one of the best cures for a breakup is retail therapy."

"You're not a doctor," said Sophia.

"That's a matter of perspective," Ava told her.

"What perspective?" Sophia asked.

"If you look from the future, I might be a doctor there."

Sophia put her hands up. "You win. I surrender."

Ava high-fived Popcorn's paw in a victory salute. "Yes! Shopping, here we come."

As the London sisters set out, first to drop Popcorn and Lily at home and then to comb the Brit-chic racks of Earl's Court, they had no idea that in the next fifty-six minutes everything in their lives was going to change forever.

LonDOs

Remembering to refresh your lip gloss even if you're just taking the dog for a walk

LIAM CARLSON

The rule that whoever is driving controls the radio

Your future self being a doctor

LonDONT's

Holy Muttrimony

Bossy little sisters

Stubborn big sisters

The rule that whoever is driving controls the radio

3

textify!

The bomb went off at Earl's Court at 4:02 P.M.

Not a real bomb, that was just how they thought of it afterward, the bombshell that changed everything, blowing them and their career up in ways they'd only dreamed of.

But it was only 3:45 when they got there. The store was large and built like a cross between a nightclub and an industrial loft with pearl-gray concrete floors and dark steel beams with massive crystal chandeliers hanging low from the ceiling. There were overstuffed gray velvet sofas scattered around and a wall of all different-sized televisions framed with ornate gold-leaf frames behind the cash registers that played music videos.

Ava and Sophia headed to the side wall which held the racks of the latest dresses. Ava had seen something in *Seventeen* that she thought would be the perfect cool-but-cute first-date dress and she wanted to check it out in person. Assuming Liam called and asked her out.

"What if he doesn't?" she said to Sophia as they browsed side by side.

"Of course he'll call."

"He might not."

"Then he's dumb. You are gorgeous! And funny."

"Sophia, he's used to dating celebrities. I'm—no one."

Sophia faced her sister seriously. "That's not true. You're Ava London and you're awesome."

Sophia was rewarded with Ava's smile. "And you're Sophia London and you're superamazing. Which I still say is one word."

Sophia laughed and recalled the day a year earlier when that had come up. It had been the first morning of their fashion magazine internship, and as excited and nervous as they'd been before they arrived, it was doubled when they walked in and saw the other girls. They all looked so polished and confident, casually throwing off the names of their Ivy League universities and design schools and favorite indie bands.

The first activity had been an introductory exercise where you were supposed to say your name and one adjective to describe yourself that began with the same letter. Rose was resonant, Catherine was cultured, Eve was eclectic. When it got to Sophia she'd been at a loss—sweet suddenly came to mind. Or sincere—but Ava had stepped in with superamazing. One of the other participants had pointed out that it wasn't a single word and Ava had sat forward with an I-Dare-You smile and said, "It is when applied to my sister."

Which was so completely Ava, unshakable in what she believed and unflaggingly loyal.

It was hard for Sophia to imagine that just a few years ago she and Ava hadn't even been close. The almost four-year gap in their ages had been big enough so that Ava was still in elementary school when Sophia was in junior high, and by the time Ava got to high school, Sophia had left for college.

Growing up they'd had separate rooms, separate friends, separate lives. Until Sophia's freshman year of college when she'd come home for winter break and she and Ava had gone to the mall to finish their Christmas shopping together.

It was the first time they'd really talked, as peers, a fifteen-year-old and a nineteen-year-old, and they discovered not just that they had a lot in common but that they *liked* each other. A lot. And they both also liked makeup. It was in the NARS section at Sephora that Sophia had turned to Ava and said, "I have an idea."

There was something in her sister's tone that made Ava nervous. It was the same tone Sophia had when she was little and convinced Ava to help her block off the road into their neighborhood and request a "toll" from each person. Sophia had always been entrepreneurial, and who knew what she was thinking up now. "The way you said that makes me a little nervous. It's not illegal, is it?"

"Yeah, you know me, I've always longed for a life of crime. No, it's not illegal, it's"—Sophia took a deep breath and said really fast—"I'm going to start making beauty videos on YouTube. Makeup tips, hairstyling secrets, fashion advice—that kind of thing. And I think you should make them too."

Ava's dark ponytail nearly knocked a mascara off a shelf, she'd shaken her head so insistently. "No way. I wouldn't know what to say in front of a camera."

But Sophia had convinced Ava to try and

"Remember how I had to force you to make your first video by bribing you with ice cream?" Sophia asked now.

Ava glanced up from the deep purple sheath dress she was holding, startled for a moment, then gave a huge smile. "Yeah and you created a monster because after that first video, the ideas just kept multiplying and—"

"Yeah," Sophia said, not needing her to finish the sentence to know what she was going to say. That had been the beginning of London Calling. But more than that, it was the beginning of their real relationship. As though before they'd been sisters by accident and now they were sisters by choice. Sisters and best friends.

"Remember how you were filming your videos in the bathroom at your sorority house and you didn't think anyone knew?" Ava said.

Sophia laughed. At that point Sophia had just been doing it for herself. She loved having a voice, even though the girls in her sorority already considered her their "fashion stylist." There was something calming about filming videos, uploading them, and having no idea who she was helping out.

She remembered how having this secret had made her feel different than she'd ever felt before—somehow free and powerful and unstoppable. So that when the cute football player who otherwise she would have flirted with immediately walked up to her at a party and said, "You look like someone I should know," she'd said back, "Nice line, but I'm on my way to another party," and turned her shoulder to him, guaranteeing he'd be panting after her for days.

For the entire first year they'd been dating, Clay still talked about how she was the only girl to ever give him the cold shoulder—"Literally," he'd add every time. How much that intrigued him and made him respect her. He chased her for weeks before she would give him the time of day, and that made him fall for her, hard. After weeks of asking, Sophia finally agreed to a date, only to cancel on him last-minute, just to seal his fate. Sophia knew she had him at that point.

Until she didn't anymore. *Enough!* Sophia mentally scolded herself.

Yes, it was true that she was convinced Clay was The One. But it turned out she was wrong. And now she was making a conscious decision to move forward and rebuild her life without him.

The breakup had been one of the hardest things she'd ever gone through, in large part because it was so unexpected. One minute they were perfectly happy. And the next, Clay was breaking up with her. He was so cold about it too. She was all dressed up for his fraternity's Valentine's Day dance, but when he arrived to pick her up, she could tell by his sullen expression that something was wrong.

"Are you okay?" she asked, putting her hand on his arm.

He pulled away and looked at his shoes, shaking his head. "I can't do this anymore, Sophia. I'm not ready to be serious."

What he *was* ready for was to go to the dance solo and make out with three different girls over the course of the night. And in the weeks that followed, he proceeded to make a series of appearances all over campus, each time with a different girl.

She'd found out later that he had cheated on her, multiple times. She had trusted him so much that she hadn't even seen the warning signs, but looking back she should have known. That lipstick in his car that wasn't hers? He had said it was his sister's . . . but now she knew.

Gossip about him followed her all over campus, and as much as she tried to avoid hearing about his exploits, she couldn't seem to escape the details. It had been agonizing. And it didn't help that she'd been so unprepared for it. She'd never seen it coming, hadn't even had an inkling of it. Sophia, the ultimate planner, the girl whose schedule was organized fourteen months in advance, taken completely by surprise.

She understood why now. After weeks of soul-searching, she knew that none of it was her fault. Clay was simply wrong for her, and in a way, it was a good thing he was out of her life, so she could find someone who was right for her. She still believed in love and wanted to find it, but sometimes it felt really far away.

Her phone pinged with an e-mail. It had the subject line: "Congratulations you're a winner!"

Great, now your heart rate is getting a lift from junk mail, she thought. But she clicked on it anyway.

Ava must have done the same thing because Sophia heard Ava's gasp at the same moment as her own. Turning to the next rack, Ava was standing there with her phone in her hand.

"Did you—"

"We—"

"And not just—"

"But—"

Giving up on words, they stared at each other in shock. The two of them had just won a super-prestigious award for being Best Webstars of the Year. Not best vloggers or best bloggers or best haulers. Best of the entire Web.

They were so gobsmacked that they completely forgot they were in public in the middle of a store until a shy voice near them said, "Excuse me?"

A little girl with thick black-rimmed glasses stood tentatively next to a rack of distressed silver leather jeans.

"Sorry," Sophia said. "We didn't mean to block the path."

"You weren't," the girl said. "I mean you were but that's not"— she swallowed—"you're Ava and Sophia London, right? Could I have your autograph on my shopping bag?"

"Of course," Ava said, smiling hugely as she took the bag from the girl and then gave it to Sophia to sign.

Sophia handed the bag back to the girl. "Thanks for visiting our site."

The girl looked at her blankly. "I don't. I mean, I hadn't until just now."

"How did you know who we were?"

The girl eyed Sophia like she was crazy and pointed behind them. They followed her finger to the wall of television monitors. Each TV was now showing a picture of their faces with a star around it.

They turned back to the girl but she was walking away, clutching the autographs in one hand and typing on her phone fast with the other.

They continued shopping, casually selecting things to try on when they became aware that the store was getting unusually crowded. A petite woman who introduced herself as the manager came over and asked if they'd mind signing a few more autographs and suddenly they were standing next to the cash registers with a line of people forming in front of them.

"What is the meaning of this?" a proprietary voice demanded from their left. "Who's blocking the cash registers?" Turning, Sophia and Ava found themselves facing a woman in her seventies swathed in a massive black fur, wearing large black sunglasses, sitting in what appeared to be a gold-plated wheelchair with a bored-looking Pomeranian on her lap. Apart from her silver shoulder-length bob, the only thing she wore that wasn't black was her lipstick, which was a pure red. Behind her stood a man with gray hair dressed in a navy-and-gold uniform with perfectly polished black boots like a chauffeur out of an old movie.

"What is the reason for this ruckus?" the woman demanded. She looked around and fastening on Sophia and Ava said, "I'm trying to buy a simple gift for my granddaughter. Why are you blocking the registers?"

"I'm sorry," Ava said. "We didn't mean to."

"We will move. We didn't mean to disturb you," Sophia stepped in to clarify.

One of the girls in line piped up with "You can't leave! You have to sign this for my friend! She will die! We voted for you every day for weeks for this award!"

The woman examined them over the top of her dark glasses. "An award? Why ever for? I can't see anything special about you."

Missy, the manager, who had come to stand next to the London sisters, said, "They just won Best Webstars of the Year."

The woman in the wheelchair pursed her red lips with distaste. "Really. So they give prizes for anything these days." Her head moved as she looked Ava and Sophia up and down. "You're sisters?"

"Yes, and we—"

"*Yes* was adequate. All of these lookie-loos"—she made a broad gesture toward several clusters of teenage girls hovering nearby and pointing at Sophia and Ava—"are interrupting my shopping trip because you are *Webstars*?"

Ava looked around. "I guess."

"And you think that gives you the right to inconvenience others?"

"No, of course not," Sophia said quickly. "This is all a complete accident. We—"

The woman's attention had drifted from Sophia to the dog on her lap, who was standing up and rubbing against Ava's outstretched hand. "Cuddles, what's gotten into you?"

Ava patted the dog. "Is Cuddles a girl or a boy?"

"That's none of your concern," the woman snapped, gathering the dog toward her.

"I have a dog too," Ava told her, trying to make peace. "He—"

"Do I look like someone who would be remotely interested in anything about you?" She turned her head slightly over her shoulder and addressed the man in the uniform. "Charles, please continue forward. Push these lookie-loos out of the way if you must. We don't have time to deal with—whatever any of this is."

Charles pushed the woman away while Sophia and Ava watched, a little bit hurt at how mean the woman had been. And when Missy came over and said, "We're incredibly happy to have you in our store, truly we are. But we're attracting a crowd, and it's a fire hazard—not to mention an interruption to other customers. We've already gotten a complaint or two, so I'm really sorry, but we're going to have to ask you to leave," Sophia was fairly sure who the complainer must have been.

It was the first time they'd ever been asked to leave a store, but Sophia found she couldn't stop smiling. Maybe she wasn't doing *everything* wrong.

LonDOs

Best Webstar of the Year awards!

Carrying a tiny brush in your purse for touchups on the go

Strawberry shrimp and cold summer noodles ordered in from Mandarette

Noise cancellation headsets

Flaming Couture sparkling cell phone case from Cellairis

LonDON'Ts

Cheating boyfriends

Being asked to leave a store before you can find a first-date dress

Getting an ominous call from your agent saying, "We heard you were kicked out of Earl's Court today; we need you to be at the office the 'next day first thing' to talk about this"

First thing meaning 8:00 A.M.

Popcorn eating the fortunes from the fortune cookies

Waiting for texts from boys

Sophia singing old songs at night in the bath

(I can hear you—A)

Ava singing new songs first thing in the morning

(So can I—S)

4

about facial

Sophia and Ava had never seen the offices of Foley+Brightman so empty, but then again they'd never been there on a Sunday morning at 8:00 A.M. before. With its sandstone walls, light wood furniture, pale green Persian carpets, and windows that gave the light coming in a slightly gold cast, the offices would have resembled a spa, except for the tension oozing off everyone in them.

That morning the only people there besides the London sisters were a handful of assistants with dark smudges under their eyes including Katie, their agent Corrina's PA. She met them at the reception desk wearing the same thing she always wore, a white blouse, black fitted skirt, and a wide belt. The just-back-from-the-cleaners crispness of her shirt was a contrast to the up-all-night-at-my-desk paleness of her skin.

She ushered them into a conference room and pointed them to seats at one end of the long beech wood table with their backs to the wall of windows that looked out over Beverly Hills.

"Corrina is just finishing up with someone," she said with artificial brightness. "It shouldn't be too long but while you wait, can I bring you anything? Anything at all?"

"No, thank you," Sophia said.

"Really," Katie pressed. "It would be no problem. Coffee? Smoothie? Milkshake? Croissant?"

When it became clear she wasn't going to take no for an answer they asked for coffee. As the door closed behind her, Ava asked, "Was that a little weird?"

Sophia was still staring after Katie. "No, it was *a lot* weird. You know what it made me think of?"

"How they bring people on death row anything they want as their last meal," Ava said unhesitatingly.

Sophia gave her a small nervous smile. "Exactly."

A clock at the far end of the room ticked audibly, as though to underscore the idea.

It had been quiet in the car as Sophia drove them from West Hollywood to Beverly Hills, partially because it was early even by Ava's standards—getting up at 8 A.M. was different than being up and dressed and ready to leave for a meeting then—and partially because there'd been something in Corrina's tone when she left her message that suggested they weren't being summoned to her office at 8:00 on a Sunday morning for a big congratulations parade.

Sophia's stomach was in knots. This was like what had happened with Clay all over again. One minute she and Ava had been blissfully happy. The next, without them even knowing why, they were in danger of losing everything.

Although they sort of knew why. A picture of them being kicked out of Earl's Court yesterday had been tweeted by one of LA's most popular fashion gossip sites . . . which happened to be run by a girl who worked on the sales floor at Earl's Court.

Though her tweet explained that it was all because of the TV appearance that aired just moments before, it didn't stop the nastier gossip sites from accusing them of getting kicked out for much more sinister reasons. The list included everything from shoplifting to punching another girl in the face while calling dibs on the last pair of Seven Jeans.

The clock ticked off one minute, then another. The toes of Ava's high-heeled motorcycle boots pointed in as she slid down in her seat, toying nervously with a piece of the fringe on the end of the gold-and-cream scarf she had looped loosely around her neck. Sophia, by contrast, sat up straighter, the hem of her yellow pleated dress perfectly straight over her knees, her ankles in her cream-and-white T-strap heels crossed, her hands resting in her lap. The only sign of her agitation was the way her fingers played with her heart ring, twirling it around endlessly.

Katie arrived with the coffees and a basket of muffins—"No reason to be hungry while you wait!" she said with excessive cheer—and disappeared again.

The clock ticked off another minute. Sophia took a muffin and began dividing it into smaller and smaller pieces. Ava pulled out her phone, checked her text messages, and sighed.

"It's only eight thirty. You can't expect a text now. He's still sleeping."

That was true, Ava knew. But . . .

"Well, look who we have here." Corrina walked through the door and slid into the seat at the head of the table, setting a thick folder and an iPad in front of her.

Before she could say anything Ava began, "I know there are a lot of crazy rumors going around, but believe me when I tell you that we didn't punch anyone, steal anything, or engage in any other illegal acts—"

"Well, why didn't you?" Corrina interrupted.

That stopped Ava cold. She and Sophia stared at their agent.

"All this attention is fabulous!" Corrina said, pointing at the screen. "We can use that in a PR campaign."

"So we're not in trouble?" Ava said.

"The only thing you're in trouble of is being on a lot more people's radars than you were yesterday. First the Best Webstar award and now all this online buzz?" She took a deep breath and crossed her hands in front of her on the tabletop. "Do you remember what you told me when you first moved to Los Angeles? What your dream was?"

Sophia said, "To have our own London Calling makeup line," at the same time as Ava said, "To have a time machine to the future." Sophia laughed, but Ava quickly amended it. "Oh right. London Calling makeup line."

Corrina went on. "And do you remember what I told you?"

Sophia nodded. "That we could aim for that but it would take at least a year or two of building our Web presence and raising awareness of the London Calling brand and even then we'd have to start with just a tie-in deal."

"Yes." Corrina turned to Katie who sprang to attention by the door. "Please bring in our visitor." Corrina said, "Girls, I want you to meet Lucille Rexford."

"We've met," an abrupt voice said as a gold-plated wheelchair was edged through the door by a man in an old-fashioned chauffer's uniform. "Not officially, but enough." The woman's hand rested on the Pomeranian in her lap. She was in all black just as she'd been when she had confronted Ava and Sophia at Earl's Court the previous day but this morning instead of a fur she was wrapped in a cashmere shawl and the lenses of her large glasses were more a smoky gray than black.

For a moment complete silence fell on the conference room. Then Cuddles, the dog, barked once, leaped off the woman's lap, and headed straight for Ava.

Ava was braced for Lucille to be upset but instead she gave a completely unexpected hoot of laughter, slapped her knee heartily with one hand, and said, "I knew it."

"Miss Rexford is the majority owner of LuxeLife Cosmetics," Corrina explained. "And she has a proposal for you." She turned to the woman in the wheelchair, more courteous than the London sisters had ever seen her. "Miss Rexford?"

"What do you call your company again?" Miss Rexford snapped at Ava and Sophia.

"London Calling," Sophia supplied in a near whisper, as though her voice had gotten scared and run away. Ava sat there with her face pale, saying nothing. Lucille scared her.

Miss Rexford nodded. "That's right. Well, no need to beat around, I hate wasting time. I want to give you your own line. London Calling for LuxeLife. What do you say?"

Ava started to choke but Sophia put up a hand and spoke first. "When you say *our own line* what exactly do you mean?"

Miss Rexford gave a very slight nod, as though indicating approval of the question. "Two palettes a year, advisory control of the content and theme of each campaign. Your images would also be featured in all the advertising."

Sophia and Ava didn't have to look at each other to know what the other was thinking: it was an incredible offer, the offer they'd dreamed of but thought they'd never get.

"Why are you doing this?" Ava asked, leaning forward as much as she could with Cuddles in her lap. "I thought you hated us yesterday."

Miss Rexford's gold bangles clinked together as she waved that aside. "Cuddles likes you. He doesn't like anyone. That has to mean something."

"You're giving us our own makeup line because your dog likes us?" Sophia said. She pronounced each word with a slight pause in between which gave the sentence an undercurrent of disbelief.

"That and because I saw how the two of you connected with your fans yesterday. And when I attended my granddaughter's birthday festivities, she couldn't stop talking about Ava and

Sophia London's makeup videos. She even forced me to sit through far too many of them!"

Miss Rexford put her hands on the table and leaned into it as though she were going to pounce. Through the smoky glasses her eyes bored into Sophia's as she said, "But none of that matters, or it shouldn't matter to you anyway, young lady. Because when someone offers you an opportunity to make your dreams come true, you don't question them. You just take it."

Sophia couldn't stop thinking about that on the ride home. There had been a pointedness in Miss Rexford's tone that suggested a lesson learned the hard way and she wondered what it had been.

A partial clue came from the Wikipedia entry Ava found as they drove home, although neither of them realized it until much later. "'Lucille Rexford, eldest daughter of Mary Louise and Joseph Rexford,'" Ava read aloud, "'inherited the LuxeLife empire with younger sister Lenora when their parents were killed in a boating accident. Twenty-two at the time, Lucille took the reins of the company, and managed to not only run it but grow it while enjoying the life of an international party girl.'"

Ava paused and looked at Sophia. "She was your age when she got the whole company. Maybe that's another reason she picked us, because she sees herself in us." Ava went back to skimming the Wikipedia entry. "It sounds like she toured the globe going to parties and being the face of the brand for a while," Ava summarized, then went back to reading. "'In 1978, ten years after the death of her parents, Rexford abruptly disappeared from both LuxeLife advertising campaigns and the high-stakes social scene she'd been the center of. Rumors abound about what caused her withdrawal but the most likely suggest a thwarted love affair. Rexford now lives a reclusive existence attended by a handful of servants in her childhood home atop Mulholland Drive and is rarely seen in public.'"

Ava looked up from her phone. "There's a photo of her here from when she was the center of the social scene holding Cuddles."

"It can't be Cuddles," Sophia pointed out.

"Maybe she's a vampire and she's found a way to preserve Cuddles and she needs our youth to keep him perpetually young."

"That's as good an explanation of why she picked us as any of the others," Sophia said with a laugh.

They'd texted Lily from the car to tell her the news and she was waiting for them in front of their door when they got home. "I've got it all planned," she announced after hugging them. "There's a big party at Mr. C tonight and I got us on the list. It's the new 3S hotspot in Beverly Hills so the scenery will be good, and since it's a party the drinks will be free."

Ava looked up from her phone, which was still Liam–text free. "Three S?"

"See and be Seen Scene. It's like 4H for the Hollywood set," Lily explained.

Now Ava was even more puzzled. "It teaches them to raise livestock and vegetables?"

"It teaches them to network and schmooze," Lily answered. "Which is how people here put food on their tables."

It wasn't clear what you were supposed to wear to a 3S spot—when they'd asked Lily she'd said, "Oh anything. Can I borrow your new kitchen tablecloth?"—so after making a quick "Thank you!!!" vlog for their viewers, Sophia, Ava, and Popcorn retreated to the closet for a wardrobe session.

They had converted the spare bedroom in their apartment into a shared closet, which Sophia had spent days organizing. "Putting all your pants together just shows you pants. Putting all your pinks together shows you *possibilities*," she'd said. In the middle of the closet there was a white fur chaise they could sit on to better appreciate those *possibilities*.

Ava sank onto it now with Popcorn in her lap, while Sophia

walked around the closet, thoughtfully eyeing the selection. The great thing about having a sister the same size as you was being able to share all of their clothes. Sophia held up a dusty-pink long-sleeve baby doll dress and a silver maxi dress and turned to Ava. "Which do you—"

Seeing that Ava was just sitting there absently stroking Popcorn's head, Sophia said, "Have you given any thought to what you're going to wear?"

Ava curled one of Popcorn's tawny ears around her finger. "I don't know. I'm thinking maybe I won't go. Just let you and Lily go on your own."

Sophia hung the two dresses on a hook and put her hands on her hips. "Hmm, let me think about that." Sophia rested her index finger on her cheek and rolled her eyes upward in an exaggerated pantomime of thinking, then abruptly leveled her head. "Yeah, that's not going to happen."

"I'm just not in the mood and—"

Sophia stopped her with an upraised palm. "You know the rule. The worse you feel, the better you have to look. Besides, we're celebrating. I know you're upset because you haven't heard from Liam, but this is bigger than any guy."

"I'm not upset because Liam hasn't called," Ava protested unconvincingly.

Ignoring her, Sophia bent and addressed Popcorn. "What would Popcorn do? Would you stay home and mope or would you get up and—"

She wasn't even finished when he leaped onto his feet on Ava's lap and started turning in circles, wagging his whole body excitedly.

Ava looked at him, and then nodded and said, "You're right." She stood up, showing the resilience that Sophia admired so much about her. "I'm being ridiculous. This is our night. I'm not going to let him ruin it."

"And just in case you feel yourself backsliding"—Sophia said, handing Ava a blue razorback minidress that she knew from experience made her sister look both adorable and alluring at once—"wear this. You always have a good time when you wear it."

"Playing What Would Popcorn Do was low," Ava said as she slipped into the dress and a pair of black ankle boots.

"It worked." Sophia grinned, stepping into the sandy-pink baby doll dress. She cinched her waist artfully with a caramel-colored belt, and slid into the pair of caramel-colored high-heeled sandals that MM had convinced her to get when they went on sale despite them still costing a dizzying amount. "It works because they make your legs look about a thousand light-years long. That's less than a dollar a light-year!"

Ava watched Sophia glance at herself in the mirror quickly, not seeming to notice how perfect she looked. Sophia always looked perfect. She knew exactly how to dress, how to smile, how to flirt. It was an ongoing joke between them that Sophia could make any guy fall in love with her, which was why it frustrated Ava that Sophia was single. Ava had watched guy after guy fall in love with Sophia, only to get ignored by her because they weren't Clay.

Maybe if I paid more attention to how she does it I wouldn't be waiting now for a text from Liam, Ava thought.

When they were dressed, Sophia balanced her phone between two platform boots and activated the timer. "I want us to remember this night, this moment, forever," she said.

She'd set the camera to keep taking pictures so they did over a dozen, smiling, laughing, one of them making scary faces, one with Popcorn trying to lick off their makeup. They were a little late to meet Lily but they were both grinning, and Ava kept smiling even after checking her messages when they arrived at Mr. C and seeing there weren't any from Liam.

"He'll get in touch by tomorrow," Sophia reassured her as they left the car with a valet.

They walked through the lobby, past an all-glass pool table, toward the restaurant which was being guarded by two men in suits with clipboards who greeted Lily by name and jumped up to remove the velvet ropes from their path. "Unless he was hit by a bus and is in the hospital barely clinging to his life or something," Lily added, as they were ushered into the restaurant.

Ava started to say, "Lily, that's horrible," but stopped abruptly. Her knees went weak and she reached for Sophia's arm.

"I think it's 'or something,'" she said quietly, staring across the floor to the spot where Liam was sitting at a table with his arms around gorgeous twin blondes. "Or maybe make that some*things*."

LonDOs

Waterproof mascara

A shared closet the size of a bedroom, with a sister the same size as you so you can wear all of her new clothing before she can

Sisters who are so free-spirited they can fall in love with any guy

LonDON'Ts

Liam Carlson

Crying over any boy, ever

The voice in your head that says flushing your phone down the toilet is a good idea

Sisters who are perfect and can make any guy fall in love with them

Gorgeous twin blondes

5

when you wish upon a bar

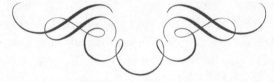

By the time Ava was done saying "stupid stupid stupid" to herself and messing up the toe of her boot by kicking the wall of the bathroom, Sophia had fixed her hair and Lily had sprayed her with something her Wiccan guide promised would turn bad energy good (apparently starting with having Lily catch her phone before it sailed into the toilet), and she was insisting they should stay rather than going home.

"Popcorn wouldn't go home," Ava said. "Popcorn would erase all memory of the disappointments of the past and go sniff around for new adventures."

"Yes, but Popcorn can't even remember if he's had breakfast," Sophia pointed out. "That gives him an advantage. Whereas you are always very clear on breakfast."

"It doesn't matter," Ava said, chin up. "I said I wasn't going to let a guy ruin our celebration and I'm not. Especially not a guy

I've just met. Even if I did sleep with him on top of me all night between the ages of twelve and fifteen."

"You'd be better off sticking with the poster of Liam Carlson and not the real thing if he's anything like the other actors I know," Lily advised. They left the bathroom and once again headed into the restaurant where the party was filling up. "I mean, they're both two-dimensional, but one of them will never wake you up with morning breath."

Ava laughed, a genuine laugh, and Sophia breathed a sigh of relief.

Lily's friend or friend's friend had reserved three stools for them at the already-getting-crowded bar, allowing them to keep their backs to the corner where He Who They Were Not Talking About And Absolutely Not Looking At was sitting.

"I also know someone who knows someone who could take care of him for you," Lily went on.

Sophia gaped at her. "Are you offering to have him killed?"

"Of course not." Lily's hand came up to her chest in shock. "Just taught a lesson. How permanent that lesson is would be totally up to Ava."

"That's okay," Ava assured her quickly. "It was my fault. I mean he must ask hundreds of girls for their number every day. I was stupid to think I could be diff—"

Ava felt hands on her shoulders and someone was spinning her around on her stool and suddenly she was facing Liam Carlson.

Who was saying, "Girl with the friendly dog! It *is* you. I'm so glad. I nearly fired my publicist when I found out she'd lost your number."

At least that's what Ava thought he was saying. It was hard to make out the individual words because his smile was doing that thing to her again where it scrambled her brains and her brains, what was left of them, were shouting LIAM CARLSON IS TOUCHING MY SHOULDER!

"You look fantastic," he went on. "Who are you here with?"

It took Ava a moment to remember—"You?" Was "You" the right answer?—long enough for Sophia to say, "Hi, I'm Ava's sister, Sophia. And this is our friend Lily."

"Nice to meet you, Sophia," Liam said politely. He turned to Lily and his head tilted to the side. "We've met, haven't we?"

"Probably," Lily told him sweetly. "I think you blew off a friend of mine." She gave him a hundred-watt movie-star smile and said, "I'm a third level ninja master so I would suggest you don't do it again if you like your arms where they are."

Liam stared at her as though he was trying to decide if she was serious or not. Still watching her out of the corner of his eye his face turned toward Ava. "You roll with a tough crew."

Ava, working hard to swallow back a giggle, said, "I'm lucky that way."

Liam shook his head in wonder. "I'm afraid my posse will seem a bit tame after yours but would you come meet them? I was just asking their advice about how to find you."

Ava turned to Sophia and whispered, "He was asking their advice about how to find me! What should I do?"

Sophia whispered back, "Go flirt with him! He likes you!"

Liam, who had been watching them like he was watching a tennis match, leaned toward Lily to whisper, "Is this some kind of girl thing or some kind of sister thing?"

"I don't know," Lily said earnestly, "but I do know three ways to make you plead for mercy using only this cocktail napkin if you hurt my friend." She smiled at him again.

Liam took a step away from her, his mouth slightly open like he was searching in vain for the right thing to say.

He was spared by Sophia saying, "Ava, go on. Lily and I will hold down the bar. Have fun."

"And be careful," Lily added, carefully smoothing her cocktail napkin.

"What did you say to him?" Sophia's eyes followed Ava and Liam across the room. "He keeps glancing back with the expression our canary at home used to get whenever my cat came into the room."

"Nothing much," Lily said a bit too innocently.

"Did he really stand up a friend of yours?"

Lily shrugged. "Or a friend of a friend. Or a godfriend of a friend. I'm sure he's stood up *someone* I know at some time. I just wanted to make sure he treats Ava with the proper respect. Fear of mauling is really the only way to make an actor behave. But it's thirsty work." She raised herself slightly in her stool and said, "Where is that hot bartender?"

She wasn't exaggerating, Sophia thought as the guy came over. He had light brown hair parted on the side, eyes a shade darker, and a crooked smile that emerged when Lily said, "Hello, sir. A double blueberry vodka on the rocks."

But what really made an impression on Sophia was the adorable Italian accent with which the bartender said, "No no, this is not the drink for you. For you I make something special."

Lily shrugged. "Whatever you say. But my trainer says I need more antioxidants so anything with berries is—" She broke off, glancing down at her phone which had started to buzz. "Excuse me, I have to go get someone past the velvet," she said, using LA shorthand. "I'll be back in a sec, save my seat."

Sophia watched her go. Turning back she met the bartender's eyes square on. She inhaled sharply.

She'd thought it was only in books that people's eyes could twinkle with mischief but his toffee-brown ones seemed to be doing just that as they held hers. Sophia noticed that his cheeks bore the faintest shadow of a beard, the kind she imagined would be smooth at the start of a date and just the right amount rough by the end when he was kissing you good-bye in front of your door to send a tingle—

"I think not," he said.

Sophia blinked herself back to the present. "What?" It was the accent that was doing it, she realized. She'd always been a sucker for men with accents and his was the audio version of thick hot chocolate with mini-marshmallows.

"The right drink, it is not the same for you and your friend. For your friend maybe a Shirley Temple. But for you—" He cocked his head to one side as though he were measuring her for a dress. "Ah, of course." He disappeared for a moment and when he came back he set a small glass filled with a light pink liquid that almost seemed to glow from within in front of her. "It is a Bellini. Slightly sweet, politely bubbly, very beautiful, a little sad. Just like you."

Sophia sat up straight with surprise. "I'm not a little sad."

"No? Forgive me. You do not sleep well last night and this makes me think you are troubled."

Sophia went very still. "How did you know I didn't sleep well?" She thought she'd done a pretty good job with the concealer and the light in the restaurant had seemed generous.

"I see many things," he said, tapping himself on the forehead and giving her a goofy grin. The grin faded abruptly. "But I am so rude. Permit me to introduce myself. My name is Giovanni and I will be your protector for this evening."

"Do I need a protector?"

He rolled his eyes heavenward. "She asks if she needs one. A princess like you in a place like this? Very much." He lowered his voice, speaking confidentially. "I know it is not kind of me to speak ill of my subjects but I must be honest."

Sophia took a sip of the drink he'd made for her. It was delicious, sweet and a little tart as he'd promised, with tiny bubbles that tickled her nose. "Your subjects?"

"*Sí.* Those who come to visit my kingdom." He spread his arms, indicating the bar. "I am afraid we have a very lax visiting policy. Sometimes I think perhaps we should stiffen our regulations but, you know, one does not wish to be a snob." He tilted the tip of his nose up with his index finger. "It is not good to have the nostrils in the air."

"Of course not," Sophia agreed with mock seriousness. "But I think you mean nose."

Giovanni clapped his hands together. "*Brava.* Already you enlighten me with your wisdom. From the first moment you sat down I said to myself, here is a woman of wisdom." He leaned toward her, bringing his face only inches from hers. The playful tone vanishing, replaced by seriousness. "You will do big things in your life, *bellissima.* Yes. Very big."

Sophia didn't know if it was his accent, or the way he was looking so intensely at her when he spoke, or that she could almost feel his breath caress her cheek, but she was suddenly having trouble swallowing.

Clearing her throat in an effort to also clear her head she said, "Are you a fortune-teller as well as prince of this realm?"

"Not prince, no no," he said, touching his finger to the side of his nose in what looked to Sophia like a very Italian gesture. "Just overseer. But yes, it is in my blood, seeing the future." He nodded seriously but the twinkle was back in his eyes. "My aunt. She has this power. Not always correct. She told my sister she was born with a broken heart and would never have love and she's been married happily twelve years with five *bambini.* So, you know."

"What about you, are you wrong?"

"No. Never, at least not with the beautiful women like you. And I say that you will do big things. Already they are starting. Aha!" he said, grinning. "I am right, no? Bigger than you had hoped. So now you know, it is settled. I say it will be so, it will be so. You can go home, and tonight you will sleep untroubled." He stood, increasing the space between them.

"It's that easy?" Sophia said.

"*Sí*. It should be. Only you make it complicated. You must to trust—" His glance flicked to the end of the bar where three white-coated waiters were standing impatiently, and he said, "Excuse me a moment, I must see to the needs of my other subjects."

"Trust who?" Sophia asked but he was already gone.

Don't be a fool, a voice in her head said, mimicking the plaintiveness in her tone when she'd said "Trust who?" *He's a bartender not a psychic. That was just small talk.*

She turned around and took in the room behind her. Lily hadn't exaggerated about the party being a See and be Seen Scene. Lily herself was near the front talking to the woman who had won the best actress Oscar the year before but the entire restaurant was filled with celebrities Sophia recognized from a screen—movie, television or, in the case of the lead singer of her current favorite workout song, video.

When Sophia and Ava had first moved to LA, parties like this had been just a dream, something you read about in a magazine. Even now, having been to a few, Sophia still felt a little like a child at an aquarium, nose pressed against the glass watching all the exotic fish circle by but separated from them, as though they were a completely different species.

Or maybe not, she thought, spotting Ava. She was at a table in the back, seated between Liam and a blond girl who was in the last movie they'd seen in a theater, looking exactly like she belonged. Ava was talking animatedly, clearly at ease which made Sophia happy. But what made her even happier was the way Liam was looking at her sister, intently, like he only had eyes for her.

Her thoughts were interrupted when a deep male voice next to her said, "Excuse me, can I ask you a question?"

Turning, Sophia saw a clean-cut blond guy in his early

twenties wearing a button-down blue-and-white-striped shirt with French cuffs. He smiled at her. "My friends and I have a bet going. They say that you're a model and I say that you're an actress."

"What's the prize?" Sophia asked, because it was the right thing to say.

"Whoever wins gets to buy you a drink," the guy said, flashing her a set of veneer-covered teeth she was sure Lily could place.

She looked at him curiously. "But the drinks are free here tonight."

He winked. "You got me. Smart and beautiful. It was just an excuse to get to talk to you. I'm Craig," he said, putting out a hand. "Tell me, what *do* you do?"

Good-looking, shows signs of having a sense of humor, Sophia's mind ticked off. *You should be nice to him, get to know him better.*

"My sister and I—" she began, then stopped. Why? Why *should* she do that? She was doing a boytox, after all. Remembering an article she'd read about the most unpopular jobs, she said, "I'm a dental hygienist."

The guy's smile didn't waver but he quickly wandered off. Two others followed him, each of whom were good-looking and well groomed and polite enough that she should have talked to them. Both of whom she sent away.

If you're not going to talk to anyone, you should go, a voice in her head said. *What are you waiting for?*

When a fourth guy began moving her way she decided she'd had enough. She'd just climbed off the stool and turned away from the bar when Giovanni's voice behind her said, "I agree. You make the right choice."

She turned back to see him leaning on the bar, chin on his palm and her heart rate picked up slightly.

"What right choice?"

"To escape while still you can. Before my charms overwhelm you."

A bubble of laughter escaped from Sophia involuntarily. "Am I in danger of that?"

He rolled his eyes. "But of course. Look how already you are sending away all other men with a flick of your pinkie." He demonstrated a pinkie flick.

She felt herself blush. That was *not* what she'd been doing. "That's not exactly—"

He put a finger to his lips. "Do not ruin the moment with words." Dipping his head in a sort of bow he said, "It has been a pleasure having you at my bar. My realm will lose the largest part of her allure with the loss of your company."

Sophia glanced around at the all-too-beautiful crowd. "I'm sure you can find an easy replacement."

"You wound me by suggesting such a thing," he said, clutching at his heart. Then he grinned boyishly, said, *"Arrivederci, stella,"* and sauntered down the bar. Following him with her eyes, Sophia watched him greet a group of girls who had just arrived with an enthusiastic *"Bellissime!"* and felt unaccountably annoyed.

Only because he was so unsubtle, she told herself. Not because she'd enjoyed talking to him. A lot. Enjoyed it more than she should have, more than she'd enjoyed talking to any guy in a long time. Not because she'd thought maybe he felt that too, maybe he'd—

What? Ask for your number?

It was a relief that he hadn't, she told herself, not a disappointment. She knew from friends that dating bartenders was a Bad Idea. They were unreliable and had terrible hours and way too much exposure to women. Their whole job was to flirt.

Exactly the way he'd been flirting with you all night. He was just doing his job.

Besides, she was boytoxing. She *couldn't* have gone out with him even if he'd asked. Even if she'd wanted to.

(Which she didn't.)

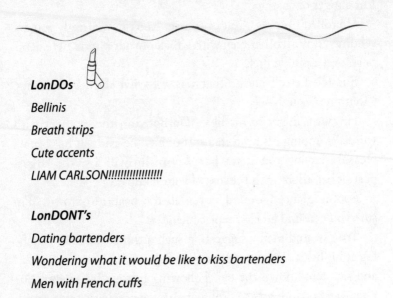

LonDOs

Bellinis

Breath strips

Cute accents

LIAM CARLSON!!!!!!!!!!!!!!!!!!

LonDONT's

Dating bartenders

Wondering what it would be like to kiss bartenders

Men with French cuffs

Men with big watches

Doubting Liam Carlson

6

one and lonely

Lily said she'd get a ride home with a friend of a friend so Sophia made her way around the groups of couples talking and dancing to the corner table Liam and Ava were sharing. "I'm afraid I have to steal my sister from you," she told Liam.

For a split second he looked like he was going to protest, confirming everything Lily had said about actors being spoiled, but instead he was very much the gentleman, saying, "I'm grateful you let me have her even this long."

He looked at Ava. "I'll send you the details about that party at Hunter's house. I'm sorry you didn't get to meet him, he should have been here by now. But you'll like him. And he'll adore you." He glanced at Sophia to explain, "My best friend is throwing a party next weekend. You should come too."

Ava stood up and he stood with her. Then he took her hand, brought it to his lips, and kissed it chivalrously.

Sophia was worried she was going to have to carry Ava out in a swoon, but she managed to stay on her feet. She'd even recovered the power of speech by the time they were leaving the restaurant. "Liam wants me to meet his best friend," she squealed as they walked past the bouncer who had let them in. "That has to be a good sign, right?"

"Right," Sophia agreed. "Did you have a nice time?"

"Oh Sophia," Ava said, stopping in the middle of the lobby and grabbing hold of her sister's wrists. "It was like being in a movie. He's—he's perfect."

Sophia replied, "Yeah, I'd say you had a nice time."

"He's funny and smart and when he laughs he gets these crinkles near his eyes that are just adorable."

Ava's list of Liam's stunning attributes carried them through the lobby and out to the valet. Sophia was distracted trying to pay attention to what Ava was saying—"he has the nicest ankles"—so when the guy she'd handed her valet ticket to gazed at her with apparent amazement and said, "You want me to get your car?" she got worried.

"Am I in the wrong place?" she asked, looking around. "Did I cut in front of someone? Was there a line I missed?"

"No," the guy told her. "I just wanted to be sure."

The front of his dark blond hair slid over his forehead, touching the edge of darker brows. He had a firm, square jaw and a faint tan, hooded eyes the same dark blue as his well-fitted V-neck sweater, and lips that curved up slightly in a look of wry amusement. Was everyone that worked here incredibly good-looking? Sophia wondered. Or was that a side effect of the boytox?

There were two other valets standing at the counter, both of them in white button-down shirts and both also quite cute. One of them reached out now, glanced at her ticket, and handed the guy in blue a set of keys. Pointing him toward the back corner of the lot he said, "You're supposed to run," and watched with visible amusement as the guy took off at a jog.

"Is he a trainee?" Ava asked. "Is that why he's wearing a different shirt?"

"Yeah, something like that," the guy who had handed over the keys said in a sort of strangled voice. "We're still trying him out." At that the other valet made a strange choking sound.

Ava watched him with concern. "Is he okay?"

"He will be."

The trainee valet pulled the car up then and got out, holding the door open for Sophia. "Are you sure you don't want to stay and get to know me better? There's a lot—"

Sophia yawned enormously. "I'm sorry," she told him, blinking. "What were you saying?"

Behind him, the two other valets burst out laughing.

The trainee shook his head. "Man, I must need some better material. Drive safe, ladies."

As they pulled out, Ava turned to Sophia, beaming. "That was a really good night. I *love* LA."

Sophia was thrilled to see Ava so happy. Even if it meant that she hummed Katy Perry's "Teenage Dream" from the moment they got home, through brushing her teeth, washing her face, changing into her pajamas, spritzing her bed with lavender water, turning out the light, and calling good night to Sophia.

"We did it, sis," she said from her room.

"Yes we did," Sophia agreed.

"World, prepare for a London invasion."

Sophia washed her face and brushed her teeth and got into bed.

And got out of bed and put on fuzzy socks and went to her computer. As tired as she'd been at Mr. C, she suddenly felt restless. It was like her body was tired but her mind would not stop clicking along. She pulled out her vintage pale pink chair and turned on her computer, trying to decide what her next vlog would be about.

Sophia checked her e-mail and saw that she had a slew of unchecked Facebook messages. She logged into the site, and that's when she saw them. A dozen pictures of Clay that had been tagged by a mutual friend, all of them different variations of him being wrapped around the same girl. In one they were kissing. In another they were hugging. In the next they were hugging and kissing. But the worst parts were the comments. "You and your new GF are SO CUTE!!!" "So happy you finally found The One." "You two are the perfect couple—great pic!"

It was just like being back at college, when she'd try to do her own thing and forget about Clay, only to have one of her sorority sisters pass along the latest piece of gossip. That he'd been spotted at a party making out with so-and-so, or hitting on a group of girls at the campus bar.

But seeing these pictures for herself hurt all over again.

"Sophia, I just thought of something else Liam said to me that was so cute!" Ava gushed from the doorway of Sophia's room.

Sophia turned to her, her eyes dark and sad.

Ava said, "Oh my gosh, what's wrong?"

Sophia gestured at the monitor and as Ava glanced over her shoulder, she said, "Looks like Clay has a new girlfriend."

"I thought he didn't want to be tied down. Wanted to play the field and all that?"

Sophia shut down her computer so she wouldn't have to look at him anymore. She turned to her sister and shrugged. "I guess he found The One."

"Ouch," said Ava.

"Yeah, super ouch," said Sophia.

And with that Ava wrapped her arms around her sister and gave her the world's biggest, longest hug.

When Ava finally took a step back, she said, "I think I have an idea. You know how they say the best way to forget an old love is to find a new one?"

"But I'm still doing a boytox, remember?"

Ava nodded knowingly. "Just trust the doctor—and get some rest. You'll need it for our early morning adventure tomorrow."

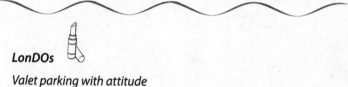

LonDOs

Valet parking with attitude

Liam Carlson's ankles

Doughnut holes for breakfast

Liam Carlson's wrists

Secret morning adventures with the ones you love

Liam Carlson's ears

LonDONT's

Ex-boyfriends' new girlfriends

Liam Carlson's name written on every surface in the house with hearts around it

7

glossed and found

Sophia wasn't sure she would ever forgive Ava for waking her up at the crack of dawn, bundling her out of bed and into the car. Even with her second coffee in her hand it seemed like a grievous offense, especially since the place Ava had gotten her up to visit was both ugly and completely locked up.

"What can possibly take place in a windowless building at eight A.M. that requires my attention?" she asked, peering at the squat cinder-block building they were parked near.

"I don't understand why there's no one here," Ava said, drumming her fingers on the steering wheel but not answering Sophia's question. "Online it clearly said they open at eight and it's eight-oh-seven now."

"Really? It feels later than that. Eight-oh-nine at least," Sophia said. "It's so nice to be seeing the underside of the morning."

"Isn't it?" Ava agreed.

Sophia laughed. "I was being sarcastic."

"And I was purposely misunderstanding," Ava told her brightly. "That way we both win."

Sophia made a sound that was like a groan and rested her forehead on the top of her pink-and-silver personalized coffee tumbler.

A battered gold Ford Bronco with a surfboard hanging out the back swung into the parking lot and creaked to a stop near them.

"Great!" Ava said brightly. "That must be them now."

Sophia took in the battered truck and looked quizzically at her sister. "When I asked if you had hired someone to fake my kidnapping and you said 'yes' I assumed you were only kidding."

"That's not what we're doing. At least not today. Come on."

It took Ava a moment to recognize the guy who got out of the Bronco. At the Pet Paradise event his hair had been combed back and he'd been wearing sunglasses. This morning his hair was windblown and he was wearing dark-framed glasses with clear lenses. He had on jeans, Vans, and a T-shirt that said I ♥ TV. But there was no question it was the guy who had rescued Popcorn from traffic. The guy who had been so mean.

Of course, Ava thought. *It would have to be him.*

She was not going to let that get to her though, she thought as she and Sophia got out of their car and followed him toward the front door of the cinder-block building. Maybe he'd just been having an off day when they met. Probably he was really nice. Even more likely, he wouldn't remember her at all.

Alternately, he'd remember perfectly and greet her by saying, "Have you come to put more animals in harm's way?"

Ava felt her cheeks get hot. "I didn't put my dog in harm's way. That was an accident."

"Careless," he murmured under his breath.

"I was—" Ava stopped. "It wasn't—" She stopped again. Out of the corner of her eye she saw Sophia perking up considerably, apparently enjoying this, which made her even more annoyed.

"You have no right to make me feel bad about that. You don't know what happened and you don't know me. I care about animals as much as you do. I'm a super-serious animal lover."

He said, "Wow, that's a nice little speech."

"It's not a speech, it's a fact."

"Really?" His eyes behind the glasses got wide and Ava noticed that she'd been wrong, they weren't brown but instead a really dark green. "Then you should sign up to volunteer here at the shelter. They're really short staffed and can use all the super-serious animal lovers they can get."

Too bad such nice eyes were wasted on such a jerk. "That's an excellent idea," she said. "I will."

"Sure," he sneered, giving her an I'll-believe-it-when-I-see-it kind of look.

She gave him a just-watch-me kind of look back. They stayed like that, staring at one another for a few moments.

If he hadn't been so annoying he might even have been cute, she thought. Or would be if you were into surfer hipster types who looked hot in glasses and filled out their I ♥ TV T-shirts like underwear models. But that wasn't her type and he was annoying so she barely noticed how well defined his chest was, or the way the muscles in his forearm rippled when he held out his hand to Sophia.

"I'm Dalton." He smiled at her as they shook.

"Sophia." She smiled back at him.

"Are you two—?" he asked, tipping his head toward Ava.

"Sisters," Sophia told him.

He nodded. "So it's like good cop–bad cop, only good sister–bad sister."

"I'm not a bad sister," Ava insisted.

"I didn't say you were," Dalton said.

"You implied it. You made it sound like I—"

He stood there impassively watching her as though she were an alien species. "Go on."

Ava's hands curled into fists as she searched for words. *"Grrr."*

"Did you just grunt?" He looked at Sophia. "Did she just grunt?"

Sophia was laughing so hard she couldn't answer.

"You are very frustrating," Ava told him.

"Me? I'm just standing here." He glanced at his watch, an old Timex on a Velcro band that had been patched with duct tape. "By the way, you've been here nearly ten minutes and you still haven't signed up to volunteer."

Ava made another noise that was not exactly a word but he ignored it, turning to Sophia instead. "Why did you come here this morning?" he asked Sophia. "Since it clearly wasn't to volunteer."

"Show me where to sign up!" Ava said. *"Show me."*

Dalton kept his attention on Sophia who was laughing openly now. "I don't know," she told him. "It was Ava's idea."

"But it was *for* you," Ava said. Then to Dalton: "We came because Sophia needs a kitten."

Sophia stopped laughing completely. "No I don't."

"Yes," Ava said definitively. "You do. Because it will cheer you up. You can do as much boytoxing as you want but I know your heart is still mending and a kitten will help."

"I'm not getting a kitten."

"We're not leaving here without one."

Dalton cleared his throat. "May I make a suggestion?"

Both London sisters turned to look at him. "What?" Ava demanded.

"I'm going to open the door of the shelter and leave you two on your own. You can come in and see the kittens we have, or not, it's up to you. The volunteer sign-up sheet is on the front desk."

He jiggled the key in the lock and was just pushing the door open when he stopped and faced them again. "You know, we did just get a new tiny kitten who could really use a loving home. I know you're not interested"—he said that to Sophia—"but maybe you know someone who would be? He's only a few weeks old, but he's partially deaf so the people who originally took him decided to just throw him away. One of our volunteers rescued him from a Dumpster—"

Sophia swallowed hard. "Maybe we should see him. In case we know someone who might want him."

Dalton held the door open. Sophia went first, then Ava. "Did you do that on purpose?" she whispered.

He gave her a deadpan look. "I don't know what you're talking about."

"Thank you," she said. She smiled. "Really."

"Don't thank me." He followed her in. "Sign up—"

"Give me the forms," she said, nearly ripping the clipboard out of his hand.

She'd barely finished filling in the sign-up form when Sophia emerged from the back of the shelter, cradling a little white puffball of a kitten no bigger than her hand in the crook of her arm. She looked up at Ava and there were tears in her eyes. "Isn't he wonderful?" she said.

Although Sophia insisted on holding him in her lap, Dalton carried a box for the kitten out to the car. "What are you going to call him?" he asked.

"I don't know yet," Sophia said, tickling him under his chin. "Maybe Winter since he's white. Or Marshmallow."

"Or Magic," Ava suggested, looking at how her sister was glowing.

Dalton shrugged. "You could always name him after me."

"It wouldn't be fair to name him Trouble," Ava said, turning on the engine. "He seems too nice for that."

"Maybe your sister should name it after you then."

"What? Smarty Pants?" Ava said.

"That's not what I had in mind." Dalton put his hand through the window and caressed the kitten on the head. "Be good."

"What did you have in mind?" Ava asked.

Dalton backed away from the car and slid his hands into the back pockets of his jeans. "You'll figure it out. Nice meeting you, Sophia."

"You too."

"Could he be any more annoying?" Ava demanded as they drove home. "What do you think he meant?"

"I don't know. Bossy. Nosy. Sneaky." Sophia looked up. "No wait, I've got it. Best little sister in the world."

Ava's chest suddenly went tight and her eyes welled up.

"Thank you," Sophia said. "For taking such good care of me."

LonDOs

Sophia's new kitten (even if she can't decide what to call it)

~~LIAM CARLSON!~~

Guys with long eyelashes

~~LIKE LIAM CARLSON!~~

Guys with nice forearms

Little sisters

Big sisters

Getting home and learning we've been invited to the Tastemakers Dance!!!!

~~LIAM CARLSON'S TEXTS~~

LonDON'Ts

Boys who wear I ♥ TV T-shirts

Surfers

People who deface other people's writing

White fur mysteriously showing up on black BCBG minidresses

Bashing into the coffee table while making up a celebratory We Are Teen Tastemakers!!! dance

Sisters who instead of leaping up to get the first aid kit, sit on the couch saying to their new kitten, "Look how silly Ava is," and laughing so hard they get the hiccups when people bash into coffee tables

Sisters who should be working but instead are distracted all afternoon by texting boys

What?

(That is not funny)

(Really? Because I kind of thought—excuse me, gotta go)

8

slapaccino

Sophia might not have been able to decide on a name for her kitten but Popcorn clearly had a few ideas of his own. Based on his behavior those included "Get away from me," "Why would someone do this to me," "The imposition," "The unwelcome visitor," and "Don't forget to take this out with the trash."

Naturally, the kitten adored him.

"There's probably a lesson here for us," Sophia observed a few days later, watching Munchkin tag along at Popcorn's heels despite Popcorn's indifference.

"The lesson would be—"

"The more you give someone the cold shoulder, the more they'll follow you around. It's about being aloof. "

"Or in Popcorn's case, awoof," Ava offered.

Sophia nodded but didn't seem to be getting the joke. "And less available. Like I bet Popcorn wouldn't text all the time."

"Oh, I get it. You think I spend too much time texting Liam."

"No," Sophia corrected. "I think you spend *all* your time texting Liam."

"Are you jealous?" Ava asked her playfully.

Sophia picked up Ava's phone and read aloud, "'LIAM CARLSON: Just had carrot ginger smoothie. Yummy. What r u doing?'" Sophia put the phone down. "Um, no."

It was Thursday, which meant pizza night, and since their call for the Tastemakers' photo shoot wasn't until three the next day, they'd stayed up late watching old episodes of *Are You Afraid of the Dark?* So when the phone rang a little before eight the next morning, even Ava was a bit groggy when she went to answer it.

She listened for a minute, then stumbled toward Sophia's door. "It's Katie. The person in charge of the Tastemaker's shoot called and they want to know if there's any chance we could be there by nine thirty. Someone had a scheduling conflict."

"Do we have to?" Sophia asked with her head still buried in her pillows.

"She says we don't but it would generate a lot of goodwill."

"How far is it?"

"Half an hour. We'd need to leave in about an hour."

Sophia took two deep breaths and hauled herself up into a sitting position. Eyes still closed she said, "Okay. I'm awake. Tell them we can do it. But I want a lot of goodwill."

When they arrived there was a little confusion about where they should go. Someone seemed to have neglected to tell the PA about the switch, and she spent ten minutes on her headset trying to verify that they really were supposed to be there then Which meant they were late by the time she whisked them over to the trailer set up in front of the snack bar.

Outside the trailer were two men sitting in deck chairs smoking cigarettes and drinking coffee. Sophia and Ava recognized both of them. The older one, wearing his signature straw cowboy hat and python boots, was Ohlfons Yaz, makeup pioneer from

Iceland. The younger one with bleach-blond hair and a tattoo of a spider on his neck was Troy Goddard, the bad boy of French hairstyling. Together they were, oh god, one of LA's top hair and makeup teams.

Ohlfons got up from his chair, put the cigarette out in the coffee cup, and tossed it sideways into the garbage can.

"You're late," Ohlfons said in an intimidating foreign accent. He snapped his fingers. "Come."

Ava and Sophia exchanged looks. So much for goodwill.

Inside the trailer he pointed each of them into a seat.

"I just wanted to say it's such an honor for us to have a chance to work with both of you," Sophia told them. "We're really big fans of your work."

Ohlfons sniffed. "How touching." He took up a position behind their chairs, crossed his arms, and glared at them in the mirror for a full minute.

"Is something—" Ava started to say.

Ohlfons made a quick karate-chop gesture through the air with one hand. "*Pfut!* Quiet. I am thinking."

They waited in silence for another full minute, his glower growing deeper and deeper. Ava tried to get Sophia's attention to see if she thought this was ridiculous too, but Sophia was watching him with rapt attention as though he was a magic trick that was about to dazzle her.

Moving behind Sophia's seat, he took her chin in his hand, turned her face left and right, and scowled. *"Bland bland bland,"* he pronounced in his complicated accent. He sighed and gave a dramatic shrug. *"Fine.* We'll do what we can."

Ava was outraged. She sat forward in her chair and was about to say something when Sophia caught her eye in the mirror and shook her head once, definitively. Ava scowled at her but Sophia was immobile.

He repeated the head turning with Ava, muttering to himself

about how an artist deserved better material, then he strapped on a leather holster filled with makeup brushes and set to work. "So you think you can do my job?" he asked as he mixed lip pigments together on a little palette.

"Not at all," Ava assured him. "We just—"

"Quiet. I do your mouth now."

Hair went a little more smoothly if only because Troy's French accent made his English entirely unintelligible, and their "New Wave nautical" outfits—MM had done the styling for the shoot and delivered on his promise that he'd put them in something good—were supercute.

But they couldn't escape the latent undercurrent of hostility that seemed to follow them everywhere. Even the production assistants lowered their voices and turned toward one another furtively as they walked by.

As they walked from the trailers toward the tent that held the staging area for the shoot Sophia said, "Are you having flashbacks—"

"To the first day of high school?" Ava nodded. "Yeah."

They were being shown from the trailers to the staging area for the photo shoot when they ran into MM. "Here are my princesses!" he said, giving them each a kiss. "Sorry I couldn't come find you earlier, we had a problem with the monkeys."

"Monkeys?" Ava and Sophia asked in unison, but with very different levels of enthusiasm.

"Not for you—sorry Little London—they're for someone else. Don't ask me why—" He stopped, stood back with a hand on one hip, and looked from one sister to the other. "Okay, what happened? Tell Uncle MM what is going on."

"Nothing," Sophia said, shooting Ava a warning glance. "Everyone is just—tense."

"Which means everyone has been a little snobby to you, right?"

MM translated. "Take that as a compliment. It means they're jealous. Just remind yourself of that whenever they do it."

Ava made a face. "Somehow that never makes me feel any better."

MM adjusted the bow at the hem of Ava's sweater and patted her on the cheek. "They just don't know what to make of you, princess. To them, you're hothouse flowers."

"Ohlfons said we were *bland, bland, bland,*" Sophia told him, trying to imitate his accent. Doing fake accents was one of the skills Sophia wished she had but didn't, and her imitations usually fell completely flat, but miraculously not today.

MM gave a bark of laughter. "Well, he should know. His real name is John White and he's from Topeka, Kansas. Doesn't get much blander than that."

Ava gaped at him. "That's not true."

"I swear on my new Varvatos work boots," MM said, bending down to touch them. "They're lickable, right?"

"Completely," Ava agreed.

MM looked them over from head to toe, made two minor adjustments, and left them at the mouth of the tent. "Will you two be okay? I've got to go organize the 'Mumbai militia' look for the next model but I'll come check on you as soon as I can."

"We'll be fine," Sophia assured him.

"Thanks to you," Ava confirmed.

They ducked through the white plastic flaps of the tent into a wide-open space. Pallets of equipment in black boxes were lined up along the sides of the tent and a bank of tables with computers ran down the center. Thick cables in all colors snaked across the floor of the tent like a tropical root system. The front of the tent had no wall and opened instead to a panorama of Los Angeles, sweeping from Hollywood all the way to the ocean.

Although it was daylight there were three massive lights

directed at the open space, where a rapper named Trapper Keeper was finishing his shoot. Careful to avoid tripping on any of the cords, Ava and Sophia found two seats against the far wall of the tent and sat down to watch.

Trapper Keeper was wearing a one-piece suit of long underwear with a tuxedo printed on the front and he was being pelted with rose petals being blown in his direction by a wind machine as a woman with bright blue hair moved around him getting pictures.

The art director, a tall man in a fedora with a scarf looped around his neck, paced up and down behind the bank of computer monitors, a plaid-shirted assistant following at his heels. The art director had a plastic bottle of Tums in one hand that made a clicking noise like maracas when he walked. He stopped abruptly, flipped the Tums open and tilted it directly into his mouth, chewed, grimaced, and called to the photographer. "That last series were winners. I think we've got it. We can strike this set." He turned to his assistant. "Get Ohlfons and Troy in for touch-ups."

Ava and Sophia had been on photo shoots before, but this was by far the most elaborate, and it was fascinating to watch as a crew now swarmed over the set and made it disappear like ants at a birthday picnic. Ohlfons and Troy came in and started talking to the photographer with the blue hair, taking surreptitious glances in Ava and Sophia's direction.

"They're just jealous," Ava said to herself. She shook her head. "No, still not making me feel better." She turned to Sophia. "I'll do the dishes for a week if you go up to Ohlfons and say 'Hi John. Been to Topeka recently?'"

"You do the dishes anyway because you can't stand to see them in the sink," Sophia reminded her. "Look at that, I think we get to pose with telescopes."

Ava slumped in her chair. "We could have had monkeys."

"Telescopes are a lot easier to work with," Sophia pointed out.

"But I love animals." Brightening up, Ava said, "Liam is an animal lover too. That's the two hundred and eleventh thing we have in common."

Sophia shot her a worried glance. "Promise me that you will never ever tell another person that. Especially him."

Ava got to work making sure the hem on her skirt sat exactly straight across her thighs. "Sure. Okay."

"You already told him."

"We're up to number three hundred and six."

"What's that? Breathing? Chairs?"

"Duh, no," Ava huffed, elbowing Sophia. "Movies with talking animals."

Sophia was just lowering her head into her hands when their attention was diverted to a group of people who swept through the middle of the shooting area and into the tent.

Leading them was a tiny girl in massive high heels with her blond hair in old-fashioned curlers. She held a lit cigarette in one hand and a Slurpee in the other. She wore tight leather pants, four-inch black studded pumps, and a white tank top with nothing under it sheer enough to allow you to read her famous tattoos, including the one that said WHITNEY ♥ LIAM FOREVER.

The art director rushed up to her, his scarf and his assistant following close behind. "Whitney, darling!" he cooed, giving her a kiss on each cheek. "My god, don't you look delicious."

Whitney was surrounded by her own small posse which appeared to be made up of one terrified-looking assistant and four reporters. She gestured to them now, telling the art director, "I was just saying, I don't think anything is sexier than curlers and a cigarette. I mean, it just screams debauch, trailer parks, broken homes, making out at the Laundromat, the whole nine. Sexy sexy sexy."

The art director and indigo-haired photographer who had joined them both bobbed their heads in enthusiastic agreement.

Sophia leaned toward Ava. "Did she really just say that curlers and a cigarette are sexy?"

"Yes," Ava confirmed. "And housing projects."

"I wonder how many things she and Liam—"

"Stop right there," Ava warned her.

"What's important is the real," Whitney went on, making a fist with her tiny hand. "Authentic. That's what Tastemaking is about. Risk taking. Going beyond, above, below. Not being afraid to break the norms, ask hard questions, say unpopular things. Am I right?"

The art director gripped the container of Tums to his heart. "As always, darling. Trenchant. Beautiful."

Whitney nodded, her eyes half closed like she was in a trance absorbing the praise. Then they snapped open and she looked around. "What's going on here? Where are my monkeys? Why isn't this ready for me?"

The art director gave her a brittle, nervous smile. "But darling, you said you wanted to move your shoot to the afternoon."

"Whittle Whitney changed her mind," Whitney told him in a baby voice. "Don't tell whittle Whitney you don wan her." She snapped back to her regular voice. "Because I can leave and not come back."

The art director chewed the Tums he'd just poured into his mouth and grimaced. "No darling, of course we do, it's just that we have the London sisters ready to shoot next. I know, why don't you—"

Whitney pivoted on her heel and stared at Ava and Sophia. "This is what I have to fight against? The dummying down of fashion discourse? It's appalling that anyone like those two"— extending an arm with a tattoo of both a teddy bear and a bald eagle, she pointed at them—"should be considered Tastemakers. What kind of taste do they have? I'll tell you: average."

Whitney turned back to address her crowd at large. "As you

all know, *I've* done something with my life." She pounded herself on her chest twice with her little fist. "I've been nominated for awards. I've made people weep. If you want a role model, pick someone who has lived. Who has loved. Who knows that makeup isn't what you put on your face to look pretty, it's what you do when you dare enough to piss someone off. That's why I'm an 'it' girl." She zeroed in on the art director. "I'm going to my trailer. I'll be ready in forty-five minutes. I hope you are." Switching to her baby voice she pursed her lips and said, "Whittle Whitney hates to wait."

She was nearly at the entrance to the tent when she realized the only person following her was her assistant. She turned around. "Well?"

One of the journalists said, "We're just going to stay and get the London sisters' reactions."

Whitney shrugged. "They are the precious minutes of your life, not mine. Waste them how you want," she said, and left.

The reporters turned toward the London sisters for a response. Ava and Sophia's shock that Whitney was the one getting the monkeys, followed by their shock that she even knew who they were, had partially distracted them from what was going on. But they quickly became aware that the entire atmosphere on the set had shifted, becoming almost eerily silent yet with a hot pumping undercurrent of expectation, like an audience at a prizefight waiting for the first round to begin.

Sophia felt Ava stiffen next to her, heard her breathing quicken, and saw the fixed, almost glassy look in her eye as panic gripped her.

"It will be okay," Sophia whispered, gripping her sister's hand. "Don't worry."

Ava nodded, once, but she still had the haunted look in her eyes and Sophia knew why.

When Sophia's sorority sisters had found out about her videos they'd been not just supportive but thrilled for her. They'd spread the word and blogged and tweeted their favorite moments. But when people at Ava's school found out, they had been merciless. It had started with a few stupid comments, people walking behind her and mimicking her videos, or asking questions like "Ava, what if my eye shadow doesn't match my shoes?" But it had escalated from there to constant taunts and threats and then to violence. For the first time in her life, Ava's resilience seemed to falter, and she refused to leave her room, sitting in a corner in the dark.

All she'd wanted to do was disappear, be invisible. To make the jeers and the insults stop by not standing out at all.

Fortunately she was able to transfer to a new school where her new classmates were a lot more accepting. But the bad memories couldn't be erased, and they all came flooding back to her now, the same desire to hide, the same sense of her complete unworthiness. Who was she to be a Tastemaker, to be a Webstar? They were right, she was a fraud, she didn't deserve this, she was nothing, no one—

Sophia linked her fingers through Ava's and stood, making Ava stand with her. She put on a lovely smile and, looking at the reporter who had asked the question, said, "Whitney is right. My sister and I aren't famous actresses or models. We're just normal girls. Whitney said our taste was average. Bland is what one of the makeup artists here today called us." Ava saw Ohlfons stiffen. "They're both right. Which is why our being here is both a privilege and important—we're not here as ourselves. We're here representing regular girls everywhere. The fact that we can be here shows that anyone can be a Tastemaker."

One of the reporters rolled her eyes. "Sure but do you really think that puts you in the same category as someone like Miss Frost?"

Sophia said, "Absolutely not. I agree with Whitney Frost that we are in a totally different class than she is."

That surprised the reporter. "You do?"

Sophia nodded majestically, like a princess interacting with a commoner. "Yes. We have some and she doesn't."

The art director gave a whoop of laughter and the Tums fell out of his hand, then he checked himself, like he couldn't believe he'd done it. But by then everyone else had started laughing too.

Only Ava, whose fingers clasped with Sophia's was the one thing keeping Sophia's hand from trembling uncontrollably, knew how much the display of poise had cost her sister. But when the photographer and art director and crew and even Ohlfons started clapping, it was clear that whatever the cost, it was worth it. The London sisters had a whole new group of fans.

In the car going home Sophia and Ava couldn't stop smiling.

In her trailer at the shoot, Whitney Frost was also smiling. She'd been smiling since, standing outside the tent, she'd heard Sophia's speech and the applause that followed it. It was a lovely, innocent smile.

Anyone who knew her knew it always meant trouble.

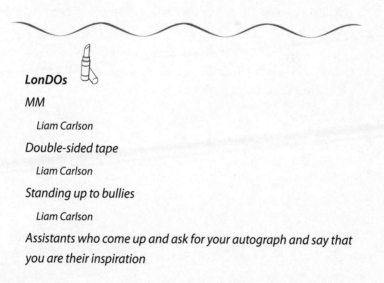

LonDOs

MM

   Liam Carlson

Double-sided tape

   Liam Carlson

Standing up to bullies

   Liam Carlson

Assistants who come up and ask for your autograph and say that you are their inspiration

Liam Carlson

Photographers who pull you aside after your shoot to say it was a pleasure working with you and she hopes you go far

Liam Carlson

Watching Pumpkin/Fairylights/Sapphire the kitten who shall not be named playing with Popcorn

Liam Carlson

Party at Liam's best friend's house!!!!!!!!!!!!

LonDON'Ts

Fake accents (except on special occasions)

Fake baby voices (no exceptions)

Curlers

Cigarettes

Bullies

"It" girls

Writing really small and thinking other people won't notice

Having to go naked to a party because your sister put dibs on every item in the closet

(You're exaggerating. I left you the bridesmaid dress you wore to cousin Meredith's wedding and all the workout clothes)

(That dress has a hoop skirt)

(What's your point?)

9

hairstyles of the rich and famous

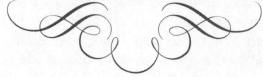

"You can stop texting now, we're here," Sophia told Ava as she rolled the car to a stop.

"I just want to let him know we're here."

"Won't he be able to see that for himself?"

"He will but—oh my god." That last part popped out of Ava's mouth when she finally looked up from her phone and saw the house they were in front of. She was still agape when the valet opened her door and offered her his hand to step out.

"I'm pretty sure I've stayed at hotels that are smaller than this house," she said, coming around the car to join Sophia and Lily.

"It's an exact replica of some chateau in France. Sharky Ralston had it built for his third wife."

"Sharky?" Sophia asked.

"That's his nickname. He's an entertainment lawyer. Real name is Ronald, father of Hunter, who isn't much of anything except a playboy."

"And Liam's best friend," Ava chimed in loyally.

"How many wives has, um, Sharky had?" Sophia wanted to know.

Lily grimaced. "I can't remember what number the current Mrs. Ralston is. But I do know she's renowned for her skill at doing seating arrangements."

Sophia and Ava exchanged their is-this-really-happening look and followed Lily up the marble stairs.

They found themselves in a huge marble hall with pointed arches like in an old European church. The ornate architecture continued inside the home. In front of them was a massive room with a high wooden ceiling, a stone floor, and a marble fireplace big enough to hold a whole other party in. One wall was made up of tall windows that opened out onto a stone patio beyond which they could see formal gardens.

"I guess that's why they call them French windows," Sophia said, nodding at the view.

Lily sighed contentedly. "This is going to be fun. Let's play my favorite game."

"Whose Boobs Are Those?" Ava asked.

"No that's my second favorite. My first favorite is FTB. Find the Bar."

They stepped down into the main room, following the flow of the crowd toward a bar that had been set up along one side. Tuxedoed bartenders stood behind ice-beaded silver buckets holding champagne and white wine. Yellow orchids with red centers twisted out of crystal vases, looking both exotic and regal against the dark wood paneling of the hall. When Ava asked for a ginger ale the bartender poured it into a cut-crystal glass that refracted the light in rainbows. When she clinked glasses with Sophia's and Lily's crystal champagne flutes, the sound it made was musical.

"Remember last week when we were looking at *Vogue* and saw that orange plastic minidress and wondered who could afford to spend forty-eight hundred dollars on something like that?" Sophia asked. She tilted her head to the left. "Now we know."

Lily scoffed. "That's nothing compared to what she spent for her shoulder implants. Those are Dr. Zeiss's. He's turned an entire mountain town in the Swiss Alps into a private clinic. Since everyone there has had plastic surgery, it's like they all share a secret so they can go out, dine in restaurants, and have spa treatments while they recover rather than hiding until their bruises fade. It's where I want to spend my honeymoon."

"The red Valentino dress you were swooning over in *InStyle* last week is behind you," Ava told Sophia. She glanced around from the people and the dresses up to the sumptuous coffered ceiling. Her eyes were wide with wonder. "This is—it's—" Ava groped for the right word. "Magical."

"I agree," a voice said next to her and she turned and saw Liam. He put his hands on her shoulders and smiled down at her. "Beautiful is exactly the right word."

"I was talking about the house," Ava said with a laugh.

"I wasn't." He shifted his megawatt smile to Sophia and Lily, greeting them both, then moved it back to Ava. "There are a million people I want to introduce you to," he said, and putting his arm around her shoulder led her away.

Sophia listened to Lily as she explained the difference between Dr. Young's and Dr. Singh's chin implants, and watched Liam introduce Ava to a group of girls. He'd been nothing but charming and appropriate with Ava, and yet Sophia still felt apprehension about him. Or about her with him.

"I know that you really really like Liam," she'd told her.

"Add about sixteen reallys to that and you might be getting close."

"Okay, but don't you think you should move a little slower? Just to make sure he's not trouble? There are a lot of rumors—"

"Yeah, *rumors*. I'm going to be fine. Trust me."

"I just don't want you to get hurt."

"You can stop worrying about me. I'll be fine."

She will be, Sophia told herself. Ava was always fine. The memory of a family trip to Italy when she was twelve and Ava was eight came flooding back to her. It was warm back at home in Georgia, but it was winter in Rome. A sunny but crisp day, and they had decided to go sightseeing. Her father had the guidebook and was in charge of picking where they went. Her mother, who had an uncanny sense of direction, was in charge of getting them there. And Sophia was in charge of Ava.

They'd just come out of a café where they'd had lunch and Sophia was admiring a fountain. Women were carved from marble, with water spilling out of urns they were holding. She turned to point it out to Ava—

—and couldn't find her. Anywhere. She'd vanished.

They searched the piazza and asked the people in the shops that lined the piazza if they'd seen anyone. They checked down side streets. The only clue they'd managed to find was one of her pink knit gloves, lying in the street near the curb on the far side of the square.

Sophia could still remember the feeling of the wool as she crushed the glove in her hands. What if Ava had been hit by a car? What if she'd been kidnapped? It was her fault, she was the one who was supposed to be watching Ava, being the responsible big sister. She was the one who was supposed to stay with her. If she'd done her job she would be holding her hand, not just one soiled glove.

They'd spent the rest of the day in a frenzy, talking with huge arm gestures to the police, asking the shopkeepers again if they'd seen a little girl, making copies of Ava's passport photo to hand out, going to the embassy. Finally, exhausted, they'd headed back to the hotel.

And there was Ava, sitting in one of the chairs in the lobby drinking tea with the concierge. She'd found her way there all by herself and was surprised it had taken the rest of them so long. "Where were you guys? I've had like a million glasses of tea." She'd leaned over to confide in Sophia, "That lady wouldn't let me leave."

Sophia remembered being so relieved the only thing she'd been able to say was, "Here's your glove."

Ava had taken it, laughing happily. "Thanks! I was wondering where I lost it."

And that was Ava—somehow, she was always okay, always got where she was going, always arrived happy and on top. Nothing seemed to bother her or make her anxious, as though she just believed everything would work out. And somehow it did. Right down to her glove. It was one of the marvels of her sister.

"Hey, come here often?"

Sophia looked over at the guy who had spoken. Over and up, actually, because he was at least a foot taller than she was, even in heels. He raised his eyebrows flirtatiously at her as he took a sip of his drink. He was wearing a gray-on-black striped shirt, black jeans, and a massive Rolex. Her mind flashed to MM saying, "The bigger the watch, the bigger the *watch out!* factor."

"It was a joke?" the guy with the Rolex went on, smiling with slightly less confidence as she just stared at him. "Because this is a party so obviously . . ." His voice trailed off.

"Pardon?" Sophia said, giving the word a slightly foreign inflection. "I am sorry, my einklish he is not so grand. Good-bye, yes?" She started to move away but he stopped her with a hand on her arm.

"That's okay. I like foreigners. Where are you from?"

"Me, I am from—" Where was a place he never would have been from and wouldn't want to talk about? "Iceland."

"No way. I was in Reykjavík last year for a deal but I toured around a lot. Where do you live?"

"I'm sorry I still am not in understanding." She gave him an apologetic smile. "But I have idea. You hold here." She took his hand from her arm and patted it. "I go and get my friend to make the translation for talking. Yes?" She backed away, still smiling, and then, when it was clear he wasn't following, turned and walked down the first corridor she saw.

A steady stream of caterers passed her in both directions and she followed them upstairs, more out of curiosity than anything. But she must have taken a wrong turn because soon she was out of caterers and in a hallway with a different feeling from the rest of the house.

It was wide like the hallway below and paneled with dark wood but instead of the panels being ornately carved, they were smooth and modern. And instead of the tapestries from the ground floor, the walls here were hung with photographs. Not family photos but professional photographs by artists. She recognized at least three from different museums she'd visited, but it was an unfamiliar one that caught her attention.

In it a man in a business suit, with the same confidence as the guy who had been talking to her downstairs, stood on a busy street corner holding a hand-lettered cardboard sign that said I'M DESPERATE.

She hadn't heard anyone come down the hall but a guy's voice next to her said, "It's not subtle, but it is effective."

Nodding, she turned to see who had spoken and her breath caught in her throat. "I know you," she said, feeling herself blushing. "You're the—"

"Valet. From the other day. Only, I'm afraid I tricked you. I'm not really a valet. I just wanted to talk to you." He held out his hand. "I'm Hunter."

"And I'm—"

"Sophia London," he said. He put up his hands. "I admit it, I'm guilty of Googling. When Liam started talking about Ava, I looked you two up. Talking nonstop, I might add."

Sophia blushed with pleasure, although she wasn't sure whether it was because he'd Googled her or that Liam was apparently as crazy about Ava as she was about him. "My sister seems to have the same affliction. It's impossible to have a conversation with her—"

"—because they're always texting," Hunter finished.

Sophia didn't know what to say. The only person who had ever been able to do that with her was Ava. "Exactly."

"Of course," he said with a sigh, "now that I've met the London sisters I can't blame him."

Sophia blushed a little more.

"Congratulations on the Viewer's Choice Award," he went on. "Impressive. You two have achieved a lot."

After the way everyone had acted at the photo shoot—at the beginning anyway—it was really nice to have someone say that. "Thank you," Sophia said. Then realizing where they were, she added, "Wait a second, this is your house."

Hunter shrugged modestly. "Well, my dad's. Although this collection"— he gestured around to the photos—"was really more my mother's thing."

"It's amazing."

"Do you like photography?"

"I—I don't know much about it," Sophia said.

Hunter regarded her with a faintly amused expression. "Ah. I'm no expert but I'd be happy to walk you through what we have if it wouldn't bore you."

"Not at all," Sophia breathed. "I'd love it."

They walked down the corridor with him throwing out names as though they were close personal friends, not some of the top artists in the world. The pictures weren't pretty or artsy, they weren't anything that you would see on a poster. They showed people in deliberately awkward positions or landscapes that were not picturesque but somehow still beautiful. Hunter had started off talking a little about each one but he gradually got quieter and as they neared the end they were looking at them in a companionable silence.

He broke it saying, "Mom really liked to support female photographers. She'd even let them stay here and use the darkroom."

"You have a darkroom?"

"We do." He narrowed his eyes. "You didn't answer before when I asked if you liked photography."

Sophia took a deep breath. *What are you afraid of?* a voice in her head asked. And as though to answer she faced Hunter and said, "I love photography. I've always wanted to try it but it seems so hard." It was the first time she'd admitted that to anyone. "I mean there are apps and everything," she said, rushing ahead, "and it's not hard to take a *good* photograph, but to take an exceptional one, one that says something—" She stopped, shaking her head and staring at the photo in front of her.

It showed a woman in profile being cradled in the crook of a man's arm. The arm was muscular and somehow you knew he was younger and she was older, and that whatever had passed between them stood for love but was going to end in tragedy, that they had read fortune cookies to each other and stolen kisses in doorways but she was going to go back to a two-story house with a three-car garage and a six-figure-income husband and he was going to go back to bartending.

Or something, Sophia's mind added.

"The image is so simple but what it makes you see and think is so complicated," she said, struggling to explain. "It's like—"

"—each picture is a poem," Hunter said.

Sophia faced him. "Exactly. That's exactly what I was thinking."

He smiled. "My mother said that. I can't take the credit."

"She sounds like a very interesting woman."

"She was. She died when I was fourteen." Hunter pulled a buzzing phone from his pocket. "That's the caterers. They need me to open the wine cellar. I'm afraid I have to go. Let me walk you back down to the party."

"Thank you. I was afraid to admit it, but I was a bit worried about getting lost."

"The house isn't that big," he told her. "We've never lost anyone for more than three days."

They were laughing when he left her back in the main room. "It's been really great talking to you, Sophia."

"You too. I hope—"

He held up his phone which was buzzing again. "I've got to run."

"Right," she said but she was talking to herself. So this was the second guy she'd had a nice time talking to in a week who had not asked for her number. Was this some kind of boytox side effect? Did she need to change her hair?

She felt herself being seized from behind and pulled down into an awkward lollipop-and-cigarette-scented hug. "You. Are. Adorable," a little-girl voice said in her ear and then the arms released her and she was facing Whitney Frost. Whitney was wearing red five-inch heels, gray fur skinny jeans with a matching top, and holding an enormous spiral lollipop.

"I'm— What?" Sophia really hoped she'd remembered to put antibacterial gel in her evening purse.

"Seriously," Whitney said, sticking out her tongue and taking a long, sensual lick of her lollipop. "That was so great at the photo shoot. Amazing PR. You and your sister both. Cute as a button."

Sophia was still struggling to understand. "I thought you were mad that we were chosen. I thought—"

Tipping her head back Whitney laughed a little-girl laugh. "You thought that was real? Adorable again! Why would I be mad? Especially now that we're practically related."

Whitney pointed with her lollipop to the side of the room where Liam was standing with his arm around Ava.

Sophia was at a loss, which seemed to amuse Whitney even more. She wrapped her hand around Sophia's arm and said, "Sweetheart, nothing in Hollywood is real. The whole thing was just for show, for the magazines. The whole thing at the photo shoot and the whole thing with me and Liam. Just for show. You'll see."

Then she leaned in conspiratorially. "And there's nothing the press loves more than a good old-fashioned love triangle. Think of it—hard-partying heartthrob jilts his glamorous cover-girl girlfriend for the ultimate girl next door. Who wouldn't run with that story? It's brilliant!"

"Ava and I aren't looking to be tabloid stars. We're trying to build a serious business—"

She was interrupted by Whitney's high-pitched laugh. "You are just too cute—no wonder Liam likes your sister. You're both adorable!"

Before she could say anything more Whitney had disappeared, the only sign of her the lollipop she held above her head as she navigated through the crowd, like some kind of candy-coated shark fin.

When Sophia turned around she was stopped by the arrival of the tall guy with the Rolex.

"*Komdu sæll!*" he said to Sophia, beaming with pride. "Did I pronounce it right?"

Sophia stared at him for a moment then said, "No," and ducked into the crowd. She could still hear him calling, "But I

looked it up on Google," as she moved through the party in pursuit of Ava.

LonDOs

Ginger ale in real crystal glasses

Mini hot dogs wrapped in puff pastry

Korres lip butter glaze

Being invited to be Liam Carlson's date to the preview party for his new movie!!!

Stopping for burgers and apple pie at the Apple Pan on the way home from the party

New heels from JustFab.com

Summer Glow cell phone case from Cellairis

Getting a private tour of the Ralston photography collection from Hunter Ralston

LonDON'Ts

Whitney Frost touching you

Whitney Frost saying "You'll see"

Leaving home without antibacterial gel

Pretending to be from Iceland

Having someone pursue you even after inventing the most ridiculous accent

Sisters who wait until they are getting ready for bed to mention that they had "a nice time" and "may have flirted a little" with Hunter Ralston who is "not ugly"

Someone (who continues to remain nameless) having shredded all the toilet paper in both bathrooms

10

picture perfect

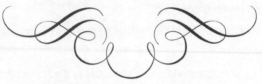

Sophia was in the middle of a dream when something heavy landed on her rib cage and jabbed her with a dozen razor blades.

Sophia opened her eyes to find Popcorn crouched on her chest with the kitten sitting on his head. From beneath the bed she heard a moaning noise and looking down she saw Ava curled in a ball crying with laughter.

"Oh my god, Sophia, you should have seen it. I was dangling Popcorn over you and out of nowhere Superkitty comes and leaps on his head. I dropped Popcorn and he fell but the kitty stayed on like a pro surfer and—"

"I know the rest," Sophia said, pulling down the covers to check for visible bruising.

"It was hilarious." Ava wiped tears from her eyes.

"I'm so glad I could amuse you this morning. Did you wake me up because you're now in the habit of making me get up at ridiculously early hours or—"

Ava was still chuckling. "Yes, I just woke you up because I missed you. Oh by the way, *góðan dag*. That's good morning in Icelandic."

Sophia set her jaw and narrowed her eyes. "You'd better be kidding."

"Your company is great but not that great," Ava assured her. "I woke you up because a messenger delivered this and I wanted to see what it was before I went to the shelter to volunteer."

Ava set a large brown box, about a foot square, on Sophia's lap.

"Whoa," Sophia said, sitting up. Ava handed her a pair of scissors from her desk and Sophia slit the tape on the package and opened the flaps. Inside there was a book and another smaller box. She lifted the book out first and felt her face flush with pleasure.

"Greatest Female Photographers," Ava read from the cover.

Sophia reached for the box and flipped the lid up. She exhaled sharply, falling back against her pillows. Inside was an old Nikon camera, six rolls of film, and a note. The paper was creamy with a brown border—subtle, sophisticated, and masculine.

"This was my mom's. She took some of her favorite pictures on it and she'd be happy to think it was being used. Let me know when you need the film developed. Yours, Hunter."

Ava stared at her. "What did you do to this guy?" she asked.

"Nothing," Sophia breathed. "I thought he wasn't interested."

"Yeah, that's the vibe I get too. Totally not thinking about you at all. Why did he send you a camera?"

"I told him I was interested in photography."

Ava stared at her. "You'll barely admit that to me."

"I don't know, it just came out."

Ava's eyebrows climbed high up into her hair.

"You look nice," Sophia said, trying to change the subject.

"You know what this means," Ava said, not falling for it. "It's so perfect. You and Hunter and Liam and I can double-date. Hunter has a boat he keeps at the marina and we can sail over to Catalina and—"

"I'm not going out with Hunter. I'm boytoxing."

"Are you going to keep the camera?"

Sophia thought about it. "Yes. I am."

"Good." Ava smiled. Paused. "Do I really look okay? I was going for something earnest and volunteer-y but still cute in case Liam was there too."

Sophia surveyed Ava's denim short shorts, knee socks, Tretorn sneakers, and pink T-shirt with the rainbow on it. "You nailed it."

"Are you sure? Because now that you're up if you want I could show you two or three other possibilities and—"

Sophia pantomimed taking a nail from between her lips and hitting it on the head with a hammer.

Ava got a pained expression. "You know how you're not that good at accents? You might be worse at mime."

"And you are an expert mime?" Sophia queried.

"I am actually. Come on, Popcorn," Ava said, then mimed pulling him and herself out the door by a rope.

"If the makeup thing doesn't work out it's nice to know you have a fallback," Sophia called after her.

"Ha ha, very—"

"Mimes are silent." Sophia smiled to herself as she listened to Ava growling under her breath. A few minutes later the front door closed and the smile moved to the book and the camera.

Hunter had written his number on the bottom of the note and impulsively Sophia dialed it now. He answered on the second ring. "I see you got my package."

"I don't know what to say."

"Say you're going to spend the rest of the day taking pictures. A camera is no good unless it's used."

"What if the pictures are bad?"

"That's why film is so perfect because you don't know. It means no second-guessing yourself or making yourself nuts about some small thing. You take the picture and move on. And if none of them are good, we'll destroy the film and start over."

"You make it sound so easy."

"It is easy," he said. "Do you know what you want to take pictures of?"

"I have an idea I'm just not sure how to—" But even as she said that, the answer came to her. It had been in front of her the entire time.

"Maybe we should meet for lunch and talk it over. I could drive—"

Not even realizing she was interrupting him she said, "I figured it out. Thank you so much, Hunter. Bye!"

She hung up and dialed Lily. Lily would be the perfect person to help her with this.

The first clue should have been the coveralls. Even before she met with Estelle Ramirez, the shelter director, Ava was given a set of shapeless one-size-fits-none blue coveralls and told to put them on. So much for the cute outfit, she thought. But what they meant didn't really sink in for a little while.

Ava hadn't really known what to expect. She'd sort of pictured sitting at the front desk and helping people find puppies or rabbits or kittens, bringing families together, that kind of thing.

"No allergies? No phobias? No stints in a mental ward?" Estelle asked straight off. Estelle was Ava's height but gave the impression of being somehow more massive. She had dark hair streaked with gray and cut short and a square face and build. Dressed in all khaki, she seemed more like a general than an animal shelter director.

"I used to be a prison warden," she explained as they walked to her office. "That's what gave me my deep love for animals." She laughed at her own joke, and Ava joined in.

Her office consisted of a side table and a folding chair set up at one end of the custodial closet. "I'd ask you to sit down, but then I'd have to stand," she said, laughing again. "We're a bit short of space. Short of space, short of help, short of money. Short of everything except animals. That's why it's a godsend you've come to volunteer like this."

"I'm glad to help," Ava told her. "Anything I can do."

Estelle peered up at her with a funny little smile. "I'll keep that in mind."

Now Ava was nodding in answer to her questions. "That's right. No allergies, phobias or, um, visits to mental wards."

"And no injuries? Limitations on motion?"

"You mean like can I lift and carry a dog? Or get on my hands and knees to play with a rabbit?"

Estelle blinked. "Sure. Something like that."

"Yes." Ava nodded vigorously. "Absolutely."

When she'd led Ava to a large room lined on either side with cages that held cats, Ava had pictured herself spending the afternoon frolicking with them, making sure they got attention and positive interactions.

"Boys and girls, meet Ava. Ava, meet the residents of the Beverly Wilshire," Estelle said, naming one of Los Angeles' fanciest hotels.

Several of the cats meowed. "Beverly Wilshire?" Ava asked.

"We like to give our guests a feeling of class," Estelle explained. She nodded to a locker in the corner. "You'll find what you need in there. You can either take them out and put them in the crib"— she pointed to a cage with no top that sat in the corner—"while you do it, or you can work around them."

"I'm sorry, I'm not sure I understand. What am I doing exactly?"

"Cleaning the cages. Not the most glamorous job but the most necessary. They can't do it themselves. It'll remind you of how lucky you are to have thumbs."

Ava wasn't sure how cleaning the cages made her appreciate her thumbs, especially once she'd been at it for over an hour. They were filthy beneath the layer of kitty litter and the bars looked like they hadn't been touched in years. There were some hard to reach corners and no brushes small enough. Still, she thought she was making good progress and getting the hang of it.

Until Dalton arrived.

He was in jeans again, and a T-shirt and glasses again, but today his T-shirt said CHEWBACCA IS MY HOMEBOY. Could he be any more of a geek?

He didn't say hi or how are you or anything a normal person would say, just came in and stood watching her.

"Why are you doing this?" he asked finally.

"I told you. I care about animals. I want to make a contribution to society, do my part to—"

He rolled his eyes. "I asked why you were doing this, not for a public service announcement."

"Fine. If you don't like my reasons, why are you doing it?"

"That's none of your business."

"You just asked me," she pointed out.

"You're right, I shouldn't have. I'm not the kind of guy you want to have anything to do with. And you are certainly not the kind of girl I want to have anything to do with."

"Why, because I'm not in treatment for rage issues?"

"Good one." He glanced around him then, as though noticing the room for the first time. "How long have you been here making your *contribution*?"

"Two hours," she told him brightly. She wasn't going to let him think for a second she wasn't enjoying it.

"And you've done how many cages?"

"Four. So I'll be done with the whole room by the end of my shift."

He peered into the cages, then back at her.

"What? Did I do something wrong? Is there a wrong way to clean?"

"Yes and no." He frowned. "You know there are three other rooms like this, right? And that you're supposed to do all of them?"

Ava rocked back on her heels. "What? No. That's not possible. No one said anything about anyplace except the Beverly Wilshire."

"There's the Hollywood Roosevelt, the Chateau Marmont, and Bonaventure." He ticked off the names of some of LA's other swanky hotels. "It's only supposed to take you an hour to do each room."

"How is that possible?"

"For starters, most people don't polish the cages. Especially not the outsides. And—" He glanced inside and did a double take. "Did you rake the kitty litter?"

"I wanted it to look inviting."

He stared at her and shook his head some more.

"Why are you looking at me that way? What's wrong with me?"

"Nothing," he said. His tone was unexpected and unreadable. "Nothing is wrong with you." He headed for the door, talking to her over his shoulder. "I'll take the other three wings if you finish here."

"I can't ask you to do that."

"You're not asking, I'm just doing it. Next time you'll know." He walked out the door leaving her "thanks" hanging in the air after him.

Not polishing every bar cut down on the cleaning time, and Ava had to admit the cats seemed just as happy with the unraked litter as the raked. She finished with ten minutes to spare and went to see if Dalton needed any help. The other three wings all looked pristine, but there was no sign of him. Walking by Estelle's office Ava asked if she had seen him and was told he'd left half an hour earlier.

Of course he had, Ava thought. Why would she have expected him to say good-bye?

Sophia wasn't home when Ava got there so she sat on the sofa to text Liam and wait for—

She woke up an hour later with her phone poking into the small of her back, sandwiched between Popcorn and the kitten, at the sound of Sophia's key in the door.

"Hey, how was your day?" Sophia asked as she bounced into the house. "Mine was terrific."

"That's great," Ava said, meaning it but also a little jealous. "What did you do?" Ava started thumbing through her messages.

"Lily and I were out all day taking pictures."

Ava stopped looking at her messages. "You and Lily?" she repeated, now a little more jealous.

"Yeah. It was amazing. I think we got some great shots." She grinned and crossed her fingers. "At least I hope so."

"What did you take pictures of?"

Sophia grinned even more. "You'll have to wait and see!"

"But Lily knows."

"Of course. She was there." Sophia disappeared to hang up the jacket she'd been wearing and came back in wearing a cardigan. "I was thinking we could order takeout. Unless you want to cook?"

Ava looked up from her phone. "Liam says we should order from Coffee Shop."

"Really? What does Liam say we should order?"

Ava started typing and Sophia reached out and took the phone from her hands. "I was kidding."

"Yeah, I knew that," Ava said, reaching for the phone which Sophia was holding just out of her grasp. "I was writing something else. To someone else."

Sophia touched the screen on Ava's phone and read: "'What should we or—'"

"Give me that!" Ava said, grabbing for it. Sophia shook her head. "No more texts tonight. We're going to have a nice family dinner."

"I hope you're including Mr. TV in that family."

"Of course."

When they'd depleted their DVR and finished dinner Sophia yawned and said, "Not it. That means it's your turn to do the dishes."

"Just because you say that doesn't make it true. I'm pretty sure it's your turn. Besides, I'm exhausted from all my good deeds."

"Okay, let's compromise. I'll get up and get the Oreos. But we have to agree to abide by its decision."

"Done."

It was a topic of heated debate in their family who had invented Pull the Oreo—most historians (anyone that mattered) sided with Mama, who had just the right kind of practical wisdom to be its inventor, but there were a few (Popcorn, Ava) who thought its emphasis on chocolate suggested their dad—but it had become the default way to decide otherwise intractable London family issues from "who has to take out the trash" to "who gets the last piece of Grandma's berry berry double crumble pie" and everything in between.

Ava and Sophia assumed the official positions for Pull the Oreo—each one holding one side of the cookie in her fingertips—and counted in unison. "Three . . . Two . . . One . . . Pull!"

"Rats." Ava flopped back onto the couch with the losing—noncreamy—side.

Sophia ate her half, murmuring about how delicious the creamy center was, which was one of the rights of the winner. But watching Ava listlessly nibbling the edge of her plain cookie took some of the sweetness out of the triumph. "It looks like volunteer work is really tiring."

"You have no idea," Ava said. "I spent five hours cleaning cages."

"Aha. That's what that smell is." Sophia sighed and brushed crumbs from her hands. "Well, since you spent your day helping others, I'll do the dishes to help you. But only this once."

"Really?" Ava sat up, suddenly much more energetic. "Thank you thank you thank you!"

She leaned in to give her a kiss but Sophia quickly turned her face away. "I'll take your gratitude from afar until you've showered. Twice. Go now. *Please*."

While Sophia was distracted by not breathing, Ava stealthily swiped her phone back and padded happily into bed.

LonDOs

Volunteering for a good cause

Taking pictures on real film

Oreos

The Vampire Diaries

Mac and cheese takeout from Coffee Shop

MAC long-wear eye shadow in "All That Glitters"

Sophia humming "My Favorite Things" in the bath

I See London Legs Ahoy Meet-n-Greet at the Beverly Center tomorrow!

LonDON'Ts

Sitting on the couch in the same clothes you wore all day at the pet shelter

Sisters who won't rub your feet when you spent all day volunteering for the good of the world

Sisters who don't shower after spending all day volunteering for the good of the world

Sisters who keep secrets

Sisters who can't go more than seventeen seconds without saying the words "Liam Carlson"

Someone white and fluffy sticking his head into mac and cheese takeout (That means you, SIR SHEDS A LOT)

Boys who say there's nothing wrong with you like it means there's something wrong with you

Almost getting arrested for creating a public nuisance with your camera

(Where?!? And how "almost" is almost?)

(You'll see . . .)

11

male call

"Popcorn woke up starving and told me he must have pancakes," Ava said, poking her head around the door of Sophia's room as soon as she heard her alarm go off. "I'm just waiting for the ingredients to be delivered from Yummy. Should I save some pancakes for you?"

"Mmwfmemwmfmwmffmffmf," Sophia said, her face pressed into her pillow.

"What's that? Popcorn can't talk? You think I'm the one craving pancakes? Get out of here! Or actually, get out of bed. It's almost nine and we have to be at the Beverly Center by ten thirty for Legs Ahoy."

"Mumfpffoofmufphhhfummufff."

"No problem, you're welcome. And yes I totally remembered to order more coffee for you."

Sophia's hand came up in a sign of thanks.

"But don't forget to get up."

Sophia's hand came up again, this time waving Ava out.

Ava was in their cheery yellow kitchen signing the receipt for the Yummy.com delivery girl when she heard the girl gasp, and saw her reach out with one hand to steady herself on the white café table. Alarmed, Ava looked up and said, "Are you okay?"

The delivery girl opened her mouth as if to speak but all that came out was *"ohemgeeohemgeeohemgee"* in a low panting moan and she'd suddenly gone very red in the face.

Ava panicked. "Sophia. Come quick. She's having seizures."

The girl shook her head. "No, I'm fine. It's just—you." She let go of the table to point at Ava. "You're the new cutie!"

"Are you sure you're okay? You're not making sense."

"Positive." The delivery girl was fumbling in her pocket as Sophia rushed into the kitchen, still holding her electric toothbrush, demanding, "What is it? What's going on?"

"Look," the delivery girl said, holding up her phone. The screen was open to a well-known celebrity gossip site, which had as its front page story, "New Love for Liam! Carlson Gets Cozy with New Cutie over the Weekend." Complete with a photo of Ava and Liam from Hunter's party.

The delivery girl glanced from the photo to Ava. "That's totally you, isn't it?"

"Yes," Ava squealed, delighted. "It is. Sophia, I'm—"

Sophia took the phone, held it up close to her face like she was scrutinizing it. She frowned. "To tell you the truth, I'm not sure it is you." She looked meaningfully at Ava. "Not sure at all. And I wouldn't want that getting around in case it isn't and someone gets upset. Would you?"

Ava didn't understand what was going on but Sophia's tone and look told Ava that the right answer to the question was the one she gave, which was, "No, I would not."

"You know how people will try to sue you for the smallest

thing," Sophia was going on, apparently to Ava but it was clear that her message wasn't lost on the delivery girl either. "Even if you only mention it in a text to a friend, the way things blow up now . . ."

"Right," Ava said, but without complete conviction.

Sophia smiled brightly at the delivery girl and led her out of the kitchen. "Sorry we gave you such a scare. I hope you're okay."

The delivery girl appeared totally perplexed. "I—I think I am. Okay, then. Uh, bye," she was saying as Sophia shut the door.

"What was that about? What's wrong with being Liam Carlson's cutie?" Ava demanded when Sophia came back to the kitchen.

Sophia's eyebrows went up. "Well, cutie, for one thing it could be the start of a big embarrassing story." Sophia sighed. "And what about Liam? Have you heard from him yet? What does he think?"

"I'm sure he's fine with it," Ava said, realizing that actually she hadn't heard from Liam all morning. Which was a little strange. Although it was still early. "He's used to stuff like this."

"Yes, but do we really want to get sucked into a big dramatic tabloid drama?"

"Why? Because I'm dating a movie star? How could that be bad press?"

"We've worked really hard to keep our personal life and our professional lives separate, and Liam and Whitney Frost are a tabloid staple. She practically told me that her entire breakup with Liam was all about the press. I think you need to consider that before getting in any deeper."

"Why would you believe anything she says? She hates us. And what am I supposed to do? Walk away from a guy who I'm really, really into because it *might* generate bad press?"

"I'm not saying that," Sophia said. "I guess . . . I'm just saying be careful. And maybe let the dust settle on his relationship with Whitney before getting too involved."

"Too late for that," said Ava on a shaky breath.

For a moment the two sisters faced one another across the kitchen table, the only sound the ticking of the clock above the fridge and the low hum of traffic from outside. The light coming through the yellow eyelet curtains was mellow and golden, in sharp contrast to the emotions coursing through Ava. Her heart felt like one of her hand weights pumping against her ribs, and her mouth was dry from nervousness. She didn't know why but instead of being ecstatic she felt suddenly . . . terrified. And not because of Liam. More because of Sophia's disapproval.

But then Sophia smiled and took Ava's hand. "Yeah, it's been hard to miss. And for what it's worth, I'm happy he makes you happy—and you know I support you in whatever you do, right?"

Ava took a deep, fortifying breath. The situation was far from perfect, but just knowing that Sophia supported her made her feel a million times better. "Yeah, I know. And I'll keep an eye on Whitney."

"I'll help," Sophia agreed. "And on the bright side, *cutie,* at least the papers don't know your name yet."

Ava's eyes got huge, but not because of what Sophia had just said. "Wow, is that the time?"

"Way to change the subject."

"I'm not, I'm being serious." Ava pointed at the clock that hung above the refrigerator. We're supposed to be at the event in a little over an hour."

Ninety minutes was the rule to get ready for an official event so they were way short, but somehow they managed to be dressed and sliding into the car—Ava wearing a lavender plaid romper with pearl buttons that she cinched at the waist with a wide brown belt and brown open-toe wedge ankle boots and a pheasant feather clipped into her hair; Sophia in a cream ruffle-front minidress with turquoise-and-snakeskin platform sandals and a stack of bangles on each arm—only one minute later than they planned.

It was a short ride to the Beverly Center from their house but long enough for worry about the absence of Liam's texts to have gone from puzzling to HORRIBLE SIGN/WORLD ENDING status in Ava's mind (ten and a half minutes).

"What's wrong?" Sophia asked around minute six.

"Nothing, why do you say something is wrong?" Ava answered, compressing the words into one quick breath.

"Because you haven't said a word since we've been in the car."

Ava stared out the window. "Am I boring? Do you think I'm boring?"

"No." Sophia chuckled. "Absolutely not."

"You're my sister." Ava slumped down in her seat. "What if Liam loses interest in me? What if I'm not sophisticated enough for him or cool enough? I don't know the right people. I can't get us onto the guest lists at the right clubs."

Sophia looked confused. "What are you talking about? Why would he care about that? Besides, if that's what he was looking for, he'd date Lily."

For some reason instead of making Ava feel better that made her feel worse. And a little annoyed at Sophia. "Not helpful," she snapped.

Sophia signaled to turn into the Beverly Center parking lot. "Why are you freaking out about this? You and he are joined at the iPhone."

"He hasn't texted this morning. Not once."

"I'm sure he's just busy," Sophia said. "Or sleeping."

"What if he's out doing something with someone else? What if he's already losing interest in me?"

Sophia put the car in park and turned to Ava. "Look at me."

She waited until Ava met her eyes. "He's not losing interest in you. You are way too interesting."

"The way you said that didn't exactly sound like a compliment," Ava said, following Sophia out of the car. "It was a compliment, right? Sophia? Hey, wait up."

The central atrium of the Beverly Center was already packed with people for the Legs Ahoy event. The event was supposed to promote their new Shaveventure line, a disposable razor with a special shave strip that allowed you to shave and moisturize your legs anytime, anywhere, without creams, lotions—or water. Sophia and Ava would demonstrate how it worked in what the Legs Ahoy people called "a challenging shaving environment," which would let people see real people using it in real time.

They were met by the Legs Ahoy representative and ushered into a hallway to wait until their official introduction. It started with the tolling of a deep resonant bell like the one on Big Ben in London. That was their cue to walk out to a poppy techno beat which became a little crackly when they reached the stage. As they climbed the stairs from opposite sides an old-fashioned British telephone operator's voice said, "London Calling."

Ava and Sophia had been put in short lab coats that covered their clothes but not much else. With the techno pop music pumping in the background, they each picked up a Shaveventure razor and marched to the sides of the stage where two of the iconic red British phone booths had been set up. Shutting themselves inside, they demonstrated the ease and convenience of the Shaveventure by shaving their legs inside the phone booth.

It had sounded good at the concept meeting and even seemed doable in the rehearsal at the Legs Ahoy offices the week before but now, on stage, it turned out to be a bit less easy than it looked. Ava peered across the stage toward Sophia's booth to see if she was having the same problems and almost choked, smothering her laughter at the what-were-we-thinking—no-what-were-*they*-thinking expression on Sophia's face. She tapped three fingers on the side of her thigh and Ava nodded, so at the count of three they both stood up, put on a big smile, and came out of their booths.

Right before going back out onto the stage, Ava had managed to steal a glance at her phone. Still no message from Liam.

She pasted a smile on her face and, taking Sophia's hand, walked to the front of the stage where they would be interviewed by the Legs Ahoy host about their Shaveventure.

The host joined them on stage and was calming the crowd so he could ask his first question when someone shouted, "Ava, what's it like to kiss Liam Carlson?"

Ava felt the blood drain from her body and her mind went completely blank.

Another voice yelled, "Ava, are you the reason Liam Carlson and Whitney Frost broke up?"

"Ava, did Liam come with you today?"

Ava wanted to curl up into a ball and hide. No, she wanted to say. Liam isn't here. Liam, apparently, is never ever speaking to me again.

Sophia moved closer to Ava and linked her fingers through her sister's.

"I guess they found out my name," Ava said.

"I guess they did."

"The real question," the Legs Ahoy host said, trying to salvage the situation, "is what Liam Carlson thinks of your Shaveventure legs. I know you've been using the product at home for a while. What's he said about it?"

There were hoots and bird whistles from the audience. The Legs Ahoy host winked at them and held the mic toward Ava who was praying in her mind for a natural disaster. Not a big one, a tiny one, one that would only affect the one square foot of territory on which she was—

"Come on, there's a better way to answer that question," a voice said, and looking behind her Ava took in the incredible sight of Liam striding across the stage. "You don't have to take her word for it, you can ask me yourself." He took her in his arms and spun her around. "Hi, babe," he said in her ear as he set her down. "Looks like we're official."

Ava felt like her heart had grown wings and was soaring. BABE! LIAM CARLSON CALLED ME BABE! "Is that okay with you?"

"Okay? It's great. Look at these crowds. Now let me feel those legs." He bent down and ran his palm slowly up Ava's calf.

The sound of the audience's titillated screams was nearly deafening.

But even better was the sound of Corrina's voice later on Ava and Sophia's voice mail. "You two are on a roll. The sponsor couldn't be happier. A surprise appearance from a major box-office star. Keep it up."

Keep it up, Ava repeated, dancing around the apartment. "Larger crowd than expected."

"Be careful," Sophia said.

Ava stopped dancing entirely and stared at her. "Why can't you just be happy for me? Why do you always have to turn everything positive into a negative?"

"Why are you so touchy? I was suggesting that you be careful of the table. Remember how you bashed into it the other day while you were dancing?"

"Oh."

Sophia picked a thread off her skirt. "But since you mentioned it, I don't think it's such a great thing to have Liam involved in our appearances."

"He's not 'involved in our appearances.' This was one time—"

"I know," Sophia interrupted. "It's just . . . I guess I saw this coming and it's exactly what I was afraid would happen, that's all."

Ava rolled her eyes. "Is that your way of telling me 'I told you so'?"

Sophia looked at her levelly. "Ava, we're a brand, London Calling. That means that what happens to one of us affects us both." Sensing Ava's protest, she said, "I'm only saying this because I care. About us and about you. Relationships are tricky and even more tricky in the public eye. The gossip magazines have already come calling, and this is just the beginning. You need to be really careful. If you and Liam are in public and he bends to tie his shoe they'll have him proposing. All they want is to sell magazines. They don't care what they say or who they hurt in the process."

"But no one's getting hurt—"

"Trust me, when you're having relationship problems and everyone around you is gossiping about them, it can be more painful than you know." At Ava's skeptical expression, Sophia sighed. "I wish you'd trust my opinion. Wasn't I right about the magazines being on your and Liam's story like red on Louboutin pumps?"

Yes, Sophia was always right. And Ava was the little London who didn't know any better. Why couldn't Sophia treat her like an adult instead of like a child? Why couldn't she respect her decisions? "Fine, then. But I wish instead of needing to be right, you could just be happy for me. You're supposed to be my biggest supporter. My number one fan. I feel like you're abandoning me."

"I'm not. I feel like you're pushing me away."

Ava stood as straight as she could, her hands curled into fists. "You know what? Maybe I am. Maybe I need a little more space. A little less of your protection."

Sophia's phone pinged and when she'd read the message she looked up at Ava. "That was Lily. She knows someone who has a table at SkyBar tonight but I told her I wasn't—"

"You should go. They'll card me. Besides, I have other things to do," she said, already typing on her phone.

Sophia hugged her arms across her chest. "Are you sure? I feel like we're—"

"Weren't you just listening to me? I want more space. Time alone. Free time."

"If that's really what—"

"God, why don't you just leave me alone?"

Sophia felt like she'd been punched. There was so much anger and frustration in Ava's tone, so much pain.

"Okay," Sophia said, more a whisper than a word. "Okay," she repeated.

When she came out an hour later, in wine-colored pleather shorts, a cream satin top, and heels, Ava was in the same place on the sofa, phone in her hands, thumbs moving.

Sophia stopped in front of the couch, hesitating.

"Ava?"

Ava glanced up now, thumbs hovering in midair, a look of impatience on her face. "What?"

"I—I just wanted to say don't forget about tomorrow. It's our big meeting with LuxeLife at noon."

Ava sneered. "Thanks, Mom."

"What does that mean?"

"It means you're not responsible for me and you don't have to treat me like I'm a child."

Sophia had to bite her lip to keep from saying—

She didn't even know what. She just knew she wanted to cry.

In her mind she heard Ava's voice, so saturated with anger but also sadness and something she couldn't quite identify, saying, "Why don't you just leave me alone?"

Because I love you. Because you're my sister. Sophia had the answers.

She just couldn't find the words.

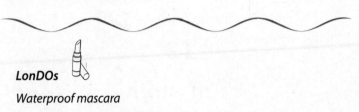

LonDOs

Waterproof mascara

Drowning your sorrows in ice cream

LonDON'Ts

Keeping secrets from each other

Not being able to drown your sorrows in ice cream because your sister ate it all drowning hers

12

ruff stuff

Ava's phone rang at 4:35 A.M. She groped for it, answering it with the light still off. "Hello?"

"Ava London? This is Estelle from Pet Paradise. Sorry to call at this hour but we have an emergency. Litter of puppies trapped by a breakwater in Malibu. Shouldn't take too long, all we need is a pair of hands. I'll send someone to pick you up in the shelter van. You don't have to bring anything; they'll have all the equipment. I know this is a long shot and you're still new but is there any chance—"

"Yes," Ava answered before Estelle finished.

She left a note for Sophia telling her she'd see her at the Luxe-Life meeting then zipped the outfit she was planning on wearing into a garment bag, packed up her shoes and travel makeup kit so she could change at the shelter after the emergency and get a ride from someone, and ran downstairs.

Her timing was perfect and the shelter van was just pulling

up when she got there. She opened the passenger door and said, "Would it be okay if I—*oh*."

"Yeah." Dalton nodded. "That was pretty much my reaction too. But," he went on, "I decided to rise above it. So, good morning, Ava London." His eyes got big as Ava loaded her duffle bag, then her garment bag, then her tote bag into the van. "And good morning half of Ava London's wardrobe."

Ava climbed into the passenger seat. "It is not half my wardrobe," she said, and immediately regretted it when she saw him bite back a laugh. He sat there, not driving, just staring at her.

She could only imagine the zingers he was lining up in his mind and she decided she wanted to get them over with. "Go on," she said. "What are you waiting for?"

"You to put on your seat belt?"

Looking down she realized he was right, she wasn't wearing it. God, he was annoying! She jammed the belt into the clasp and he pulled away from the curb.

He surprised her by staying silent for most of the ride, until they got close to Zuma. Then he said, "Have you ever done anything like this before?"

She found herself searching his voice for sarcasm but there wasn't any. "No. But I'll do whatever I can to help."

Dalton did a U-turn and pulled the van onto the rocky shoulder of the highway, right next to the ocean. "The report we got is that someone abandoned a mother German shepherd and a litter of puppies on the beach. They're trapped in the breakwater and the tide is coming in which means this could get ugly. High tide is in about half an hour. Whatever happens, I'm in charge. Got that?"

Ava nodded.

"I'm serious. This could get ugly. If I say we leave, we leave."

"Aye, aye, captain."

He looked at her. "Okay. Grab the ropes, the harnesses, the

two baskets with the blankets in them, and the muzzle stick and come with me."

The words "breakwater," "tide," "trapped," and "could get ugly" took on new meaning in person. The sun was rising behind them, painting bands of orange and blue across the sky and sending scattered points of light along the surface of the ocean. The shoulder of the road was ten feet above the beach now but Ava could tell by the lines in the wall of jagged rocks that supported it that at high tide the water would reach to nearly where they were standing. Good-sized waves pounded the sand and the tide was already moving up the beach in frothy lines.

There was a steady wind which whipped Ava's hair out of its ponytail. The air was cool but not cold, yet Ava had goose bumps. She had to lean close to hear Dalton.

"There!" Dalton pointed to a spot a little below them and to the left.

Ava made out the mother dog and, against the wall, the tinier shapes of five puppies. "They're safe."

"For now. When the tide comes up—"

Ava nodded. "—they'll be completely underwater." She understood why he'd been so insistent now.

"And so will we," Dalton stressed. "We can only work until the water reaches that wall. After that we won't be safe either. Which gives us about half an hour."

"Why are we talking?"

They tied the ropes to the hitch on the van. Dalton went down the rocks first, using the rope to descend quickly despite the basket and supplies he was holding. Ava brought the muzzle stick and the backpack with first aid supplies.

They landed five feet from the dogs, close enough to get a look but far enough to avoid overly alarming the mother. What Ava saw on the beach broke her heart. Apparently understanding the danger she and her puppies were in, the mother had dragged objects from all over the beach—a bright blue plastic margarita glass, a red Converse shoe, a Superman sippy cup, a battered green bottle—using other people's discarded junk to create a safe haven for her puppies.

Unfortunately, it wouldn't last a second against the tide, which had risen visibly even in the minutes they'd been there. Tying the ropes off among the rocks, Dalton took a step toward the enclosure.

The mother dog began to bark furiously, hissing him away. Spit frothed at the corners of her mouth and her ears were pinned back against her head.

"She's under an enormous amount of stress." Dalton said to Ava, without moving his eyes from the mother dog. "We have to calm her down. We won't be able to get to the puppies unless we get her out first."

"We don't have time to calm her down," Ava said, watching the water.

"Yes," Dalton told her, "we do."

She realized what he was saying without saying it, that the calmer they were, the calmer the dog would be. Ava took a deep breath as he took another step toward the mother.

She hissed again, saliva gathering at the corners of her strong jaw and around her sharp incisors.

"You know proper first aid for a dog bite, right?" Dalton asked casually. "Just in case?"

"No." Ava shook her head. "So don't get bitten."

"Thanks."

Ava had been watching the water but something compelled her to turn now toward the dogs. She found the mother dog staring at her.

Without saying anything Ava made a low clicking noise in the back of her throat and took a step toward the dog.

The dog stayed where she was, watching Ava intently.

Ava took another step. The dog didn't move.

Ava's heart was pounding so hard in her chest she was surprised it wasn't visible. *Sophia will kill you if you miss the meeting because you had your hand bitten off,* she told herself.

If you have your hand bitten off that meeting will be the least of your worries, another voice pointed out.

Ava's feet suddenly felt cold and looking down she saw that the last wave had covered her shoes. The next one would be higher. They didn't have a second to lose.

She took another step and without hesitating lunged forward, grabbed the mother dog by the collar, and hauled her away from the puppies in one smooth motion.

For a moment Dalton just stood there gaping but then he sprang into action. Ava crouched down next to the mother dog, talking to her and holding her attention while Dalton stepped into the walled-off sanctuary and began scooping up the puppies. He put them all into one of the baskets with the blanket that they'd brought down, and carried it toward Ava and the mother.

The water was now past their ankles.

"We did it," Ava said.

"Not yet. I think you should go up with the mother first, to keep her calm. Then I'll come up with the puppies."

Ava coaxed the mother dog into the free basket and tied a rope to it. Using the other rope she scaled the rocks as quickly as she could with the equipment bag on her back, her wet shoes sloshing and slipping down the rocks, her fingers, numb with cold from the water and the wind, barely able to hold the rope.

She was out of breath when she got to the top but she didn't waste a moment and began hauling the mother dog up. It was harder than she expected and her biceps were screaming in protest by the time the basket crested the top of the wall.

Maddeningly, it took her three tries to adequately tie the mother dog to the fender of the van because her hands were shaking so much from cold and exertion. When the big dog was secure, she stepped back to the edge of the shoulder to haul the other basket up.

Just in time to see one of the puppies slip out of the basket and go running down the beach, diagonally toward the water.

Ava could imagine the calculus Dalton was doing. He couldn't put the basket of puppies down to chase after the other dog, but if he took them he wouldn't be able to go as—

Cradling the basket in one arm, Dalton leaped forward, grabbing the puppy and raising it and the basket in the air as a wave came crashing over him.

For one terrible moment the only part of Dalton Ava could see were his two hands, one holding a basket of mewling puppies and the other holding a single pup that kept trying to twist himself away.

Then Dalton sat up, used his shoulder to wipe the water off one lens of his glasses, and got to his feet.

Ava hadn't realized that she'd stopped breathing but when Dalton stood up and started walking toward her with both the basket of puppies and the one roamer, she brought her hand to her mouth and took a deep, ragged breath. She wasn't sure if she was laughing or crying.

The sun was cresting the mountains behind them, sending a line of dancing white spots across the ocean behind Dalton and making him, with his glasses and soaking wet shirt and jeans, look like some kind of (very fit) hipster hero. Holding the basket of puppies up with one hand and the wayward puppy up in the other he gave her a huge smile and then Ava knew she was laughing.

Ava saw that the water was above his waist as he tied the basket of puppies to the rope and tugged it twice to signal she could begin hauling it up. It was lighter than the mother had been but it still took effort and her biceps and forearms stung with every pull. Finally she got them up, setting them next to their mother, and tugged on Dalton's rope.

The end came up easily. She peered over the edge—

—and was nearly knocked backward by Dalton vaulting over the top of the seawall. Only his arm, coming around her waist to grab her at the last minute, kept her from falling.

Their bodies were pressed so closely together that she could feel his heart racing and the warmth of his breath on her neck. Or was it her heart? Slowly she raised her eyes to his.

He looked away almost immediately.

"You're freezing," she said. "We have to get you out of those wet clothes."

"Unfortunately, unlike you I didn't bring half my wardrobe."

She gave him an appraising look. "And unfortunately I don't think I'm your size."

He did look at her then, right at her, and seemed like he was about to say something. That was when they realized that he was still holding her, that she was still standing pressed up against him, that her arms had gone around his waist for absolutely no reason at all.

What are you doing? she asked herself, stepping backward so hastily that she almost put her foot into the basket of puppies.

He pulled away at the same moment and nearly catapulted himself back down the seawall.

"You get the dogs—" he said at the same time that Ava said, "I'll pick up the supplies—"

Ava stopped. "You're in charge. What's next?"

They secured the puppies in the back and let the mother dog sit up front with them. Rooting around the equipment bag for some gauze, Dalton's hand closed on something unfamiliar and he pulled out a green glass bottle.

"What's this?" he asked.

"A souvenir." Ava started to lean close to him then stopped herself abruptly. "It was part of the wall the dog made. Hold it up to the light. Do you see?"

Dalton twisted the bottle around. "What's in there?"

"A message!" Ava said. "It's a message in a bottle."

"Should we open it?"

"No way," she said, taking it from him. "Besides, I need it for my meeting."

"You really do have a meeting? I thought that was just an excuse to bring a bag as big as the trailer I live in."

"You don't live in a trailer."

"Wanna bet?"

"Where are there trailer parks in LA?"

"What kind of meeting?"

Ava glanced at the clock in the dashboard of the van. "The kind I'm going to be late for." She looked at him. "Unless you'll drop me there instead of going right to the shelter. It's on Wilshire in Santa Monica."

Dalton agreed and while he drove she took her bags into the back of the van with the pups and shimmied into her clothes.

She should tell the Shaveventure people about this, she thought—shaving in a van that not only contains live animals but also a boy you're trying to avoid flashing while going 60 mph made the phone-booth stunt seem like a piece of cake.

She'd given up trying to tame her hair or put on eyeliner and was struggling with her mascara when Dalton said, "Hey. Thanks."

Ava paused with the mascara wand halfway to her eye. "For what?"

"Out there. You were great. How you handled the mother was amazing. And hauling all that stuff. I know guys who couldn't have done it."

"Really?"

"No. Well, maybe little guys. Still, it was great working with you."

"Thanks. It was great working with you too."

Ava found she was having trouble keeping her cheeks in the proper position to apply blush because she was grinning so much. Not to mention that the van seemed to hit a bump every time she got the stick near her face. She gave up on blush too.

When she was as together as she was going to get in a confined space surrounded by wet puppies—she'd given up on her belt, letting her minidress float lose around her—she ducked back into the passenger seat. Dalton glanced at her. "You look very nice."

She laughed. "Thank you. And you look very action hero-ish."

"I'm going to imagine that in your world that's a compliment."

Her smile vanished and the frown line appeared between her brows. "What does that mean?"

He shrugged. "Just that my ideal isn't to resemble some cookie-cutter tool for marketing fast cars and liquor."

"And that's exactly what I had in mind."

"It is whether you realized it or not. All of that, the movies, is really about selling something. First making people feel like they're missing something because they're not perfect like the people on the screen, and then making them feel like they can at least fill a tiny part of that void by buying whatever car or soap or shaving cream they see the hero using."

"You've thought a lot about this for someone who doesn't care."

"And you haven't, for someone who's in the middle of it." He shook his head. "Don't you ever get tired of selling stuff? Makeup? Liam Carlson?"

"I'm not selling stuff," Ava said, putting the phrase in finger quotes, sitting up straight. "Not the way you mean. I'm just being myself." She sat with her back to the door, facing his profile. "Why are you so quick to judge all the time? Why do you think you're the only one who has the right idea and understands how things really are?" She knew what she was saying was true, but somewhere at the back of her mind she suspected that maybe her frustration wasn't only with him. "Why do you care?"

"It just seems like kind of a waste."

"I'm going to imagine that in your world that's a kind of compliment," she shot back at him. "I've had enough of you, Mr. Judgey McJudgeypants. Maybe if you gave people a chance instead of pushing them away all the time you'd be able to smile once in a while."

He pulled up to the curb in front of the LuxeLife offices on Wilshire Boulevard. "Did you just call me Mr. Judgey McJudgeypants?" Ava saw that his jaw was tight.

Good. Maybe she'd hit a nerve. "Yes," she said defiantly. "And I'm not sorry." She got out of the van, dragged her bags after her, and slammed the door. *You will not turn around,* she told herself. *You will walk straight in and not look back at him.*

Which is why she didn't see it when Dalton completely cracked up. "Judgey McJudgeypants," he repeated to himself, laughing so hard he could barely see as he pulled away from the curb.

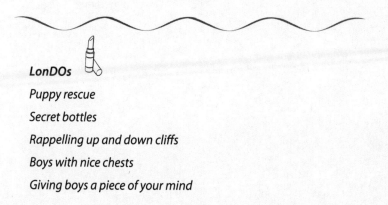

LonDOs

Puppy rescue

Secret bottles

Rappelling up and down cliffs

Boys with nice chests

Giving boys a piece of your mind

LonDON'Ts

Boys with bad manners

Being late for meetings

Not answering your phone

Not letting your sister know where you are

Not letting your sister see your photos

13

kiss and makeup

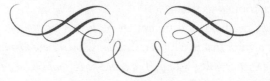

"Need help. See you @Life."

That was the note, in Ava's big loopy writing, that Sophia woke up to that morning. At the time she'd assumed that it meant someone (?) needed her help and Ava would see her at their meeting at LuxeLife.

Sophia was at one end of a rectangular conference table in a conference room that looked like a set for a show based in 1984. The carpet was dark green pile and the walls were a golden-brown veneer and the pictures on the walls, framed magazine covers, were all from before 1981. Even the ficus plant in the corner looked like a relic from another time.

Only the people around the table looked modern. To Sophia's right was Shoshanna Beck, the LuxeLife head of product, flanked on one side by two women in black and on the other by two men in black, who were simply introduced as "My Team." On Sophia's left, Corrina, the London sisters' agent, was occupying herself answering messages on three BlackBerrys at once. Not at the table but behind it, giving her a commanding view of the proceedings without having to take part, was Lucille Rexford, in her wheelchair. Today she wore a black cable-knit sweater with black fur sleeves, black leather pants, and a black fur hat. Cuddles was dozing on her lap but he'd periodically give a little bark of surprise as he was jolted awake when he started to slip off the smooth leather of her pants.

Other than that, and the clicking of Corrina's thumbs as she typed, the room was silent.

Sophia's head was a different story. *If only you hadn't gone out last night,* a voice inside whispered. *If only you'd stayed home then—*

Then another voice asked, *You could have watched Ava text?*

We could have talked. Made up.

But Ava had told you to go. To leave her alone.

I shouldn't have listened. I should have known there was something wrong, should have—

Don't even think about it, the voice warned as she started twirling her gold bird ring around her finger. It was her nervous habit, and anyone who knew her well could tell she was growing more anxious by the minute.

Sophia had dressed carefully for the meeting, wanting London Calling to make the best possible impression. She was wearing a red suede pencil skirt that came to her knees and looked both polished and chic with a matching red-and-white-striped boatneck sweater. The outfit presented precisely the polished but chic, reserved but fun, image she'd been hoping for. She and Ava were so young and while she knew that was part of their appeal, it could also work against them professionally. They had to appear twice as responsible, twice as hardworking, twice as dedicated, and twice as fun.

Being perfect but carefree was part of their brand. Being late was not.

Ava knew all of that too. Ava took their company as seriously as Sophia did. And Ava was never late.

There were three easels set up at the front of the room with large pieces of artboard on them that were covered. Sophia's eyes went to them but in her mind all she could see was Ava's note.

"Need help. See you @Life."

What if the note had been a cry for help? What if "See you @Life" meant—

Sophia cleared her throat and addressed the room. "When you use that little symbol, the A with the circle around it—"

"The 'at' symbol?" one of the team suggested.

"Yes. Right." Sophia picked up the pen in front of her to keep from twirling her ring. "That one. It doesn't mean anything else, does it?"

"It can mean whatever you want," another member of the team said. "Everyone has their own shorthand."

Shoshanna gave Sophia a look of distaste through her black cat-eye glasses and leaned forward like she was leaning into a microphone at a hearing. "Symbols don't play well for makeup lines. They're too cold."

"Oh you thought—no." Sophia shook her head reassuringly. "This isn't about our line. I'm just curious." She turned back to the team member who had spoken. "Like what? What do people use it for?"

He shrugged. "I use it for 'about.'"

"I know people who have used it for 'along,'" one of the women said.

"What about 'after'?" Sophia asked.

"Sure. I guess it could."

Need help. See you in the afterlif—

That was it. Rising from her seat Sophia said, "I'm sorry but I have to—"

Cuddles gave a little bark and Miss Rexford a little snort as they both awoke at the same time. Miss Rexford's head went left and right, and behind the smoky lenses of her glasses, her eyes blinked five times as though she was trying to remember where she was. As she got settled in her wheelchair, she seemed to realize everyone was looking at her. She snapped, "What are we waiting on? Where are you going? Let's get started."

Sophia said, "I was just going to find my sister. It's not like her to be late."

"On foot? Would you like to summon a horse brigade? Perhaps some hounds? Last time I checked it was the twenty-first century. We have phones for that."

"She's not answering."

"Ah. I don't rate your chances of being able to find her in a city of seven million when AT&T cannot as very good. We have a meeting, young lady. Let's get started."

Sophia lowered herself back into the seat.

Shoshanna nodded to the team and one of the assistants rose and flipped the covers off the two outermost easels. They held mood boards, one that said AVA and the other SOPHIA, with objects, words, and colors representing the two girls.

"Our idea for the initial season of London Calling for Luxe-Life is to play off the fact that you're siblings, one blond and one brunette, one who likes cats and one who likes dogs, different but related, with that special closeness but also tension that only sisters can have," Shoshanna explained. She nodded to the assistant again and the cover of the middle easel was flipped back.

"We wanted something that real girls could relate to, but with a slight edge. Something authentic but aspirational. So the concept we came up with is 'I Told You So.' It's a celebration of the unique relationship that sisters—and good friends—have, the push-pull, the similarities but differences, the joys, the fights, the . . ."

Sophia rolled the pen beneath one finger as she thought about the concept. She wasn't sure she liked the idea, especially for London Calling. Their brand was all about united sisters and this felt catty, divisive, and not to mention a little—

Sophia stopped rolling the pen and looked down at the note as she'd transcribed it. "Need help see you @Life." Maybe she'd been focusing on the wrong part.

Who would Ava go to for help?

Liam! She pulled her phone from her pocket. She didn't have Liam's number but she could get it from Hunter if she—

"Do we bore you, Miss London?" Lucille Rexford's acerbic voice cut through Sophia's thoughts.

Sophia turned toward her. "No, I just thought of a way to find my—*sister?*" Sophia gaped and all the heads in the room swiveled to look at the figure who had burst through the conference room door. She looked like she'd been blown there by the wind. Her hair was a wild tousled tangle, her outfit looked like it had been packed in a shipwrecked trunk, her cheeks glowed with the kind of perfect pink that only nature could achieve, and her eyes sparkled. She was wearing almost no makeup.

"Ava?" Sophia said, as though she wasn't sure. Sophia thought she knew every one of her sister's expressions, but she couldn't quite read what was on her face now. It looked like exhilaration and . . . fury?

She watched with a mixture of fascination and horror as Ava dropped her luggage—*luggage?*—against the wall and slid into the nearest seat. Sophia discreetly pointed a finger behind Ava, indicating Lucille Rexford's presence, but Ava apparently misunderstood.

Instead of turning around, she addressed everyone else in the conference room. "I'm so sorry I'm late," she said. "But I've had an incredible morning. I volunteer at a pet shelter and this morning they got a call about a litter of newborn puppies and their mother who were trapped on Zuma Beach and about to drown."

"What happened?" Sophia asked.

Ava faced her and it was like there were just the two of them in the room. "We had to rappel down the seawall to the beach. Then I calmed the mother down—she was so terrified she couldn't tell the difference between a friend or an enemy—and Dalton gathered up the puppies and then—"

"Dalton?" Sophia interrupted.

"I *know*," Ava said. "He is totally insufferable. Especially when he's talking. Or breathing. But he did the most amazing thing, Sophia. One of the puppies got out of the basket we'd put them in and he threw himself after it, saving its life." She shook her head. "It was incredible. And best of all, we found this." She set a battered green bottle on the table triumphantly. "A message in a bottle."

"What does it say?" Sophia asked.

Ava flashed an ecstatic smile. "I don't know. That's the magic of it. It could say anything. It could be a love letter or a treasure map or someone's will or a dying confession! We can imagine any story we want." Ava beamed around the table at everyone else as though expecting them to be as enthralled as she was.

But the LuxeLife team wasn't looking at her, she discovered. They seemed to be looking through her, as though she were invisible. She turned to Sophia and saw that her sister was doing the same thing.

Then there was a little bark and an imperial voice from the corner behind Ava said, "Well, at least you're not boring."

Ava jumped and turned in one motion. "I didn't know you were here, Miss Rexford."

"Evidently." Keeping one hand firmly on Cuddles, who was wriggling on her lap trying to get to Ava, Lucille Rexford's eyes moved to Shoshanna and her team. "Come with me. All of you. Not you two," she said to Sophia and Ava as they started to leave their seats. "Not you or your agent. You stay and wait."

Wordlessly but as a group, Shoshanna and the rest of her team followed Charles as he wheeled Miss Rexford through the door.

Leaving Sophia, Ava, and Corrina alone at the table. Taking, Sophia thought, their entire deal, their future, with them. Ava opened her mouth but before she could say anything Corrina pointed at her and hissed, "Not another word from you. I mean it."

Ava closed her mouth.

As they sat in complete silence for the next ten minutes, Sophia found the I Told You So concept growing on her. A lot.

I told you we had this meeting.

I told you to be more careful.

I told you that one day your reckless behavior would get us in troub—

Shoshanna and her team filed back into the room. They looked somber and wouldn't meet Sophia's eyes.

Lucille Rexford was nowhere to be seen.

As she sat down, Shoshanna pointed at the storyboards. "Somebody get those down. Out of here. We won't be needing them."

Sophia's heart sank. There had to be something she could do, some right thing that could make this all okay. "What if—" she began but Shoshanna was already talking.

Animatedly. And what she was saying was, "—just great. After listening to you"—she looked at Ava—"our original concept felt tired. Banal. We realized we didn't need to hit the sister note so hard—you're sisters, that's what binds you together. It's the glue, the backbone to the story but not the story. The story is about that feeling of possibility, of the moment between childhood and adulthood, whimsy and responsibility, that you two capture so well."

All six members of the team were scribbling furiously as Shoshanna went on. "The romance of the unknown, the things to come, the possibility of magic, of strangers in the night, old-fashioned glamour, accidents that act like destiny, lost wishes and found secrets." Shoshanna stopped and looked around at them. "Can you feel it? It crackles."

It did. Sophia's body tingled with excitement. A glance at Ava showed she felt it too.

"I'm just going off the top of my head here," Shoshanna said. "But I'm thinking a palette based around sea glass, muted grays and browns and greens, an ocean blue—"

"—or a series. The ocean at different times of the day," one of the team members put in.

Shoshanna nodded, tapping the table in front of her, apparently the sign to write something down. "Good, remember that."

"Soft wind-kissed blushes," someone else said.

"Shimmery made-for-whispering lip glosses."

Shoshanna's eyes looked up as though she was remembering a prewritten speech and then she said in the voice of an announcer, "LuxeLife and London Calling are proud to present their new line, Message in a Bottle, embracing the eternal values of friendship, romance, adventure, Old World glamour, and New World possibility."

"Message in a Bottle," Sophia repeated, like she was trying it out.

"It's good," Ava said in a hushed, almost awestruck voice.

"It's great," Sophia agreed.

Ava looked at her and Sophia saw that there were tears in her sister's eyes. "It's us."

Shoshanna was beaming. "We're still thinking about packaging, although right now we're leaning toward something smooth like sea glass or maybe sand dollars, and maybe having the lip gloss shaped like a bottle."

"Or a perfume," one of the team suggested.

"Body shimmer."

"Good," Shoshanna said, tapping the paper.

Sophia listened, fascinated by watching how the team worked, bouncing ideas off one another. But there was something nagging at the back of her mind and she finally realized what it was.

"Excuse me," she said, interrupting a discussion about whether making the eye shadows look like travelers' trunks was cute or tired. "What about Miss Rexford? What does she think?"

Shoshanna glanced down as though embarrassed by the question. "Actually, most of this was her idea. She said it reminded her of something she would have done in her youth and she hasn't been this excited about anything in a long time."

Ava got out of her chair and went to hug Sophia. "This is happening," she whispered into her sister's hair. "It's really, really happening."

"I know," Sophia said, hugging her back.

"I'm sorry about yesterday," Ava went on. "I was just—"

"Me too," Sophia told her.

And finally it felt like it was supposed to.

Or almost anyway.

LonDOs

Sisters

Detangling conditioner

Chili dogs at Pinks

Two large orders of fries

Scope Extra Strength Mouthwash

LONDON CALLING FOR LUXELIFE

Hidden messages

Liam Carlson's wrap party

Lint rollers

Being featured on the Cute Couples page of People *magazine*

LonDON'Ts

Silent treatment

Not being honest with each other

I Told You So

The third large order of fries

Riding in the car with my sister after she's eaten a chili dog

Leaving Popcorn and Clover at home alone all day with the closet door open and the dress you were going to wear to Liam's wrap party on the pouf

Being featured on the Cute Couples page of People *magazine*

14

tendril is the night

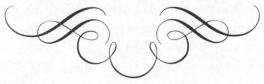

Sophia and Ava watched in silence as Lily, head back and eyes closed, rotated slowly on one foot in the middle of the wide, empty hall for the fourth time.

"What do you think she is doing?" Ava whispered to Sophia. They'd seen Lily do many, many strange things, but this was among the oddest.

"Silence!" Lily commanded in a spooky, mystical voice. "I am listening to the ghosts of guests past. They ask if you are sure you wish to enter."

Sophia shifted from one foot to the other, making the jet beads that covered her flapper dress whisper. "We're sure," she told Lily.

They were standing in the entry hall of the Magic Castle, which was supposed to be the site of Liam's wrap party. The party was Roaring Twenties themed, in keeping with the period of his film, so they'd dressed accordingly. Sophia was wearing a short flapper dress covered in jet beads, with a long pearl necklace and T-straps that Lily had lent her with a passing comment about what a good thing it was that she and Greta Garbo wore the same size. Ava decided to go as more of a sultry nightclub singer, wearing a floor-length gown with over-the-elbow gloves and putting her hair in a side-parted finger wave. Lily was a gangster, in a pin-striped suit her grandfather had once worn to play Al Capone.

They'd arrived a bit after the party had supposedly started—finger waves turned out to be more like frustration waves and then there was talking Lily out of bringing the authentic-looking tommy gun her grandfather had also lent her—but when they walked into the wide, parquet-floored front hall of the Victorian mansion that housed the world's foremost magic club it was silent and . . . empty.

And not just empty. There were no windows and no doors apart from the one through which they'd entered. The only thing besides a chandelier was a staircase against one wall with an elaborately carved banister of woodland creatures that curved up to the second floor.

"Liam said we'd have to get past the door to get in," Ava said. "But I didn't realize he meant we'd have to find it first."

That was when Lily had put her finger to her lips and gone into her human compass routine. Still in her creepy voice she now repeated, "I must ask you again, are you sure you wish to forsake the safety of the known world and travel to the precincts of—"

"Yes," Ava said in a tremulous whisper.

"Very well." Lily put her fingertips to her temples and said, "Spirits from before, spirits from today, open your portal, show us the way."

With a soft hiss the entire staircase, which turned out to be an elaborate fake, swung away from the wall and they found themselves in the middle of a rollicking party.

"I came here when I was little," Lily explained to them happily. "The password is 'portal'. Like door? The place isn't really haunted."

"Really?" Sophia told her with a look of fake surprise.

Lily elbowed her. "Little London believed it for a second. Come on, it's time to play FTB."

"Aren't you on a juice fast?" Sophia reminded her.

Lily looked scandalized. "Which part of vodka and grapefruit juice isn't a juice?"

"I didn't believe it," Ava protested. "I was just playing along."

"Excuse me, Ava?" a familiar-looking woman said as she joined them at the bar. Ava noticed that she glanced at Ava's drink—ginger ale, two cherries—before she looked at what she was wearing, which seemed strange until she introduced herself. "I'm Tana, Liam's publicist? Liam asked me to bring you over. He's right there"—she pointed into the thick of the crowd where enough flashes were going off to make it look like a minor lightning storm—"but he couldn't get away himself."

"Is that okay?" Ava asked Sophia.

"Of course," Sophia said. "You don't have to ask my permission. Do whatever you want." She turned to Lily and they clinked glasses. "To boytox," they said, like they were affirming some private club that only they belonged to.

Ava gave what she hoped looked like a jaunty wave and went. She knew her sister was only repeating things she herself had said, but somehow it didn't feel the way she'd expected—

Whatever she had been thinking completely left her mind as soon as she saw Liam. Or more accurately the way he smiled when he saw her, like there was no one in the world he'd rather be with.

"Hi," she said, gazing up at him.

"Hello, beautiful."

LIAM CARLSON CALLED HER BEAUTIFUL!

Even though they were in the middle of a crowd, with reporters listening and cameras shooting them from every angle, when
he put his arm around her and smiled down into her eyes he made
her feel like there were just the two of them there. He slipped his
arm around her shoulders and whispered in her ear, "Smile for
your fans, babe. That's what they want to see."

For a fraction of a second her mind flashed to Dalton, and
him saying, "Don't you get tired of always selling things?"

But then he added, "I can't believe I'm lucky enough to have
you as my girlfriend," and she forgot everything except the thrill
of being with LIAM CARLSON! HER BOYFRIEND!!!!!!!!!!!!!!

Sophia leaned back, closed her eyes, and let the wind rushing by
her ears blanket out all thought.

Driving up Pacific Coast Highway on a moonless night as the
passenger in a convertible Porsche was not a bad way to spend
part of a Saturday night, Sophia decided. The lights of the city
were less bright so you could actually see stars like tiny diamonds
embedded in the inky sky, and the scent and moist feel of the
ocean air wrapped around her like a blanket. She had the sensation of escaping from her life, just for a little while, and it felt
great, like a dream.

"Are you warm enough?" Hunter asked from the driver's seat
now.

"Perfect," Sophia said.

"I'll say," Hunter answered with a grin, failing to notice the
way Sophia's smile tightened slightly at the corners.

Sophia thought of what Lucille Rexford had said the day they
met her at Corrina's office. "When someone offers you an opportunity to make your dreams come true, you don't question them.
You just take it."

Maybe that was so you didn't have time to think about the consequences, Sophia thought. Like how much work it was to launch a makeup line. Especially if the person in charge decides she wants it done as soon as possible which, in Lucille Rexford's language, appeared to mean yesterday or maybe even the previous week.

"I'm sure she has many good qualities," Ava had said, tipping her shoes off and collapsing onto the couch after a sixteen-hour day at the LuxeLife offices.

"But none of them are patience," Sophia had finished for her.

It was exhilarating and exciting as well as exhausting, and it came with the added benefit that she and Ava didn't have the time or energy for any more disagreements. But she was aware that the tensions were still there.

Like that night at Liam's wrap party, when Ava had asked if she could go with Liam's publicist, Sophia's first instinct had been to say no. But Ava was right—she wasn't a child. It was her life. Sophia had no say over it.

Although she'd had to propose the toast to boytox with Lily to distract herself from the sudden urge she'd felt to cry.

Lily had to run off "to say hi to Uncle Harrison and Aunt Calista" so Sophia was alone when Giovanni came and stood next to her, holding out a white linen handkerchief and saying, "It's clean."

He smiled at her. "I of course will not comment on perfection but perhaps a little bit here." He touched the corner of his eyes. "It is a pleasure to be seeing you again, *stella*."

She realized her body had been aware of his presence before her mind, as though it had felt a little more alert, a little more alive.

She took the handkerchief with a grateful smile. "What does *stella* mean?"

"Star. It, how do you say, pants you."

Sophia laughed. "Suits." She'd thought the laughter would break the spell but it didn't.

"I am sorry to come upon you like this, without warning. In person I am taller and even more devastatingly handsome, no?" he joked.

"Oh yes," she played along. Only it was true.

He held her eyes. "I hope you will not find me imposing, but this is the second time I have seen you look sad at a bar. Perhaps you should consider a different pastime?"

"Maybe I should."

"On the other hand, I am also the possessor of good crying upon shoulders." He tapped his shoulder. "Firm, but not too firm. You see?"

Sophia laughed. "I will remember that."

"As you wish."

Out of nowhere Sophia said, "I got a kitten."

His eyebrows went up. "Yes? But this is wonderful news. Congratulations."

She nodded. "But I don't know what to call it. I keep picking a name, then changing it."

"Ah."

"I can't make up my mind about what the right name is."

"Maybe it is not time yet."

"But this is stupid. It's just a kitten. Why can't I pick a name?"

"Then it is not stupid. For some reason it is important. When you figure that out, you'll know the name."

"Just like that?"

"Yes. It is easy."

She looked at him from the corner of her eye. "You said that about big things happening. That it would be easy."

"And big things have happened, no?"

Sophia nodded slowly to herself. "They have. How did you know?"

Giovanni threw up his arms. "She asks a psychic, 'How did you know?'"

She laughed. "That's right, I forgot that you are a bartender and a psychic."

His head went from side to side. "*Sí* and no. You can keep a secret?" Sophia nodded. "Really I am not a bartender."

"What are—"

A beautiful woman in a floor-length beaded caftan with a massive jade pendant threw her arms around Giovanni. "*Amore mio,*" she said, kissing him on both cheeks. "Here you are. I have been looking for you."

She had the kind of effortless good looks only European women could have, Sophia thought, and she was sure that the woman's nearly elbow-length glossy brown hair dried naturally in the waves it had. Sophia looked down and realized she was crushing Giovanni's handkerchief in her hand.

"Sophia, this is my friend Nina from Rome. She does the design of production for this movie. She is very talented, but also a bit crazy. You must not listen too much to what she says."

Nina linked her arm through Giovanni's. "What kinds of stories is our Giovanni telling you?" she asked, caressing his cheek. "Has he spoken of his sculptures? Or perhaps the one about his family estate on the Po and his vineyards and string of polo—"

Giovanni gave her a pleading look. "*Madonna,* do you try to ruin me? I do not tell stories to this *signorina,* I would not want to bore her."

Nina laughed, but there was something in it that showed such intimacy between them, as though they knew all of each other's secret places, that made Sophia a little jealous.

"You're an artist?" Sophia asked him.

"Look what you have done," he complained to Nina. To Sophia he said, "No, no, I would never say that. I make art, yes, but as to being an artist, I'm not wise enough yet. Perhaps in fifty, eighty years. Right now I am just a sculptor."

She laughed. "What do you sculpt?"

For the first time since she'd known him, Giovanni looked uncomfortable as though talking about himself made him uneasy. "Marmosets," he said, looking away. "Tiny monkeys. It's a metaphor."

"I wish I could see one of your sculptures."

"Perhaps one day you will come to my studio and—"

Another stunning woman, this one in a red silk dress trailing a red feather boa, joined them then, shaking her short dark hair. "Of course I find you two at the bar talking to a beautiful woman," she said. She held out a hand with three large rings on it. "I am Lucretia. Nina's girlfriend." She kissed Giovanni on both cheeks and said, "Now you give her back."

Nina took Lucretia's hand and any envy Sophia might have felt—which she didn't of course because she wasn't even interested in Giovanni since the only people more unreliable to date than bartenders are artists (and psychics? That wasn't even a category!)—disappeared. Not to mention that she didn't even know him, or understand how she felt around him—sort of jangling and tingly—or why when he looked at her even when he was joking it felt somehow serious, as though he was looking not at her but into her in a way she wanted to be looked at, had *always* wanted to be looked at, and yet it was entirely unnerving and made her want to hide as well. But if she had felt any envy it was only for the connection the two women seemed to have, nothing else.

Of course she wasn't jealous of anything because she was on a boytox.

That's when Hunter had appeared and whisked her away, saying he had someone to introduce her to. It turned out to be an artist's agent who was mounting a show of young photographers. "Would you like to submit some pieces?" he asked. "If I see something I like, I'll see if I can get it in for you. It will have to be soon though; the show goes up in a month."

Sophia was stunned. "Being with you is like being with a genie who makes all your wishes come true," she told Hunter.

"A genie?" Hunter looked skeptical. "To be honest, I've always thought of myself more as Prince Charming." He lowered his voice. "And you are certainly a princess." Clearing his throat he said, "Speaking as one royal to another, are you, ah, seeing anyone?"

She nervously told him about the boytox, but he seemed more intrigued than annoyed.

"I get it." He nodded enthusiastically. "And I like it. I can work with that. To tell you the truth, I'm not sure I'm even ready for a relationship right now. My last one—" He gave a shudder. "But I could absolutely use a friend. So, as a friend, is there any chance I could take you somewhere and buy you dinner?"

"Yes," Sophia said. "That would be—that would be great. I just need to find Ava. She and I have a Come Together, Leave Together policy."

"I've got that covered," Hunter said. "I just saw Liam at the bar and told him we were taking off. He promised to tell your sister."

"Wait, you told Liam before you asked me?"

Hunter shrugged. "I'm an optimist."

Sophia laughed, a little nervously. As though sensing he may have overstepped, Hunter said, "Look, if it's really important, we can spend the next hour saying our good-byes and working our way out of here. No problem. On the other hand"—he pointed to a large mirror—"that's a secret exit that goes right to where my car is parked and—"

Sophia had gazed across the packed room toward Ava. Liam had his arm around her and they were both animatedly talking to the circle of admirers that ringed them.

Ava looked blissful. She would be fine—maybe even happier—without Sophia.

"Let's go," Sophia said to Hunter.

"I'm really glad we're doing this," Hunter said to Sophia now.

"Me too," she told him. Looking down she realized she was still clutching Giovanni's handkerchief in her hand.

LonDOs

Costume parties

Secret entrances

Boytox

Men with white linen handkerchiefs

Driving up Pacific Coast Highway in a convertible Porsche

Moroccanoil hairspray

Men with good-for-crying-on shoulders

Miniature ice cream sandwiches

Being just friends

BEING LIAM CARLSON'S GIRLFRIEND

LonDON'Ts

Hundred-hour weeks

Finger waves

Bringing weapons to parties

People who think that miniature ice cream sandwiches are not dinner

Trying to eat miniature ice cream sandwiches with over-the-elbow gloves on

Boytox

Sisters who don't call or come home all night

15

damsel in a dress

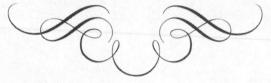

This might possibly have been the best night of Ava's life.

Sure her hand was a little sore, but it was in a good way. Because Liam had been holding it THE ENTIRE TIME. It was his party, but he'd wanted her—HER AVA LONDON HER HER HER—by his side.

And the party was amazing. Pretty much anyone she'd ever bought a poster of or *thought* of buying a poster of was there, along with magicians walking around doing tricks using cards or the gold-wrapped chocolate coins with Liam's face on them that the producers had made for the party. But the best part was how nice everyone had been to her. They'd asked some embarrassing questions about her and Liam but mostly they'd wanted to know about her and what she was working on and London Calling and how she and Sophia got started. A few people asked about Whitney Frost, but Liam stepped in and waved those questions off like it was no big deal.

She'd wished Sophia could have seen him do that, could have been part of all of it with her. But the first time she'd looked for her she was still at the bar with Lily and the next time she couldn't find her anywhere. Ava was glad she was having a good time but—

No but. She was glad. She *was*.

There was just this tiny nagging tension between her shoulder blades, like the dull ache of a toothache, hovering on the edge of her consciousness but inescapably there. She'd get the same feeling sometimes when she walked into the closet she shared with Sophia, a pricking awareness that something was out of place. When that happened, she would look around until she found the purse Sophia had put away crookedly or the dress that was in the wrong place and straighten it or move it and the feeling would go away. But real life was more complicated than any closet, even hers and Sophia's, and people couldn't be conveniently kept where you wanted them, when you wanted them.

Which was really too bad because Ava was pretty sure a lot of people would be happier if they did what she thought they should. It wasn't that she was bossy, it was just that she knew what was right and wasn't afraid to share that information in an authoritative tone. If people didn't want to listen, that was their choice (also: mistake). Or, as Lucille Rexford had put it during a LuxeLife meeting that week: "My goodness, Miss London, you certainly know your own mind."

Ava hadn't been sure how to take that—she'd gotten a lot of lectures growing up about her "tendency to expect others to conform to her will" as her second grade teacher put it after Ava had rearranged the classroom and posted a set of rules (No CHEWING NOISES *EVER*! and ALL PENCILS SHOULD LINE UP WITH THE EDGE OF THE DESK) during one recess. But then Lucille Rexford added, "Be careful or people are likely to put you in charge of something," and she'd realized it was a compliment.

And that was the trouble with her and Sophia. Sophia could be just as strong-minded and confident in her opinions. Usually this similarity gave them an even stronger bond, but every so often, like with Liam, it caused them to butt heads.

The ragtime music that had been playing during the early part of the party now changed to more current stuff, and around them people were starting to dance. Ava heard the first strains of the song she and Sophia and Lily had been singing at the top of their lungs in the car on their way to the party, "L.A. Sky," and saw Lily moving toward the dance floor.

She turned to Liam to ask if he wanted to go join her but before she even opened her mouth Liam leaned toward her and said, "Let's get out of here. Now."

His tone was vehement, and the expression on his face looked like (very hot) fury. "Sure, okay. I just have to find Sophia. She and I have kind of a rule about that."

"Can you make it quick? I hate this song."

"Yes, of course." She'd never seen him so . . . angry before. Letting go of his hand for the first time that night she pulled out her phone to text Sophia but discovered it had no service. She made a superfast circuit of all the rooms but couldn't find her sister anywhere. Back in the main room she spotted Lily on the dance floor doing the tango with a man dressed in an old-fashioned policeman's uniform and moved along in time with them.

"Come join us!" Lily said, holding out her arm.

Ava laughed. "I think three is a crowd for tango."

"Doesn't matter," Lily confided in a shout-whisper as her partner spun her out, then back. "He has no strange scars, prison stories, or hobbies. A total dud."

"Bummer," Ava sympathized. "Have you seen Sophia?"

"She left like an hour ago."

Ava shouldered her way past another couple to keep up with Lily and her Keystone Kop partner. "She left? Are you sure?"

"Positive," she said from the bottom of a dip. "She waved at me before she and Hunter took off."

Lily and her partner cha-cha'ed away, leaving Ava standing in place, hands at her sides, staring at nothing, the words "She waved at me before she and Hunter took off" blanketing out all other sound.

Sophia had left. Without her. Without telling her. But she'd taken the time to tell Lily.

Ava felt like she'd been punched.

She shivered, suddenly freezing despite the crush of bodies all around her. A hand closed on hers and Liam was beside her. "Hey babe, you ready?"

His frown was gone and he was smiling at her again and his smile warmed her almost all the way back up. "Am I ever!" she said, even managing to sound enthusiastic. "Let's go."

"I'm sorry about in there, with the song," he said as they pulled away from the Magic Castle in what after a week of looking at color boards Ava now thought of not as black but rather his onyx Land Rover. "Sometimes I just get fixated on things, you know? That band is just so overhyped."

"I completely agree," Ava said, making a note to make sure Liam never saw her iTunes Most Played list.

He smiled over at her and took one hand off the steering wheel to hold hers. "This is our first time in a car together."

Ava had the sensation of wishing there was someone she could look over at and mouth, "He just said this is our first time in a car together! How cute is that?!" It seemed like her entire relationship with him was one big OMG moment.

"Are you hungry?" he asked her.

"A little?" She didn't want to admit how many Liam coins she'd eaten.

"We could hit the Redbury or Beacher's Madhouse," he said, naming two of LA's most popular clubs. "Or—"

"Or?" Ava prompted.

They were at a stoplight. With his head against the headrest he turned to face her. "If I make a confession to you, will you promise not to judge?"

Ava put her hand over her heart. "Promise."

Liam looked at her for a long beat. "I believe you. And maybe it's better just to show you. Hold on."

"Where are we*eeeeesh*—" Ava was pressed against the door as he made an illegal U-turn.

"Sorry about that," he said, gunning it to the next light. He made a left just before it went red and then a quick right into a parking lot, roaring into a space in front of the 7-Eleven.

Ava was just starting to breathe again when he came around to open her door. "Wow," she said. "You really, um, drive."

"I had race lessons when I was prepping for my last movie, and once you've done that, it's hard to go back."

"Sure, I bet," Ava said, hoping her legs would be steady when she stepped out of the car. She looked around, fully taking in their surroundings for the first time. "I've never been on a date to a convenience store before," she said.

"I've never taken a date to a convenience store before," Liam answered. He reached up and tucked in a piece of her hair that had flown out during the drive. "But then again, I've never dated anyone like you."

HE SAID HE'S NEVER DATED ANYONE LIKE ME! Ava looked for a partner in OMG!!!!!!!!!!!!!!!!! but the only person there was a man dozing by the garbage can.

It was pretty quiet inside too. The guy behind the counter barely looked up from his copy of *Variety* when she and Liam came in, even though she was still wearing a floor-length gown and Liam was dressed as the young Jay Gatsby, his character from the movie. (Ava had heard him describe the movie that night as "A prequel to *The Great Gatsby* with a Sherlock Holmes element.")

Seeming to know exactly where he was going he took her hand and led her to the back of the store. "Ta-da!" he said, pointing to the Slurpee machine. It was the largest, fanciest Slurpee machine Ava had ever seen. "This is my confession. I love Slurpees. And this place has the best ones in Los Angeles."

"What flavor do you recommend?" Ava asked.

"I've got a magic formula. Step aside and let me work."

Based on what Ava could see—before Liam made her cover her eyes so she wouldn't give away his secrets—the magical formula involved using all eight of the Slurpee flavors to create a color that she would now describe as mud. But when she finally tried it, Liam hovering around her like a nervous parent teaching their child to ride a two-wheeler, she had to admit it was good. Although what she said to Liam was, "Completely and totally delicious. I hope you weren't planning to share because this one is all mine."

His smile lit up the convenience store. "You're the best," he sighed. "I've never known a girl I could take Slurpeeing before."

Ava winked at him over the extra-wide red Slurpee straw. "You were dating the wrong kind of girls."

"That's for sure," he agreed. "Tana says so too. She says you're good for me."

"Tana your publicist? You talk to her about us?" Ava shuddered a little from the Slurpee chill.

"Tana knows about everything going on in my life. She has to. She's the only protection I have, the only thing between me and"—he made a wide gesture that took in the store but also the general population—"everyone."

Ava couldn't say if it was his tone or his expression, suddenly more somber, but she felt the same loneliness from him now that she'd felt the first day they met. Spontaneously she reached her hand to his cheek and said, "I'm so sorry."

Liam cupped his hand over hers. "Thank you." For a while he

just looked at her. "I don't think anyone has ever understood me the way that you do. You date another star or a singer, you're just two lonely people together. But you—you're so normal. So grounded."

Ava looked away. "So boring."

"No. Not boring. So—I'd really like to kiss you."

She looked back at him. "Here? At the 7-Eleven?"

He nodded. And bent down. And ever so gently kissed her on the lips.

For four minutes.

"Oh wow," she whispered breathlessly when they pulled away.

Liam swallowed hard. "Yeah." He pointed to the parking lot. "I'm thinking—"

"Me too."

Liam handed the man a hundred-dollar bill for the Slurpee, said "Keep it" when the guy reminded him about his change, and they bolted to his car. They got inside, locked the doors—

And were kissing again. The single soft kiss on the lips became even more captivating and they lost themselves in it completely. Until another set of headlights raked the car and they realized where they were and what they were doing and cracked up.

"I guess we should get out of here," Liam said.

Ava laughed. "Yeah. And I should get home. We have an early video shoot tomorrow and Sophia will go nuts if I'm too late."

They didn't talk on the way to her house but held hands, both of them sitting way back in their seats with their heads against the headrests. Every time they stopped at a light Liam would turn his neck so he could look at her and give her this adorable, goofy smile. "How great is this, eh?"

"Pretty great."

When they pulled up at her building she stopped him before he could unfasten his seat belt. "I wish I could ask you to come up but I can't," she said. "We have a No Boys on Work Nights rule."

"But it's Saturday."

"We have that video shoot tomorrow. Besides, I don't want to wake Sophia up and—there will be other chances."

"You bet there will."

They grinned at one another for a while. "Well, good night, Liam," she said.

"Good night, Ava," he said.

And then they were kissing again, Liam's seat reclined and Ava half over the cup holders, and between kisses they laughed and stopped and looked at each other and then kissed some more.

Ten minutes later Ava said, "Well, good night, Liam."

And he said, "Good night, Ava."

She sat there smiling at him. He reached out to touch her cheek and his thumb brushed her lips and as though completely out of their control his mouth sought hers and she leaned into him and their lips brushed and Ava yawned.

Not a small yawn either, a really big yawn.

Liam pulled away with a completely different expression on his face than the one he'd had less than a minute earlier.

"I'm so sorry," Ava said, covering her mouth with both her hands and feeling her face flush with embarrassment.

Liam chuckled. "No one, not one single other girl, has ever done that to me before," he said, then yawned. They both cracked up and he shook his head. "But you're one of a kind, aren't you, Ava London?"

Ava's heart began to pound very, very hard. "I'm glad you"—yawn—"think so. Okay, I have to go."

Liam yawned again. "Yes you do."

He came around and opened her door for her. "Thank you for being a great date," he said. "They love you."

"They?" she said, copying his gesture from the convenience store.

"Everyone."

Ava was still grinning when she opened the front door. She listened for a moment to see if Sophia was up or asleep but she didn't hear anything so she was asleep. Or that's what she thought until she got into her room and found the kitten without a name asleep on Popcorn's stomach. As cute as that was, it was odd. The kitten always slept with Sophia. Ava picked him up and tiptoed into Sophia's room to put him in bed with her.

But she didn't need to bother because Sophia wasn't there.

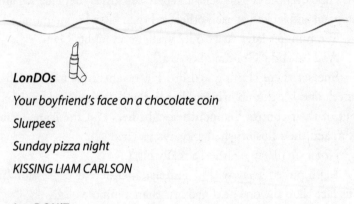

LonDOs

Your boyfriend's face on a chocolate coin

Slurpees

Sunday pizza night

KISSING LIAM CARLSON

LonDON'Ts

"L.A. Sky"

Sisters who don't come home

16

pacific coast myway

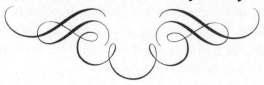

Ava checked her voice mail, sure the message was from Sophia.

It wasn't.

It was their mom. Ava promptly called her back, and got the latest scoop on life in Georgia. Ava always loved talking to her mom, but when she clicked off the phone, her smile faded fast.

Sophia hadn't left any message whatsoever. She. Simply. Hadn't. Called.

Which was fine, Ava assured herself, lighting the candle by her bed as she forced herself to go through her normal nightly ritual. They were their own people. She sprayed the sheets with scent. They didn't have to share everything, she thought as she climbed into bed.

Except that they had shared everything for the past few years. They'd been more like Siamese twins in some ways than sisters. And now, suddenly, it was as if Sophia didn't want that anymore. Ava realized she'd forgotten to brush her teeth or wash her face so she got up again.

As she stood in front of the bathroom mirror removing her twenties' eyeliner, Ava found herself thinking of the trip her family had taken to Italy when she was eight. They'd just finished having this amazing pizza for lunch and they were standing in a piazza waiting for her dad to figure out where they should go next. That always took forever, so when Ava spotted a woman with a dancing dog across the street, she'd gone to look at it. It was pretty amazing—it did this Russian dance on two legs that she'd tried to teach every dog she'd had since then, with zero success—so she had gone to get her family and show them.

Only they were gone. Vanished!

She figured that as soon as they realized she wasn't with them they would go back to the hotel to wait, so she went straight there. But they must have gotten lost because she'd been there for hours before they got there. The concierge was really nice and got her tea, but Ava hadn't learned how to ask for the bathroom in Italian so she started to feel like she might burst.

The only other dark spot was that she'd lost one of her new pink mittens. Not only did she love them, but her mother had stressed that they were pretty fancy for a little girl and she had to promise to take good care of them. And now one of them was gone. She started to imagine it as the price she had to pay for wandering off, and made a solemn decision never to wander off again.

When they finally got back to the hotel hours later, her parents had practically devoured her with kisses. But not Sophia. Sophia had looked at her like she was a spoiled brat and said, "Here's your mitten." Restoring it to her just like magic. She'd gone to hug Sophia but Sophia had just pushed her away and said, "Don't thank me. This shouldn't have happened in the first place."

Ava remembered standing there with the mitten in her hand

and the sinking feeling in her stomach that Sophia would have been happier if she'd never come back.

A feeling she was starting to have again.

At least, she thought as she climbed back into bed, the next night was Sunday, which meant pizza night. Maybe once she and Sophia had spent some time together, everything would feel better. Happier with that thought she picked up her book and started reading.

Suddenly, she was kissing Liam and her eyes were closed but she could tell from the golden light coming beneath her eyelids that it was daylight. She wondered where the time had gone and why Liam was poking her in the side but the kissing was nice. Really nice, nicer than it had been in the car. She went to take a breath and opened her eyes and woke up. But in the split second before she woke up she'd seen the face of the guy she was kissing and it wasn't Liam. It was Dalton.

It took Ava a moment to register her surroundings. Her light was still on, and her book had tipped out of her hand so it was poking her in the side. It had been a dream. Just a dream, it didn't mean anything.

She blew out the candle, put the book on her bedside table, and turned off the light. But she lay awake in the dark for an unusually long time afterward, the image of a pink mitten floating at the edge of her mind as she listened for Sophia's key in the door.

When Hunter found out Sophia had never been to Gladstone's he insisted they go there for dinner. He gave her his jacket so she wouldn't be cold and they sat on the patio that overhung the beach, shelling peanuts and listening to the surf while they waited for their blue crab cakes and curried coconut shrimp. Over dinner he asked her if she'd used the camera yet and she said she had.

"But I'm afraid to get the film developed," she admitted over the top of her strawberry daiquiri.

Hunter almost coughed out the beer he'd been drinking. "That's absurd. Why?"

"I was thinking I should stop now. If I do that, I can just have enjoyed the experience. But if I get the film developed and it's bad, then I won't be able to look back on it the same way."

"And if you get the film developed and it's good, your photos might end up in a gallery." He took another sip of beer. "If they're bad, then you use them to figure out what would work better the next time."

By the time dinner was over she'd agreed to let him get the film developed. "Do you need to go home right away?" Hunter asked as he gave the waitress his black card for the bill. "My family has a little place up the beach and it's a great place to just sit and chill."

Sophia pulled his jacket more tightly around her shoulders. "I should probably get back."

"But do you *want* to?" Hunter perched his elbows on the table to explain. "One thing I've learned from my father is that you can divide the world into two kinds of people. There are the ones whose first thought is whether they *should* do something. And the ones whose first thought is whether they *want* to. The *shoulds* tend to be the ones you can rely on because they're always thinking of someone else. But the *wants* are the ones who make exciting things happen. I feel like you might be a *want* trapped in the life of a *should*."

Sophia laughed at that, but something about it resonated. She was enjoying talking to Hunter and there really was no reason she *had* to go back yet. "I'm not sure I'm *want* material but I guess I don't have to get back right now."

She should have expected that Hunter's idea of a "little place" wouldn't match hers, but she was still unprepared for the Roman villa they pulled up in front of.

"Actually it's not a villa," Hunter explained. "The design was based on the archeological findings of the bathhouse at Pompeii. But the idea is similar."

He brought her one of his stepmother's cashmere track suits and a bottle of Perrier—"as long as that's what you *want* to drink, not what you think you *should*"—and led her onto a stone terrace that overlooked the beach. There was a mosaic-bottomed pool with lounges along one side, but he gestured her toward a set of couches around a fire pit that ignited with the touch of a switch.

"I never realized the Romans had self-starting fire pits," Sophia said.

"Of course. They were also really big on four-car garages," Hunter joked. He settled back against the couch cushions and took a sip of beer. "So, I'll tell you mine if you tell me yours."

"My what?" Sophia replied quickly. Had she been wrong about him? Should she not have come?

"Sad sad love story." Sophia had opened her mouth to object but he went on over her. "You wouldn't be doing a boytox if you didn't have one."

She was about to object to that as well, but stopped herself. Maybe he was right. Maybe her problems dating really were all about what had happened with Clay.

And maybe it was time to tell someone. Someone who didn't know her, someone whose scorn wouldn't hurt her.

So she did. Without looking up, she told him about Clay and how the breakup had taken her by surprise. How she'd thought everything was wonderful between them, how hard she'd worked to be the perfect girlfriend, and how wrong she'd gotten it.

How since then she'd been afraid to make any decisions, and was always second-guessing herself because she'd been so wrong about their relationship. And because she was afraid that if she made one mistake everything she'd built would fall apart.

And when she was done Hunter said, "I know that exact feeling. About being scared you'll say one wrong thing and send the person away." He reached out and took her hand in a comforting, but not romantic, way.

It was amazing having a guy as a friend, Sophia thought. A guy you could talk to about guys.

She said, "Okay, your turn."

"I was sort of hoping you'd forget about that."

"Not. A. Chance," Sophia told him. There were blankets at the end of the couch and she took one now and wrapped it around herself. "I'm waiting."

"Well, there was this girl," he said. "And I was crazy about her. And she was crazy about me, I thought. But it was the old story, she started doing drugs, and then the drugs started doing her, and she changed, completely. I stayed with her and tried everything I could to get her clean but she wouldn't stop. She'd moved into my apartment when things were good and I couldn't kick her out with her doing so badly. Plus, to be honest, I thought if she stayed with me instead of going back to her family she might get clean." He shook his head. "I had to go to Vegas for a bachelor party one weekend and when I came back, the apartment was empty. She'd stolen everything and sold it for drug money. She didn't even leave me my toothbrush."

"What happened to her?" Sophia asked.

"I don't know." Hunter finished his beer. "Her father was a con man, her brother a thief. We can't pick our families. So unfortunately she'll never get the help she needs from them."

"No," Sophia said, having pulled the blanket a little more tightly around her shoulders at the word "family." Family had always been everything to her but recently she'd been feeling as though hers—or anyway, Ava—had been slipping away from her. And, like with Clay, she couldn't really understand why.

Sitting side by side they watched the sunrise over the ocean.

It was a magical moment, maybe even more magical, Sophia thought, because they were just friends.

"Thank you for being the perfect date, um, friend," Hunter said as he dropped her off.

Sophia kissed him on the cheek. "Thank *you* for being the perfect friend." She riffled around in her evening purse and pressed something into his hand.

"What's—you had these with you all night?" he said, staring at the three rolls of film lying in his palm.

Sophia nodded. "I told myself I didn't have to give them to you. And I was going to chicken out. But I realized that I trust you. I want you to get them developed. Please."

"You are likely to make me crazy, Sophia London," Hunter told her. He jiggled the rolls of film together in his hand like dice then said, "I have some tickets for a charity benefit tomorrow night. It's a forty-five-course champagne tasting."

"Forty-five courses?"

"Some of them are very small. And you don't have to taste it all. Just take a sip here and there of the brands that intrigue you. Anyway, would you and Ava want to come? Liam will be there and there will be lots of Hollywood types—actors, stylists—the kind of people whose support could really help take London Calling to the next level. Especially with your launch around the corner."

Sophia felt like Hunter just kept offering her the keys to the kingdom. The kind of personal access he was offering to celebrities and especially stylists would be invaluable. But she had to say no. "That sounds amazing, truly, but Ava isn't legal to drink. I'm not sure I'm legal to drink forty-five courses of champagne. Even just a sip here and there."

"What about your friend Lily? Either she's legal or it's not stopping her."

Sophia nodded slowly. It really was an opportunity too good to pass up. "I'll ask her. I bet she would enjoy it."

"And I would enjoy having you around. As a friend." He pointed to his cheek. "Plant one of those on here and then get upstairs to bed. Not that you need the beauty rest."

Sophia was still wearing the warm-up suit and carrying her dress in a garment bag Hunter had given her as she tiptoed up the stairs to the apartment. It was 6 A.M. That meant she could still get three hours of sleep and be ready before they had to leave for the video shoot.

She couldn't believe she'd stayed out all night the night before something as important as the video shoot. She was tired, but she also felt exhilarated. And lighter than she had in ages.

Determined not to wake Ava she slid her key into the lock and turned it as slowly as possible to make the minimum sound. She had the doorknob in her hand when it was wrenched away from her. The door was flung open and Ava, wild-eyed and holding a pen and a slipper over her head like she was poised to attack, yelled, "Don't even think about it!"

After Sophia's heart started beating and Ava lowered her weaponry to her side, Sophia said, "So your plan just now was—"

"To attack whoever was trying to break in."

"With a pen and a slipper."

"We don't exactly have an arsenal in the living room. Besides, I also had the element of surprise on my side."

"That you did," Sophia said. Ava backed up and Sophia followed her in. Glimpsing the pile of blankets on the couch, she said, "Why were you sleeping in the living room?"

"Because someone didn't come home last night and I got tired of listening for the sound of someone's keys from my bedroom." Ava set the slipper and pen down.

"Popcorn has a set of keys? Since when?" Sophia asked, purposely misunderstanding.

"That is really not funny," Ava told her, and Sophia had the sense that Ava was close to tears. "Where were you? Whose clothes are those? Why did you leave the party without telling me?"

Sophia decided to take the last question first. "I tried to get your attention but you were distracted."

"Would you like me to introduce you to a neat little device called an iPhone?"

"There wasn't any service at the Magic Castle," Sophia pointed out.

"What about after? Were you on an airplane? Because I'm pretty sure there is service in most of CALIFORNIA."

"I didn't think I needed to. Hunter told Liam we were going to dinner."

"Well, Liam didn't tell me."

"That's not my fault."

Ava said, "How do you know Hunter really told him? Maybe it's your boyfriend who's not a good guy, not mine."

"I never said Liam wasn't a good guy," Sophia protested. "And Hunter isn't my boyfriend."

"Ah. He's just a guy you spend all night with and come home wearing his pajamas."

"They're his stepmother's."

"Was she there?"

"No, but—"

Ava crossed her arms.

"We just stayed up talking." When Ava's expression didn't change, Sophia felt her face getting hot with frustration. She picked up the bag with her dress in it and turned toward her room. "You know what? I don't care if you believe me."

"But we always go and come together," Ava said, her voice quiet and soft and—sad. She evened up the sides of the two magazines on the coffee table. "That's the rule. You can't just change the rule. I'm not some mitten you can just pick up and put down at will."

"Mitten?" Sophia was genuinely confused. "The other day you

accused me of smothering you and now you're accusing me of not paying enough attention? What do you want me to do?"

"Nothing," Ava said, carefully lining up the pen and the slipper with the magazines on the coffee table. "Just do what you want and I'll do what I want."

Sophia heard an echo of Hunter saying "I think you're a *want* trapped in the life of a *should*." "Perfect," she said to her sister. "Look, I'm tired and I want to get a few hours of sleep before we have to leave for the LuxeLife video shoot. Can we do this later?"

"There's nothing to do," Ava said. "We are totally done."

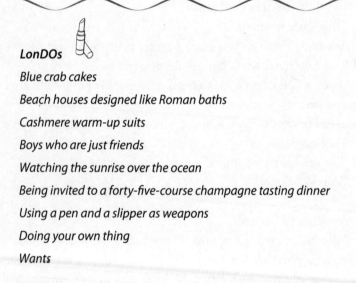

LonDOs

Blue crab cakes

Beach houses designed like Roman baths

Cashmere warm-up suits

Boys who are just friends

Watching the sunrise over the ocean

Being invited to a forty-five-course champagne tasting dinner

Using a pen and a slipper as weapons

Doing your own thing

Wants

LonDON'Ts

Relying on boys to relay messages

Forgetting to take advantage of our unlimited texting plan

Come together, leave together

Sleeping on the couch

Discovering chocolate coins with your boyfriend's face on them in your evening purse

Shoulds

LonDOs addendum

Our LuxeLife video shoot

17

knight fever

Sophia had said it casually, like it didn't matter at all. "Oops, I'm so sorry, I totally forgot. I have to go to this dinner tonight."

Until that moment, when they'd just come home from their video shoot, the day had gone great. Despite their rocky morning, the shoot had gone well. Really well. The art director was thrilled with the images.

"If he could only see us now," Ava muttered under her breath. She and Popcorn were sitting on the couch scrutinizing her eyebrows in a hand mirror. Ava was very tempted to get out the tweezers and have her way with them but she knew better than to Tweeze when Tense.

"What?" Sophia asked, coming into the living room in a red-and-purple color-block minidress. "Can you zip this for me?"

"Of course, madame." The subservient tone in Ava's voice was only half humor.

Sophia didn't notice. "I really am sorry to be missing pizza night." She turned and was facing Ava now. "But I think it's important for me to go to this. Hunter just read me a partial list of the guests and pretty much every stylist you've ever heard of is on it, as well as every celebutant. If I can build a bridge between even one of them and London Calling, it will be huge."

"I know," Ava told her, annoyed by the marketing lesson. "I said I understand." And she did. She understood why Sophia was going, and why she couldn't go too.

But that didn't mean she liked it.

Sophia disappeared into her room but came out again a moment later as though she'd been shot out of a cannon. "Max Houck is going to be there too. Isn't that amazing?"

"Who's Max Houck?" Ava asked.

Sophia frowned. "I thought I told you but I must have told Lily instead." Ava wasn't sure if she was glad or mad that Sophia was too preoccupied to notice the hurt expression she didn't quite manage to keep off her face. "Max Houck has a gallery in Santa Monica that specializes in photography and their next show is new LA photographers. Hunter introduced me to an art agent who might be able to get me in, but even if I don't, getting to meet Max Houck in person . . ." Her voice trailed off like she didn't have the words to describe it.

"Good luck then," Ava said, mustering all her enthusiasm. And trying to squash the jealousy she felt when Sophia had so blithely forgotten which of the people closest to her she'd mentioned this amazing opportunity to, the insane woman who lived down the hall OR HER SISTER.

"Thank you," Sophia said, coming over and kissing Ava on the cheek. She moved back and did a pivot so Ava could take in the dress, the black platform sandals, black motorcycle jacket, and yellow patent-leather clutch. The dress had a sort of mod feel so

Sophia had pulled the top of her hair back into a high ponytail. "Am I okay?"

"You look fantastic," Ava said, meaning it. "I can't imagine a better brand ambassador for London Calling." There was a knock at the door and Ava went to get it as Sophia touched up her lipstick.

"You're not Hunter," she said to Lily who was standing there in what looked like a gray leather dress but could have been a bunch of garbage bags she stapled together.

"No," Lily said, batting her eyes, "but I'm cuter." She looked beyond Ava. "We better go, Sophia. Hunter's limo is downstairs waiting for us."

"I'm on my way."

"You didn't tell me Lily was going too," Ava said as Sophia stopped to give her a kiss on the cheek.

"I didn't? I guess I didn't think it would matter." Sophia frowned. "Does it matter?"

"No," Ava lied. "Absolutely not."

When they left Ava marched straight to the bathroom and pulled out her tweezers. With Sophia and her new BFF Lily at the Very Important Champagne Tasting, Liam busy at some kind of "command performance," and MM and Sven still on a yoga retreat, she had all night to work on her brows. She held the tweezers up to the light and said, "It's just you and me, babe."

From the door of the bathroom there was a low growl and Ava looked up to see the kitten and Popcorn standing there, staring at her.

"What?" she said to them, gesturing with the tweezers.

Both Popcorn and the kitten's eyes followed it, then returned to her. The kitten gave another little growl.

"Are you saying you don't think I should tweeze?" As a test, Ava made a gesture like she was putting the tweezers away.

Popcorn started wagging his whole body. "Okay," Ava said. "Sure."

She talked to Popcorn a lot but she never really expected him to reply. And certainly not on a topic like—

That's when she looked at the clock and realized she hadn't taken Popcorn out all day. So much for attaining a new level in human-animal bonding.

Still, he'd probably saved her from making a very grave mistake. "Just for that we can walk anywhere you want," she told him as she hooked his leash on.

Anywhere he wanted turned out to be down Third Street. Ava didn't usually take him there because it was so busy, but the smells must have been phenomenal because it was always the direction in which he pulled.

They'd only gone two blocks when there was a honk and a familiar-looking beat-up gold Ford Bronco swerved to the curb beside her.

"Hey good looking," Dalton said, clearly addressing Popcorn. To Ava he added, "I saw neat pictures of you in a magazine."

The way he said it, it was absolutely not a compliment. "Thanks."

He frowned. "What, no snappy comeback? No jazzy name for me?"

Ava felt like a flower that someone had pressed between pages of a book. And then stomped on. "I'm not in the mood."

Dalton's frown deepened. "That is not the Ava London I know. I think you've been keeping the wrong company. No offense, buddy," he said quickly to Popcorn. He looked up at the sky like he was trying to make up his mind about something, and let out a long breath. "I know I'm going to regret this but some friends of mine are having a kind of happening tonight at a loft downtown."

"A happening?"

"It's like a party, but more artsy. You can come if you want."

A happening, Ava repeated to herself. "I'd love to! What should I wear?"

"What you're wearing now is fine."

Ava looked down at the cream crochet top she was wearing over her flowered denim-shorts romper and beige suede platform sandals, then back at him. "I can't go to a party like this."

Dalton shook his head. "I knew I was going to regret this. I have to run an errand. Go home and change. I'll pick you up in half an hour. And if your sister's there, feel free to invite her too. There's room in the car."

"She's busy," Ava said, a pang of sorrow hitting her straight in the gut. Fortunately, she didn't have time to dwell on it. She'd never gotten dressed in half an hour before in her life, and there wasn't time to focus on anything except making herself look cute.

She rushed it, but the doorbell was still ringing before she was done. She answered it and couldn't figure out why Dalton was looking at her funny. "Is something the matter?"

"No, you just look really pretty," he said. "You and your sister must have some gorgeous parents to have gotten such good genes."

"Right," she said brushing the comment off. "I just need to go finish my lipstick. Give me one more minute."

As Ava perfected her lipstick, it rolled through her brain that Dalton had mentioned Sophia twice. First inviting her to the party, and then complimenting their shared genetics. She had to wonder if he was just being friendly, or if he might be a little interested in Sophia. Or maybe a lot interested.

When she came out he was sitting on the floor with Popcorn and the kitten in his lap going through her iPod. And sneezing.

"Are you okay?"

"Just a little allergic to cats." He sniffled.

"I'm so sorry, I had no idea," Ava told him, airlifting the kitten from his lap into Sophia's room. "You're allergic to cats but you still work at a pet shelter."

"Yeah. I wear a mask," he explained, but not really. Ava started to ask him more but he hit play on the iPod and "L.A. Sky" came on. "Do you like this song?"

Remembering Liam's reaction to the song, Ava said, "That's Sophia's mix. Personally I think the song is overrated."

Dalton shrugged. "Really? I think it's kind of catchy."

He twisted to point at a photo on the console table behind the couch. It was a picture of Ava when she was about five, on a Big Wheel with pillows strapped to different parts of her. "My best guess was that you were trying out for the kids' version of *American Gladiator.*"

"Why wasn't there a kids' version of that show?" Ava asked.

"I know," Dalton said. "One of life's great mysteries. So what were you doing?"

"We had this neighbor who always had a big bowl of candy in their front yard." Ava walked around the bar that separated the living room from the kitchen to feed Popcorn and the kitten but kept talking. "They said I could come by anytime and take some, but not more than five pieces a trip. Our house had a long steep driveway and their house was at the bottom." She finished feeding Popcorn and the kitten and circled back into the living room. "If I walked down to get the candy, I'd usually finish it by the time I walked back up. It didn't seem very economical. So I thought— why not take my Big Wheel? It would be easier and quicker, right?"

"Or you could just have—never mind," Dalton said. "Was it quicker?"

"It was. A lot quicker." She picked up the photo and looked at it. "I got there *before* the Big Wheel because it spun out of control and sort of catapulted me down the driveway. I landed pretty much in front of our neighbor's steps. It was like flying."

"Into the ground," Dalton said. "So after that lesson you decided it would be better in the future to respect gravity and walk?"

"*Or* I decided if I strapped pillows to myself for protection I'd be fine."

Dalton winced. "Did it work?"

"Totally. Until my mother saw. Apparently that wasn't what she'd had in mind for the mustard-yellow velvet cushions from Great-Aunt Gretchen's sofa."

Dalton's head bobbed up and down with dawning comprehension. "You've always been this way, then."

Ava was wary. "What way?"

"We should go," he said.

"What way?" she asked again as she trailed him to the car.

"A danger to yourself and others."

"I'm not a danger to others," she protested.

"That's where you're wrong, Ava London," he said, opening the passenger door for her. "That's a compliment in my world, by the way. Buckle up."

The sun was just setting when Sophia, Lily, and Hunter arrived at the Buffalo Club for the champagne tasting. Chinese silk lanterns embroidered with flowers hung over the garden, bathing it in a golden glow.

Hunter took it in and smiled. "Perfect picture lighting."

And within ten minutes he had introduced Sophia and gotten her photographed with two top celebrity stylists and the editor of *Elle*.

"He's good," Lily conceded after Hunter had maneuvered Sophia near but not next to a potential new "it" girl. "That way if she gets big, you're there, and if she doesn't, it was an accident. Party pictures are the new letters of introduction," she explained. "Aristocracy is over—this is the age of the photocracy. People see you with people they want to be seen with and then they want to be seen with you."

"That's almost Zen," Sophia said.

Lily adjusted the twist tie that was structuring the razorback look of her dress. "I'm like that all the time now. It's the juice fast. I've never felt so clearheaded before."

Sophia's eyes got huge. "I forgot about your juice fast. I'm so sorry, I never would have invited you to something like this."

"Don't be silly," Lily told her. "Champagne is totally a juice, just a fermented one. I'll be fine. In fact, I think I need some juice right now."

Sophia watched her go in pursuit of a serving woman with a tray of champagne flutes, passing a blossom of people clustered around Liam. Photos of him and Ava from the wrap party the night before had begun trickling onto gossip blogs that morning, and when Sophia had seen them a tight little knot formed in her stomach. There were just a few photos, and they were, as all the stylists at the video shoot squealed to Ava, "sooo cute!" But what if there were more? Not all as flattering? What if one was bad or embarrassing or—

As more pictures "surfaced," though, Sophia realized that Liam was as protective of his public image as she was of Ava. Watching him now, smiling warmly first in one direction then the other, with flashes twinkling around him like fireflies, Sophia recognized his professionalism and found herself thinking that he might just be worthy of Ava. *Might*.

She only became aware of the person standing at her elbow when he said, "A true prince of the photocracy, as your friend so accurately called it. Although I'm less confident of her claims about champagne."

It was amazing that she hadn't noticed him, Sophia thought, since he had apparently been there for a while and was dressed in a bright green corduroy suit, a purple gingham shirt, and round glasses with orange frames. He smiled at her through them and held out his hand. "You're Sophia London. I'm Max Houck. It's a pleasure to meet you."

"You—" Sophia touched her fingers to her heart. "You know who I am?"

"Of course I do. And I want to say congratulations."

Hunter had joined them then, and Sophia noticed he was wearing the satisfied expression of a schoolboy who'd just pulled off a great prank. "Thank you," she said, looking from Hunter to Max. "For what?"

Max spread his hands. "We love your work. We're putting five of your photos in our show. And, with your permission, we also wanted to use one of them as the poster."

Sophia hadn't even had a sip of champagne yet so she knew she wasn't drunk, but what she was hearing made her think she had to be. "Are you—" She turned to Hunter. "Is this true?"

He nodded, grinning.

"But how? How did you even see them?"

"I had the film processed today," Hunter explained. "I looked them over, submitted the images I thought Max wouldn't be able to resist, and the rest you know."

Sophia marveled at him. "Do you do this for all your friends?"

"I do what's required." He slipped her an envelope. "Here are eight-by-tens of your photos for you to admire. The ones in the show are considerably larger."

"Thank you," she said and leaned in to kiss him on the cheek. But he turned at the last minute and she kissed his lips instead— a little longer than might be considered strictly friendly. But it was a special occasion, she decided, and she was very grateful.

She took out her phone to text Ava but the dinner gong sounded and there was a rule about no phones at the table. Sophia saw the wisdom of this almost immediately. Or at least immediately after her tablemate, "Call me Pat from Texas," forced her to drain her second and third glasses of champagne in one swallow after declaring, "Down the hatch!"

By glass number six not only did Sophia have *a lot* of ideas she wanted to share with many people via her phone, but she was also feeling a little light-headed. She excused herself to find the bathroom and get off a few texts—"Dear Clay, I never really liked your cologne I just said I did to be nice," for starters and then one to Ava, "Please answer Liam's texts, he keeps asking where you are and I am not your secretary"—but on her way she spotted Giovanni working behind the massive mahogany bar at the end of the garden.

"Stella mia!" he greeted her happily, leaning across to kiss her on both cheeks. "You have been enjoying the champagne?"

"Yes," she confirmed, steadying herself with one hand on top of the bar. "But I might have reached my enjoyment limit."

"I know exactly what you need." He pulled out a bottle of San Pellegrino and a shot glass and set them in front of her, like an old-time barman in a Western.

Sophia took a shot of San Pellegrino and shook her head back and forth. "Much better," she conceded. "How do you always know exactly what I need? Oh right." She tapped a finger to her forehead clumsily. "You're psychic."

"Sí," he confirmed, setting up a tray of filled champagne glasses for the next course. He offered her one but she waved it away. "You are having a nice time?"

Sophia nodded enthusiastically. "There are so many important people here."

He puzzled over that, repeating the words to himself. "But is that the same as a good time?"

Sophia reached out and tapped him on the nose with her finger. "You are being tricksy, *stella*."

"No, you are the *stella*," he corrected. "I am just the admirer of stars." His star-admiring gaze moved behind Sophia and he said, "I think your friend also has enjoyed the champagne."

"Champagne gives me wiiiiiiings," Lily sang as Liam and Hunter, between whom she was draped, deposited her on a bar stool. Only she missed it entirely and ended up on the floor. "Mmm comfy," she said, leaning her head against the bar.

"It looks like someone had a little too much juice," Sophia said, then started giggling to herself. Which made her hiccup. "Uh oh."

"Uh oh," Lily said too.

Hunter stood looking down at Lily. "Can you get her up and onto one of these stools at least? She's making a scene."

Sophia patted Lily's head while she considered this. "I think it might be better"—she hiccupped—"to take her home."

"I agree," Liam said.

"My limo won't be back for another hour and I doubt anyone here is in any shape to drive," Hunter told her.

Giovanni had gotten very busy polishing glasses when Hunter came over but now he said, "I have the great misfortune to be exactly sober enough to drive. And I believe I am no longer needed here. If you would permit, I would be happy to take the sleeping one home."

"I should go with you," Sophia said, almost managing to get it all out without hiccupping.

"It's not even ten," Hunter protested. "Let the bartender take her and you stay with me. Don't be a *should*."

Sophia put her hand on Hunter's chest. *"Mmmnice,"* she said. She hiccupped. "When I hiccup"—she hiccupped again—"it's a sign that I've had enough. It would be better for me not to meet anyone at all, then to meet them"—hiccup—"like this. That is a *want* speaking." She leaned toward Hunter, angling to whisper in his ear. "You really have a very nice chest."

"Thanks," Hunter said, unable to stay mad at her. "You too."

Sophia found that to be just about the funniest thing she'd ever heard. As she and Giovanni helped Lily out to his car, she kept repeating, "Did you hear what he said? I didn't think he had it in him."

"Me either," Giovanni agreed. They got Lily into the backseat of his dark green convertible Fiat Spider, and he held the door for Sophia to climb in the front.

"You don't like Hunter," Sophia announced when he'd pulled away.

"Right now, with two beautiful ladies in my charge, I have the more important things to think about."

From the backseat where Lily lay sprawled with one metallic Miu Miu slipper dangling off to the side, came the sound of her singing, "Champagne gives me wiiiiiiiiiiings."

"This is a popular song?" Giovanni asked.

"Not on this planet," Sophia told him.

"You are funnier than the Hunter," he said.

"You too." Sophia tipped her head back and looked up at the sky. Two rides in convertibles with two different men in two days—she had to hand it to Lily, boytox really was something. The Fiat Spider was not as smooth as the Porsche but the leather of the seats was supple from years of use and everything looked more handmade, less like it was manufactured in a factory.

The cars resembled the men, she thought. Hunter was sleek, contained, reliable. From his smooth shave to his fitted sweater, he exuded an aura of control and order down to the smallest detail. He'd even refolded his napkin after dinner, Sophia had noticed, reminding her of Ava.

Giovanni was different. Like his car he had an Old World air of refinement, impulsiveness, and charm with an undertone of having been around a bit. She could picture him getting up in the middle of dinner, sweeping everything off the table, and pulling her down on top of him to—

"You are alright, *stella*?" Giovanni asked her. "Perhaps you are not getting enough of the air?"

Sophia felt her face and realized she was blushing. "I'm fine. Great."

"Champagne," Lily sang. "Gives me wiiiiiiiiiiiiings!"

That made Sophia think of something from when she was much younger, all the way back to before Ava was born. "When I was little, I thought I could fly," she told Giovanni.

"From what I have seen of you, I am guessing you put this to the proof."

"To the test," Sophia corrected. "It was BA—before Ava—so I was only three. I spent almost a whole day making a set of wings. They were blue with feathers and rhinestones at the tips."

"Champagne! Gives me wiiiiiiiiiii—" A hiccup came from the backseat.

Giovanni said, "And so?"

"I put them on and got a running start"—she paused—"and tripped on a rock in the path. I never got to fly, but I got this scar." They were stopped at a light and she lifted her chin to point to the faint mark beneath it.

Then quickly, like she'd only at that moment realized what she was doing, she tipped her chin back down and covered the scar with her hand. "I never show that to anyone," she said, sounding almost surprised at herself. "That's—that's how I learned about makeup in the first place, to hide my scar."

"But this is not a scar, this is a badge of honor," Giovanni said. "And also I must confess this—it is not very easy to see. But did you never try to fly again?"

She shook her head. "Ava was born the next month and then there was her to think about. I didn't want my parents to have to worry about both of us. Plus I wanted to be a good role model for her. As older sister, I had a responsibility to protect her. I couldn't run around putting myself in danger, I had to keep her safe."

"Her or yourself?"

Sophia was starting to feel a bit more sober. "What do you mean?"

Giovanni laughed it away. "Nothing. I never mean anything."

A tiny frown creased her forehead. "Would you mind not telling anyone what I told you tonight? About my scar?"

"I would never mention this."

She added, "Especially not Hunter?"

"Why especially not him?"

"He's so perfect," Sophia said. "I wouldn't want him to know."

"I am not sure I understand this word 'perfect' with the Hunter."

"Why do you call him that? The Hunter?"

"Is his name, no? And it pants—no, you say—it *suits* him."

Sophia gave an uncomfortable laugh. "I hadn't thought of that."

Giovanni pulled the car to the curb with one smooth motion and came around to open the door for her. He insisted on carrying Lily up the stairs and waited politely outside until Sophia had tucked her in. As Sophia closed her door they could hear the faint strains of "Champagne gives me wiiiiiings."

Then he and Sophia walked to her door. She fished the keys out of her evening bag and like a gentleman in an old movie, Giovanni took them from her and used them to open her door.

"Thank you," she said, standing in the open door. "For being our knight in shining armor."

Giovanni gave a small, formal bow.

Sophia suddenly realized she didn't want him to leave. "Hunter brought me some copies of my photos," she said. "The ones that are going to be in the show. I'd love your opinion of them if you want to come in."

He said, "If you are sure?"

She nodded and he followed her into the apartment. Ava's

door was ajar but she could sleep through nearly anything. She had only glanced at the photos herself so she was excited to look at them.

She pulled a mock-up of the poster and her pictures out of the white envelope and fanned them over the table. Giovanni picked up one, then another. She tried to focus on the pictures rather than on his face but it was hard. Finally he turned to her and smiled.

"They are very pretty," he said. "You should be proud."

For some reason the word "pretty" stung. "What's wrong with them?" she demanded.

"But there is nothing wrong with them," he said, looking confused. "They are very easy to look at."

"You mean they're dull."

"Absolutely I do not. They are not dull. There is motion, a story. I mean that you took them with your head. Another time you should think less, just do."

"Why? So I can end up as a waiter?" Even as the words were out of her mouth she regretted them, but she was too upset to apologize.

What made it even worse was how unruffled Giovanni was. He simply said in a mild voice, "But are you not already waiting always? To make sure it is safe? Always peeping before you are leaping?"

Before she could object he put her keys in her hand, his fingertips barely brushing her palm.

"Good night, *stella*," he said, and showed himself out.

He hadn't even tried to kiss her.

Which was right, of course. She wasn't disappointed at all. She didn't even like him. Besides, she couldn't wait to tell Ava about her photos being in the show. She knocked on Ava's door—but the room was empty. Ava wasn't home.

Though given the number of outfits strewn over the bed, she had been dressing with a purpose and in a hurry.

LonDOs

Glasses 1 to 3 of champagne

Being part of the photocracy

Getting your first gallery show

Gallant Italian waiters

Fiat Spiders

Dior Crème de Rose lip balm

LonDON'Ts

Glasses 4 to 6 of champagne

Juice fasts

Anything "pretty"

Sisters who don't text their boyfriends

Sisters who don't bother to come to pizza night

Sisters who don't bother to come home

18

lofty glambitions

"You might strain something if you keep that up," Dalton said, watching Ava's neck swivel from one side to another as they drove through downtown Los Angeles.

"I've never been here before," she said. "I thought it was just office buildings and that opera house." She gazed wide-eyed through the window. "Look at all these cute restaurants. And there is totally a line to get into that club."

"Edison," Dalton said. "It's popular with bankers who want to act like hipsters."

"Which is not a compliment in your world," Ava said, correctly translating his tone.

Dalton pulled into a parking lot that was filled with parked food trucks doing a brisk business.

"You hungry?" he asked. "I know it's probably not the fancy feasts you're familiar with."

"I had a Slurpee for dinner last night."

"Well, it's nice to know that's the score to beat." He looked around, and then pointed at a pink truck. "I think we'll start with that one."

"CANDY'S CANDIES." Ava read the awning that hung from the rainbow-colored truck. Then her eyes moved to the sides of the truck and she gaped. Instead of metal with a window you could order through, Candy's Candies was made up of a hundred square plastic containers, each filled with a different candy.

"Yeah, I don't know why after that story this just came to mind."

"I haven't seen this one in years," Ava said, pointing at a yellow-and-blue package in the second row. "Or this one," she said, pointing to something in a red wrapper. "Oh and these are Sophia's favorites."

"Nerds Rope?" Dalton was skeptical.

"You'd be surprised. It's that sweet and salty mix she so adores."

"And you?"

Ava didn't have to think hard. "I'd say that my favorite candy is One of Everything Please. But I guess we can just start with this part of the truck," she said, putting her arms around a three-by-three-foot square of boxes.

"You heard the lady," Dalton told Candy. "And add a Nerds Rope."

They strolled around the parking lot, weaving between knots of people standing up and trading bites of food with serious or blissed out or seriously blissed out expressions on their faces. Ava spilled some Pop Rocks onto her tongue, then held Dalton's nose until he opened his mouth and let her put some on his too.

He tried to close his mouth but she said, "No, ew haf to do it like dhiss," demonstrating by talking with her tongue out.

"Whai?"

"Is moah fuhn." She pointed at him with his blue popping tongue sticking out. "Ha ha ew luk fuhnee."

"Tahks wohn tah no wohn."

Ava swallowed. "Sophia's at some fancy forty-five-course dinner with Hunter Ralston but this is definitely way better."

"Hunter Ralston?" Dalton said, and Ava noticed he suddenly seemed a little tense.

"Yeah, they're at a party tonight. Why? Is something wrong with that?"

"Apart from my tongue cramp? Nothing." But given the tense set of his jaw, Ava didn't believe him. "Let's go inside."

Ava started to notice that some of them would nod or wave at Dalton and he'd do the same back, but it was all really low key, without interrupting one conversation for another, or stopping to introduce one person to someone else they just had to meet. Now they sort of worked their way to the front of a crowd until they got to a garage door that had been rolled up. There was no rope and no guest list that Ava could see, just a really, really big bouncer who could have eaten even Sven's muscle-bound self for an after-dinner snack.

The bouncer was repeating, "Be cool, no pictures okay," and stamping the wrists of everyone who went by but he interrupted himself when he saw Dalton to shake his hand.

From there they went up a set of metal and concrete stairs past a roll-down door with a jellyfish spray painted on it and another tagged with OCCUPY EVERYTHING. Each floor they climbed brought them closer to the music they could hear until they reached the top-floor loft which was where the party was.

"This is insane," Ava said, drinking it in with her eyes. If it was possible to make a contrast with the dark wood paneling and old-timey-mansion feel of the party the night before, this would have been it. The space was decorated with flowers, giant fake butterflies, and swings everywhere. Ava saw someone riding around on a tricycle and looking closer she realized it was the lead singer of one of her favorite bands. "Isn't that—" Ava said, pointing to a guy standing by himself by the wall. He'd made a splash the previous year when his biceps almost got an Oscar nom. "And over there—"

"No pointing," Dalton told her, gently nudging her finger down. "And no staring. That's the difference between a party like this and parties where the celebrities are paid to appear," he explained. "People come here because they want to."

Ava thought of what Liam had said about having a "command performance" that night. Suddenly she realized there were no photographers here.

Based on the number of high-fives and greetings he got, everyone knew Dalton and was happy to see him. "How cheery for you to have so many friends," Ava said.

"It's a wonder, such a Judgey McJudgeypants like me," he answered.

"You're never going to let that die, are you?"

"Die? I'm having it embroidered on my hand towels."

There was a band playing, and as Ava watched, members of the crowd got up and joined them. Some of the people who climbed up onstage were people she recognized as famous musicians and she also recognized some of the songs. She and Dalton talked and danced and laughed and after some coaxing she even agreed to share her cotton candy puffs with Dalton. She felt invisible but in a good way, like she was part of something, something . . . *happening.*

Ava noticed a guy with a long beard and a set of headphones dangling from his neck signaling to Dalton. He looked slightly familiar but she was sure she'd remember if she'd met anyone with a beard like that. She pointed him out to Dalton who nodded back to him. He put his hand on Ava's shoulder and bent down to say in her ear, "Sorry, I have to leave you alone for a little while," and disappeared.

Only to reappear a few minutes later onstage with the guy

with the beard. Who she now recognized as a famous singer. They each had a megaphone in their hands and began doing a back and forth duet of "L.A. Sky," the song Dalton had asked her about earlier.

The song she now realized was his song. His band.

The crowd went wild and Ava joined them. She felt a little guilty because she knew Liam would disapprove but Liam wasn't there. Liam was command performing. She wondered if Liam ever went to parties like this. Probably they were the kind of thing he needed to be protected from.

Or, she amended, watching the A-listers scattered through the crowd dancing to the next four songs, that he *thought* he needed to be protected from.

Dalton's band played four songs, then one encore. The crowd loved them and they seemed to love the crowd. Dalton left the stage by diving headfirst into the crowd, who carried him hand over hand right to where Ava was standing.

A spotlight caught them together and for a second she thought he was going to put his arm around her. But he was just lifting it to wave to everyone. Then he ducked down and grabbing Ava by the elbow, led her out of the crowd.

They kept going to a spiral metal staircase that occupied an empty corner of the loft. She had no idea how long they had been there so she was astonished when they came out onto the roof and she saw the first signs of dawn breaking over the city.

The roof had been marked with labyrinthine paths lined with snow globes, all leading toward what looked like a little house someone had just planted there. On one side of the house there was something that appeared to be a shooting range with a line of garden gnomes as the target.

She stared at him. "I thought you said you live in a trailer."

"I do." He pointed to the little house. "That's a trailer."

"On top of a building. Surrounded by—" Ava didn't quite

have words to describe the pathways. In the early morning twilight the globes showed a faint pink glow.

"I'm not in charge of the landscaping."

"Who is?"

"Here's one half of the team," Dalton said as a huge slobbery mutt came bounding toward them. He brushed by Dalton but then headed for Ava, rubbing his head insistently against her hand.

"Nice, Slipper," Dalton said. "That's what I get for years of care and feeding? The literal brush-off?"

Slipper ignored Dalton and instead started herding Ava toward the house. As they walked, she looked out at the unbroken panorama of the city. The view was amazing. She'd never seen Los Angeles from that angle or, since it was nearly dawn, at that hour.

There was an old-fashioned WELCOME mat in front of the door, which Dalton pushed open without a key.

"Wow," Ava said, her hand going to her heart without her even realizing it. "That reminds me of home. Not home here," she rushed to add, "*home* home where my parents are. The cozy little house in Georgia with the pretty flower garden and the porch swing. No one locks their doors there." She grew quiet for a moment before asking, "Is it really safe in Los Angeles?"

"Well, we are on top of a roof," Dalton pointed out. Then he said, "You're homesick, aren't you?"

The question took her by surprise but not as much as the realization that he was right. She was homesick. She missed, maybe not home, but that feeling of *being at* home.

Feeling her chest tighten she realized: she missed Sophia. "A little," she said, turning her face into the sun in case her eyes might be a tiny bit wet. "How can you tell?"

Not fooled, Dalton reached out and caught her tear with his thumb. "Your Southern accent came out a little bit. Come in, I'll make you breakfast. California style."

"I can do it, I'm a good cook," Ava said.

"I'm a better one," Dalton told her.

Ava put her hands on her hips. "Want to bet?"

"I wouldn't do it," admonished the sleepy-eyed girl in floral pajama bottoms and a peach camisole who joined them in the kitchen then. She looked like an ad for California girls with a perfect heart-shaped face, clear blue eyes, slightly tanned skin, and just-past-her-shoulders hair in that blond color that only kids have. Kissing Dalton familiarly, she held out a hand and said, "You must be Ava. I've heard a lot about you."

"And you must be Dalton's girlfriend," Ava said, trying to sound chipper. Because of course he had a girlfriend who looked like her, perky in all the right places and skinny in all the others. And of course she didn't care. She was dating Liam. Liam Carlson!

The girl in the pajamas laughed and punched Dalton on the shoulder. "You doofus, you didn't tell her?" She smiled at Ava. "I'm his little sister, Hotchkiss. Most people call me Kiss." She shook her head at her brother. "You're such a dork. Ava, how do you put up with this dork?"

"I find it works best if I do all the talking," Ava said, wondering what Dalton had told his sister about her.

"Great minds," Kiss said, gesturing with a finger between her and Ava.

After they'd done the dishes, Ava asked if she could have a house tour.

Dalton said "No" but Kiss said, "Of course," so Ava went with that.

She saw Kiss's room, which barely looked lived in and had a stack of boxes against one wall. "Did you just move in?" Ava asked.

"A few months ago," Kiss said.

Dalton laughed.

"Fine," Kiss said. "Six months ago. I just haven't gotten around to unpacking."

The walls of Dalton's room were lined with surfboards, over forty of them of different lengths and widths. Some were beautifully painted, others were completely battered. There was one that looked like a shark had taken a bite out of it, and another with the signatures of all the Bee Gees. "Dalton and I come from a long line of surfers," Kiss said. "Most of these are antiques, boards collected by our father and our grandfather."

"They're amazing," Ava said. "Like totems to worship."

"Only that would be the worst thing for them," Kiss said. "All those boards need regular love and attention or they'll dry out and die."

"That's a lot of surfing," Ava said.

Kiss nodded. "Dalton thinks they're our legacy but to me sometimes they seem more like a prison sentence, forcing us to be like our dad."

"Who's made you surf in the past year?" Dalton objected.

"Who gave you permission to speak?" Kiss asked. She looked at Ava who was struggling not to laugh. "You better get him out of here, he's getting feisty."

It was a little after eight when Dalton's gold Bronco pulled up outside of Ava's building. "Your sister is seriously great," she said.

"Yeah, I did pretty well in the sister lottery," he agreed. "As did you." He went quiet for a moment and seemed to grow more serious. "Can I ask you something?"

Ava's heart started to pound really fast. They were facing each other across the seat in his truck, knees and hands almost touching. The dream she'd had the other night of kissing him seemed dull compared to what it was like sitting here with him.

"Yes," she said, hoping to look alluring.

"Is your sister really into Hunter Ralston?"

That wasn't what she was expecting. It took her a second to

recover but in that moment, she made up her mind. Her thoughts flipped back to Dalton and Sophia laughing that day at the shelter when Sophia adopted her kitten. Dalton casually asking her to bring Sophia to the party. Dalton commenting on Sophia's prettiness. Dalton buying the Nerds Rope after she'd said it was Sophia's favorite. Dalton getting upset that Sophia was out with another guy.

Dalton was definitely interested in her sister. She should have known. And she was happy for Sophia. Dalton was a great guy. Besides, she already had a totally awesome boyfriend.

"I'm not sure," Ava said. "I mean she says she's doing a boytox which means she's not dating anyone but I'm sure if the right guy were to come along—" *There*, she thought. *That was a good sisterly thing to do. Good karma.*

But that didn't seem to please Dalton. With an intensity in his eyes she'd only seen when he'd berated her for letting go of Popcorn, he said, "Please tell her to be careful. Hunter Ralston is a vindictive liar. He's like a spoiled child with an infinite toy budget to woo friends with. He treats people like playthings because no one ever said no to him. I just don't want her to get hurt."

"Sure, no problem, thanks." Ava said the words as one breath, squashing them together in her haste to leave. She couldn't believe she had been thinking of kissing him when all he'd been thinking of was Soph—

"Thanks, Ava," he said when her hand was on the door latch. "I had a super time. You're a great person to hang out with."

She had to bite her lip to keep from crying. Because those were exactly the words in exactly the tone she'd want to hear from a boyfriend. But not from her sister's future boyfriend.

"Yeah you too," she said, flinging open the door and sprinting into their apartment complex. Behind her she heard him say, "Wait, you forgot the Nerds Rope," but she didn't stop.

* * *

Sophia was in the living room when Ava burst through the door at 8:15. She'd moved to sleep on the couch so she would know the minute Ava got home because she was so excited to tell her about—

"Don't say anything," Ava ordered, crossing the living room. "I know you're going to yell at me for staying out and ask where I was and remind me that I have responsibilities and tell me how much I'm letting you down and I don't want to have that conversation with you. I can't handle it right now." Ava nodded once, as if that settled things, and went to her room.

Sophia stared after her, shocked. She hadn't been going to say any of those things. Picking up the mock-up of the poster for her gallery show that she'd left on the coffee table, she went and knocked on Ava's door. "Are you okay?"

"Please just leave me alone."

Ava's tone, even more than the words, worried Sophia. It held a core of anger with sadness wrapped all around it. It sounded confused.

Deciding to give it one more attempt, Sophia tried the knob on Ava's door. It was locked.

They never locked their doors. Ever.

But what stronger message could Ava have sent that she didn't need Sophia than locking her door?

Sophia glanced down at the mock-up of the poster she held in her hands. She'd been so excited to share it with Ava and now—

She could leave it on the kitchen table, she decided. There. Perfect. Now even if she didn't get to tell Ava about it in person, she'd find out.

But as she crossed the living room to get her bag, she caught sight of Ava's locked door. Changing her mind, she stuffed the poster into her bag and left.

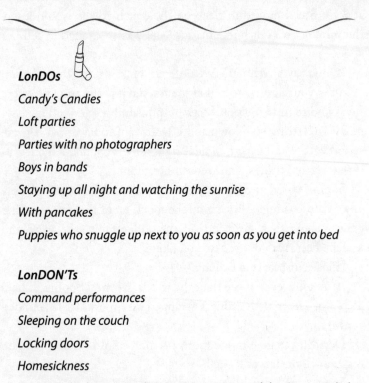

LonDOs

Candy's Candies

Loft parties

Parties with no photographers

Boys in bands

Staying up all night and watching the sunrise

With pancakes

Puppies who snuggle up next to you as soon as you get into bed

LonDON'Ts

Command performances

Sleeping on the couch

Locking doors

Homesickness

Puppies who keep snuggling up next to you until they've snuggled you off the bed

19

miss understandings

The first thing Ava saw when she woke up was the stamp on her wrist from the party and she felt a surge of happiness. Followed almost immediately by a dull ache of sadness when she remembered Dalton's last words. "You forgot the Nerds Rope." Which was followed, when she picked up her phone and saw ten text messages from Liam, by a pang of guilt. Quickly followed by annoyance since the whole reason she ended up hanging out with Dalton was because Liam was off having fun at a party that she wasn't invited to.

Not quite ready to text him back, she went to check on the London Calling Twitter feed and gaped at the number of new tweets about them. It had skyrocketed overnight. Had some video from their shoot leaked? Or worse? Warning bells and Sophia's words about what the press could do with even one bad picture of her and Liam filled her head. Taking a deep breath she started scrolling through the tweet mentions.

"Congratulations @London1!"

"@London1 Can't wait to see them."

"You rock @London1."

London1 was Sophia. Ava checked on Sophia's recent posts and saw that she'd put up a vlog that morning.

"Hi guys!" Sophia started. "This is just a quick one because I'm so excited." She was smiling, and she seemed excited, but her eyes looked tired.

From waiting up for you, a voice in Ava's head told her, and a whole new wave of guilt washed over her.

"Obviously, I'm not afraid of cameras," she said over a montage of photos. The first one showed her in the bumblebee costume she wore last Halloween, and the last photo was taken just a few months ago. In it she stood on the beach laughing and splashing her toes in the water, the sun setting behind her. "But what very few people know is I've always dreamed of being on the other side of the camera. And now I have my chance." She held a piece of paper up to the camera close enough for Ava to read MAX HOUCK GALLERY PRESENTS: LAHYP—LOS ANGELES' HOTTEST YOUNG PHOTOGRAPHERS. Below that was a list of ten names including number three: SOPHIA LONDON.

Ava gasped. She couldn't believe it. Couldn't believe that this dream of Sophia's was coming true so spectacularly.

Couldn't believe she'd had to find out about it from their Web site like a complete stranger.

Ava felt hot tears burning in her eyes and couldn't tell if they were happy tears, for Sophia, or tears of frustration and hurt for herself. How did this happen? How could they have gone from being best friends to being uneasy roommates?

She watched the rest of the vlog with her knees hugged to her chest, and stayed in that position, staring at nothing, after it finished.

Her phone rang and as if saying you've-been-at-this-long-enough, Popcorn nuzzled his face into her lap. Checking the caller ID she saw it was Liam. For the sixth time.

"Where have you been?" he demanded when she answered.

"I'm sorry. I—I wasn't feeling well." It wasn't a lie, she told herself. She absolutely did not feel well at all. The fact that she wasn't leaping up and down thinking LIAM CARLSON IS CALLING ME was proof of how unwell she was.

"I'm sorry, babe," he said. "I miss you. I was hoping you'd have brunch with me. Are you too sick for brunch?"

Somehow although she could exaggerate the truth, she couldn't lie outright. "No," she said. "I could do brunch." Besides, it would probably be good for her to get out of the house. And of course to see Liam.

She and Popcorn met him at the Ivy. He was already at a table on the patio when they arrived but he leaped up and met them outside, kissing Ava and taking Popcorn's leash to lead them in.

Ava couldn't help but be charmed, especially when she smiled and Liam's face lit up. "That's what I was looking for," he said, linking his pinkie through hers.

"Liam, over here," one of the paparazzi who were always outside the Ivy called.

Liam waved him away good-naturedly, saying, "Cool it guys, can't you see I'm trying to spend time with my special lady?"

"Sorry about that," Liam told her and even as she said, "Don't be, it's part of your job," Ava heard a voice in her head asking if he really did want some quiet time with his special lady, why chose a restaurant that always had photographers in front? Dalton's voice, she realized.

An unfair voice, Ava thought as Liam pulled out a chair for her at a table in the middle of the patio.

"I took the liberty of ordering some biscuits for Popeye."

"Who?"

"Your dog?" he said, picking up Popcorn under the legs and saying, "How quickly they forget about us, huh, dude?"

Popcorn whimpered. "His name is Popcorn."

Liam's face fell. "Isn't that what I—oh god, sorry babe. Sorry Popcorn. I'm not supposed to tell anyone but my agent sent me a script for a Popeye prequel and I was reading it this morning— slip of the tongue." He got serious. "You won't tell anyone what I just told you though, right? It's still in the hush-hush stage."

Ava mimed turning a key on her lips and locking them down tight.

Liam laughed. "Wow, beautiful and a mime too."

Ava flashed back to the morning a few weeks earlier when she and Sophia had been joking about miming. She remembered Sophia lying in bed with her kitten on her chest, remembered the way they'd laughed together. Remembered her opening the box from Hunter with the camera in it.

Remembered that afternoon when she came back from taking pictures with Lily and wouldn't say what they were of.

She tuned back in to catch Liam saying, "—says it's a good niche. And you can't say it doesn't sound cool, to be the prince of prequels. So that's the angle we're going to push. What do you think?"

"It does sound good," Ava agreed, gratefully catching the gist of the conversation. "The prince of prequels—it *is* a good angle," she repeated, but her voice sounded forced even to her own ears.

Liam was looking at her intently. "What's wrong, babe?" He took her hand and cradled it between both of his. "I can tell there's something weighing on you. I wish you would confide in me."

He really was the best boyfriend. If she wasn't as all-caps crazy about him now as she had been at first it was just because it was real now. Deeper. More solid.

Ava waited for the waitress to take their order. Her eyes on their joined hands, she said, "I—Sophia and I have been fighting. A lot. We never used to fight but recently it's like we can't be in the same room together without it feeling like there's a minefield and one wrong step will cause an explosion. I don't know what to do. I feel like I'm losing my best friend."

"We won't let that happen, will we?" Liam asked Popcorn, who, with Liam's assistance, shook his head. He turned a serious face to Ava. "I had hoped this wouldn't happen, but I have to say, I'm not surprised."

Ava stared at him, wide-eyed. "You're not? Why?"

"It happens a lot when one person gets more famous than another. It happened with my friends. Hunter, he's cool, but we used to have another friend who kind of lost it when my career blew up. He couldn't be supportive. Instead of being happy for me when my picture started showing up places, he acted like I'd done something wrong. I felt like he was always judging me, always angry unless I did what he said. Like he was the only one who knew what was right. Finally we stopped hanging out."

Ava shook her head. "That's not what it is. London Calling has always been our top priority, and that's why she's been worried about getting caught up in the gossip mill."

Liam stroked Popcorn's head and nodded pensively. "Maybe— or maybe you're just too sweet and trusting. The way I see it, she's jealous of all the attention you're getting from dating me. So she tries to hold you back, to punish you."

"Jealousy's never been an issue with us, so I don't think that's it. But there's got to be *some* reason she's been leaving me out so much. Doing things with Lily and not telling me about them. Maybe she feels left out of our relationship, so she's trying to leave me out."

"You're trying to understand her because you have a kind nature," Liam said. "But I've seen this plenty of times. She's jealous,

babe. The only power she can have is the power to rip you down."
He reached across the table and put a hand on Ava's shoulder.
"You can't let her do that. You deserve to be a star. Promise me
you won't let her—or anyone—stand in your way."

Popcorn, still in Liam's lap, barked in apparent agreement.

"Of course I won't," Ava said uneasily. "But—"

"No buts. You have to make her realize that you don't need
her, and that you'll leave if she doesn't start treating you with the
respect you deserve. That's why I had to leave *Heaven Is Next
Door*, and it was the best move I ever made."

"Don't knock that show. It's what got me sleeping with you,"
Ava teased as the waitress came with the coffee (for Ava) and the
strawberry-kiwi-coconut smoothie that wasn't on the menu but
they were sure the chef would be happy to whip up and of course
they could add a sprig of mint as a garnish (for Liam) they had
ordered. "Or at least, poster you."

Liam grinned while the waitress set down their drinks, then
followed her with his eyes until she was out of earshot. "Let's
hope she doesn't have a blog or you're going to have some denials
to make."

Ava inhaled sharply. "You don't really think she does, do you?
Sophia would kill me, especially with our launch coming up so
soon."

"I was kidding?" Liam gave her a bemused smile. "Wow, Sophia really does have you wound up." He turned his chair so he
was facing her, his knee touching her leg. He put his pointer
finger under her chin and tilted it up so he could look right into
her eyes. "I know this is hard. But I also know what I'm talking
about. You have to take a stand. You can't let her walk on you.
Trust me."

Ava gave a little nod and got busy lining up the creamer, the
sugar bowl, and the small silver stirring spoon alongside her
saucer. "I do trust you," she assured him. "It's just, even though

everything you've said makes sense, somehow it just doesn't seem like Sophia. At least not the Sophia I know."

Liam threw up his hands, a move Popcorn took as a cue to jump off his lap. "As you wish. You know her and the situation the best. I'm just telling you how it looks to me based on what you've said." His crossed leg vibrated up and down with tension. "Do what you want, but take my advice about one thing?"

"Of course. What?"

"She seems to be giving you signals that she wants some space?" Ava gave a tentative nod. "So do that. Give her some space. Don't ask her questions about what she's doing or where she's going. Don't be needy. Quietly let her know you're fine on your own."

"Okay," Ava said, nodding. "That makes sense. I can do that."

Liam smiled at her. "Good girl." He pulled her toward him and gave her another one of those devastating kisses on the lips where she forgot where she was and who she was . . . and the fact that there were half a dozen paparazzi outside on the sidewalk.

Until Popcorn started barking. "Speaking of someone who feels left behind," Liam said, reaching down to pull him back into his lap. But Popcorn growled at him. Ava laughed and picked him up. "Don't you start being jealous," she told him. "There's plenty of me for two men."

"And another quote we hope the blogging waitress didn't hear," Liam said.

"You told me she doesn't have a blog!"

"Kidding again."

When he dropped Ava off, Liam said, "Now what are you going to do?"

"Give her some space."

"Right. Remember less 'we,' more 'I.'"

"The I's have it," Ava joked. But her smile vanished as soon as she turned away from him, and her stomach felt hollow even though she'd just had a burger and fries and most of Liam's fries because he had to slim down for an audition for *Rocky on the Block*, a *Rocky* prequel.

She had begun to hate coming home, the oppressive tension in the first moment that she and Sophia saw each other. The air was pregnant with meaning, with unspoken accusations and judgments. Leftover phrases from every bickering exchange they'd had clung to the atmosphere, ready to be reactivated at the slightest brush. The more hostile they felt, the more polite they acted.

Ava hated feeling like every conversation she had on the phone was being scrutinized, every move she made studied and observed. One night she and Sophia had both been on their laptops in the living room. She'd had her phone on her lap so she'd know when Liam texted. And every time it vibrated, Sophia would sigh in annoyance. Until, not able to take it anymore, Ava retreated into her room. Since then she'd started going straight to her room, leaving Sophia and the kitten the living room to themselves.

Today she took a deep breath and opened the door of the apartment. "Sophia?" she said in the softest possible voice.

There was no answer.

A wave of relief washed over Ava, then ebbed when she walked into the living room and saw Sophia on the couch.

She had her computer propped on her lap, and the little white fur ball was curled up at her hip. She was listening to music with headphones so she hadn't heard Ava come in and for one insane moment Ava thought of fleeing. What was happening to her?

Sophia looked up and pulled out her earbuds. "You're home," she said in a completely neutral tone.

Ava kept her tone neutral as well. "I am. But I won't bother you. I'm going to work in my room."

Sophia looked at her nails, not at Ava. "I'm just organizing my vlog ideas for the next week."

Ava clutched the strap on her purse tightly. "I watched your vlog this morning. The one about the gallery show. Congratulations. That's really exciting." Her tone was so flat that the word "really" almost sounded sarcastic.

Sophia nodded. "Thank you. I tried to tell you about it this morning before I posted the vlog but you—rushed off to bed."

"I was tired," Ava said.

Wanted to say: "You must not have tried very hard."

"Did you have a good night?" Sophia asked.

Wanted to say: "Why didn't you come home? Why didn't you text? I was so worried and so afraid to show it because I didn't want you to feel like you were being smothered. I don't know what you want from me."

Ava said, "I did. I assume yours was nice."

Wanted to say: "Did you and your friend Lily have a nice time? Did you meet all the important people you wanted to meet? Did you make good connections for London Calling?" And also: "What was the food like? What were the other people like? How many courses did you get through? Would I have liked it? Were there good desserts?"

"Very nice," Sophia told her.

Wanted to say: "I wish you'd been there. I met two stylists who are interested in previewing Message in a Bottle. Also one of the top three animal psychics in the world, according to him anyway. They had these little mac and cheese squares dipped in bread crumbs and deep fried that you would have been crazy about. I wanted to sneak some out and bring them home for you but we left sort of suddenly. It turned out champagne is more 'fast' than 'juice.' Giovanni drove us home. He—he has a nice car."

Ava said, "I'm going to go work on some content for the site in my room."

Wanted to say: "Unless you want to show me your photos and tell me about your show."

"Well, bye." Sophia put in her earphones.

Wanted to say: "What did I do? Why are you being so distant? Please don't run away."

Ava clutched the strap on her purse. "Bye."

Wanted to say: "What did I do? Why are you abandoning me? Please don't leave me alone."

Later that night, Sophia sat on the ledge of her window with Puff(ball?) in her hand and searched for a star. "Not just any star," she explained to the kitten. "It has to be brighter than the stars around it, and have a slight bluish tint or else the magic doesn't work."

Sugar(puff?) reached out his tongue and licked the end of his nose which Sophia took as a signal that he understood.

The lights of Los Angeles were bright but usually if you looked long enough you could find a good candidate. "There," she said, holding Puff(Daddy?) up. "I think there's one there." She studied it for a few minutes before deciding for sure. The way Sophia saw it, you didn't get a lot of wishes on stars in your life total, so you had better make sure each one was as correctly executed as possible.

When she was satisfied, she began the ritual she had invented when she was ten and used, only in emergency situations, since then. Staring at the star she intoned, "I wish I may, I wish I might, have the wish I wish tonight." Then she closed her eyes. "I wish for things to be back the way they were," she said. "I want my sister back."

LonDOs

Calamari at the Ivy

Burgers at the Ivy

Berry crumble at the Ivy

Liam holding Popcorn

Kissing

Not being needy

Four days until the LuxeLife launch!

LonDON'Ts

Finding out news about your sister from a Web site

Finding photos of your sister making out with Liam Carlson on a Web site

No, make that every Web site

With the caption, PRINCE OF PREQUELS' PUBLIC PUCKER

Four days before the LuxeLife launch

20

star light, star slight

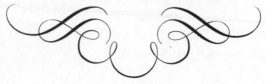

Sophia's dream evening that night would have had her in her pajamas and in bed by nine. At the latest. Two straight days of rehearsals for the LuxeLife launch had left her longing for a hot bath, a bowl of pasta, and TV she could fall asleep in the middle of.

But Hunter had other plans. He wanted to take her out for a celebratory dinner in honor of her gallery show.

"Could we do it another night?" Sophia asked him when he called as she was walking through the door that evening. "I'm afraid I'm not going to be very good company."

"You'll be great. Come on," he urged. "How can you say no to your number one patron? Besides, I bet you haven't laughed in over twenty-four hours."

She stifled a yawn and settled onto the couch. "That's probably not quite—"

"I knew it," Hunter said triumphantly. "I'll pick you up at eight thirty. You won't regret it."

Sophia set her phone down on the coffee table next to the living room couch and kicked off her shoes. If she had been a little less tired she might have protested a little more, but basically he had her. She *hadn't* laughed in well over a day, unfortunately.

Well except for when the choreographer suggested adding "Just a simple spin-jump-moonwalk-moonwalk-freeze!" combination and she and Ava had leaned over to whisper, "Can you really use the words 'simple' and 'moonwalk' in the same sentence?"

They had both cracked up. Their eyes met in the mirror and for one instant they forgot what was going on between them and everything was how it used to be. But then reality flooded back, rushing between their gazes like a swollen river and sweeping the laughter away.

But that moment only underscored how little laughter there had been. And it did feel a little rude to say no to Hunter after everything he'd done for her. What was one—*yawn*—dinner? A few hours? She owed him so—

Sophia woke up with just enough time to change into a white gauzy dress and touch up her mascara before Hunter knocked at the door. When she opened it he looked her over from head to foot, reached out, and tucked a hair behind her left ear. "Perfect. You're like a doll."

"I feel more like a throw pillow."

Hunter put on a fierce impression. "I'm supposed to be the one doing the entertaining. Stop that."

Their reservation was at Mr. C—"Because technically this is where we first met," he explained—where the maitre d' showed them to the best table in the house. As soon as they sat down a bottle of Dom Pérignon in a frosted silver bucket, a plate of toast, and a ramekin of caviar arrived at the table.

"It's the Boy Scout in me," Hunter explained. "Always call ahead."

Sophia frowned slightly. "I thought the motto was always be prepared."

"Not in Los Angeles."

Sophia laughed.

The waiter poured the champagne and set the glasses in front of each of them.

Hunter raised his. "To Los Angeles' newest darling, Sophia London. May all your enterprises rise to the heavens like the gilded bubbles in your glass."

Sophia began to giggle, thinking that sounded like something Giovanni would say. Only Giovanni would be smiling at her instead of frowning, the way Hunter was.

"I was being serious," he said.

"Oh. I—" She stopped laughing. "I'm not good with strong emotion. Thank you. That was lovely." She pressed her lips together to keep from cracking up again. Sitting there holding the fancy champagne and talking in bad metaphors, Hunter seemed suddenly less suave and more pompous. "Very—thoughtful."

Apparently satisfied, he smiled at her over the top of his champagne flute and took a sip. "I meant it." He twirled the champagne flute around in his fingers, studying the gilded bubbles she imagined, then put it down and leaned toward her.

"Sophia, I've really enjoyed the time we've been spending together. And I think you've enjoyed it too."

"Absolutely," she agreed.

"You're—well, you're the whole package. Beautiful and smart and accomplished. Perfect. Everything I want in a girlfriend."

She felt a rising tide of panic. "I'm flattered. And if I were going to date, you would be exactly who I'd want. But I'm not."

"You *weren't*," he corrected. "You can start anytime you want, can't you?"

The panicky feeling intensified. She knitted her fingers together in her lap. "I suppose but—" She swallowed. "I can't be that person for you. The perfect girl. You see me as someone I'm not."

"That's the point," he told her. "You are to me."

"But not to myself."

"Don't you want to be with someone who adores everything about you?"

Didn't she? Wasn't that precisely what she'd said she always wanted? "Of course. But I—I have to adore me too."

"I can adore you enough for both of us. Sophia, think about it. We're perfect together."

"That's very sweet," she said.

"I don't want to be sweet," he said roughly. "Sweet is what you call kittens and puppies. I'm a man, and I need you to see me that way."

"What are you talking about? I told you from the beginning I wasn't looking for a boyfriend."

"And I thought I was fine with that, until I fell for you. Hard." A wistful smile played on his lips. "I hoped you felt the same way."

"I . . . I don't know how I feel, Hunter. This is so . . . unexpected. I feel like there's no way I can start a relationship right now, with everything that's going on. But I couldn't stand to lose you as a friend."

"Yeah." He shook his head. "That's the thing, I don't think I can handle being 'just friends' with you anymore. Deep down, I don't think you want that either." And without giving her time to object, he grabbed her and pulled her in, covering her lips with his.

Hunter kissed the way he did everything: with precision, skill, and control. When he released her, it took Sophia a moment to catch her breath. She brought her fingers to her lips and met his eyes.

He grinned. "I told you. You can't say you didn't feel something between us."

"I did," she said. She could smell his aftershave on her skin. "I—I think I need to go home."

She stood up, pushed her chair back, walked around the table, crossed the floor, and entered the lobby. She was conscious of her body, of each motion being performed with fastidious exactness. Her mind focused on that, she imagined, so it did not have to focus on the shock of Hunter's kiss.

She stepped out to the valet parking desk. "Would it be possible—"

"I beg your pardon," the valet said.

Sophia realized she was whispering. "Would it be possible," she tried again and it still came out that way, as if she'd lost her voice. The valet leaned closer to hear. "To get a taxi," she said.

"Sure."

He lifted the whistle he had around his neck and was about to blow it when Hunter came out and said, "She doesn't need a taxi. I'll drive her."

"Are you sure?" Sophia whispered.

Hunter looked hurt. "Of course. Why wouldn't I be?"

"I don't know, I just thought—" Sophia resisted the urge to glance back toward the restaurant. "Thank you."

Hunter cleared his throat and with a sad smile said, "What are friends for?"

"Excuse me, Sophia?" She swung around at the sound of Giovanni's voice behind her. "I believe you require these." He handed her the wrap and purse which she must have left at the table when she fled. As she took them he said in a lower voice, "You are okay?"

Sophia couldn't deny the spark she felt when her fingers grazed Giovanni's. She nodded at him, the memory of how she'd treated him the last time they were together making it hard for her to meet his eyes. "Of course I'm okay," she said.

Hunter pulled fifty dollars out of his wallet and held it toward Giovanni. "Thanks for bringing those out to her, champ."

Giovanni ignored both Hunter and his money, keeping his focus on Sophia. "You are sure you are alright? If you would like, I can drive you home."

Tension crackled hotly between the two men but Sophia found herself feeling suddenly chilled. Gratefully, she saw Hunter's car being pulled around toward them. She gave Giovanni a smile and said, "Thank you, I'm fine," and slid into the passenger seat.

Studying Hunter's ideal profile as it was outlined by the headlights of oncoming cars, Sophia wondered if maybe he was right and they really were perfect for each other. When she'd been little, she had always imagined that being a grown-up meant candlelit dinners with champagne and a handsome prince who would gaze lovingly into her eyes and tell her she was perfect. And, as though he'd read her childhood fantasy, that's exactly what he'd given her.

So why had she run? Why didn't she say yes? What was wrong with her?

By the time they reached her house, the tension in the car had dissipated and what little was left evaporated when Hunter turned off the ignition and said, "Well, I'd be lying if I told you that turned out the way I'd planned."

Sophia checked his expression, saw he was grinning, and grinned back. "I'm sorry—" she began again.

He shook his head. "No, it's my turn to give you an apology. I—I shouldn't have kissed you. You weren't ready for that. I rushed you. That was unfair and I'm sorry."

"Thank you."

"It's just—spending time with you, I can't help it. I know

you're not ready, I do, and I'll wait. But—" He looked at his hands. "I wanted you to know what I think of you. What I really think of you."

Again, like with her girlhood fantasy, he was saying all the right words, doing all the right things. She knew he wanted her to say that she'd made a mistake, that she did want to move their relationship to the next level. *Do it,* she told herself. *What do you have to lose? He's done so much for you. He adores you. What more do you want?*

Sophia smoothed the hem of her dress with her fingers. "I think you're pretty perfect too. You're exactly how I used to imagine my boyfriends. But I do need more time."

He looked at his watch. "It's nine thirty-five. Is ten minutes enough?"

She laughed and let him walk her to her door.

"Good night," he said, giving her a kiss on the cheek. "I'll be waiting."

She should be falling head over heels in love with him, Sophia thought as she watched his broad shoulders disappear down the stairs.

The chill she'd felt earlier returned, and with it a sense of being hollow. Not fragile just . . . empty. Lost. She stood in the dark on the landing listening as Hunter's footsteps faded, listening to the low hum of traffic that never stopped, taking large gulps of the warm night air.

And shivering uncontrollably.

Ava was in bed, making a careful study of her ceiling, when her phone rang. Too lazy to turn her head, she reached for it and dragged it toward her and held it up over her eyes. Dalton.

"Sophia isn't here," she said when she answered. "And I don't know where she is."

Dalton sounded confused. "Are you worried about her?"

"No, we have separate lives." Ava kept her tone breezy, mature. "I leave her alone and she leaves me alone."

"That's a lot of leaving," Dalton said.

Ava brushed that off. "Whatever. I just wanted you to know."

"Sure." Dalton paused. "Are you feeling alright?"

"I'm fantastic," Ava chirped. "Why? Why wouldn't I be?"

"No reason," he said, sounding like he had something caught in his throat. "You're acting totally and completely normal."

"Of course I am." Why was he being so weird?

"Okay. Well, now that we have that established"—he went on, still sort of choking—"I was actually calling because we're scheduling slots for the shelter's phone-a-thon and I was wondering if you'd take a shift. Or ten. You can do it pretty much anytime you want. No one seems to be signing up."

Ava pushed a pillow under her neck. "What happens if no one does it?"

"The shelter closes."

"Oh," Ava said. And started to cry.

Dalton sounded alarmed. "Ava? Are you okay?"

She sniffled. "It's just thinking of all those homeless animals with no one to love them. Abandoned. Left all alone in the world." She started to cry harder.

Now Dalton sounded even more agitated. "You know you're not alone in the world, right?"

Ava heard Sophia's key in the lock. "I have to go," she told Dalton.

"Wait, are you—"

She switched off her light, pulled the covers over her, and turned her back to the door, pretending to be asleep. If Sophia wanted to see her, she could make an effort.

* * *

Sophia had stopped shivering by the time she entered the apartment, but she still felt chilled. Confused. Lonely. The sensation had been a dull ache for days, but tonight it had exploded, like fireworks over a city, illuminating how empty she was inside.

Standing outside of Ava's door, she hesitated. Then, afraid to try the knob, afraid of finding it locked again, she pivoted and went to her room.

She didn't turn on any lights but undressed in the dark and, still in the dark, went into the bathroom. She washed her face, washing off the smell of Hunter's cologne, the feel of him kissing her, wanting to wash away the whole night if she could. Then she wrapped herself in her robe, gathered Snowfall—who smelled very clean—into the crook of her arm, and went to stand by the window.

"Remember the day we met?" she whispered into Snowbear's fur. "If it wasn't for Ava, who wanted to cheer me up and knew exactly what I needed, you and I never would have met."

An ache started to build in her chest. The happy memory only reminding her how different everything was now.

As she looked through the window at the Los Angeles sky, the reflection of a face stared back at her. A girl with long blond hair and blue eyes. A girl people would call pretty and sometimes even beautiful.

She knew it was her face, all the pieces were there. But looking at it felt like she was looking at the face of a stranger.

***

LonDOs

Watching Hoarders *with Popcorn and Snowflake*
Grilled-cheese sandwiches and curly fries

Trying to teach Popcorn to walk on two legs

Clorox Disinfecting Wipes

Lush Comforter Bubble Bar

Being in bed by 9:45

LonDON'Ts

Popcorn and Snowangel practicing their sharing skills—with your grilled-cheese sandwich

Thinking that if one order of curly fries makes you feel good, two orders will make you feel better

Popcorn's reaction to attempts to teach him to walk on two legs

Snowman's foray into art

21

kiss off

Third Street Promenade in Santa Monica was in the process of being transformed into a massive pedestrian aquarium for the Message in a Bottle product launch. Nothing of this scale had ever been attempted for a makeup line before, and the press was covering it like a breaking news story. It didn't hurt that both London sisters had recently made the front screen of all the major gossip blogs, as well as the covers of several weekly magazines.

Sophia hadn't realized that there were photographers at Mr. C the night she and Hunter were there, or that her dress was quite as low cut from the side, which was the angle the photographer favored while getting pictures of their kiss, her face afterward, and her flight from the room.

Ava was flipping through the latest copy of her favorite gossip magazine, which had somehow managed to do an entire spread on the incident even though it had only happened three days earlier. They were sitting side by side in the hair and makeup trailer that had been put up next to the stage. The occasional ping of a hammer from outside and the low hum of the generator were the only sounds inside the trailer. Except the swoosh every time Ava turned a page of the magazine. Or turned back to a page. And then forward. In fact, as far as Sophia could tell, Ava had now looked at the article about the dinner with Hunter sixteen times.

When she turned the page again, Sophia had had enough. "You don't have to gloat."

Ava looked up from her magazine. "Okay. About what?"

"About that." Sophia waved her fingers toward the paper. "About me being the one to end up with the embarrassing photos that launched a thousand gossip stories about my relationship."

The frown line appeared between Ava's eyes. "Do you really think I'd sit here and be happy that something you dreaded happened to you?"

Sophia was taken aback by the heat in her tone. "I didn't, but then I saw you flipping back and forth, over and over, and—what else could I think?"

"You could think I was cheating on the Jumble," Ava said, holding the paper up to show Sophia the Jumble on one page and the answer on another. She dropped the paper. "Or you could think the worst of me. It's nice to know which one you'd choose."

Sophia bit her lip. "I'm sorry, I'm just nervous."

"Really? I'm not. This is only the biggest moment of our lives, as you keep reminding me. I'm not nervous or concerned at all."

Sophia started to laugh. "When you describe it like that, it doesn't sound like such a good idea. Ava, I said I was sorry."

"Sometimes sorry isn't enough." Ava batted tears off her face. "Sometimes sorry is just the beginning."

The door of the trailer opened then to admit a procession of MM, Sven, Lily, and a delivery guy carrying a box filled with eight cans of hairspray and six gas masks. He put the box down and backed quickly toward the door, keeping his eyes warily on Lily.

"What's wrong with him?" Ava asked.

"He asked what we were doing with the hairspray and gas masks and Lily said, 'Hunting.'"

Lily shrugged. "People shouldn't be nosy."

The gas masks and hairspray were to create the elaborate updos that Ohlfons—who had called and begged to work with them again—had designed for Ava and Sophia. They were going to be costumed as mermaids with a Victorian feeling, and appear onstage as though they'd arisen out of the sea on a massive glass bottle.

Lily was studying the storyboards and gave a low whistle when she got to the last one. "Whoever thought of this was a genius," she said, pointing to the drawing depicting how the bottle Ava and Sophia were seated atop was going to be pulled along the stage by six shirtless sailors.

"Just wait until you see the dance number," Ava assured her.

"According to the *Los Angeles Times*, LuxeLife is putting six million dollars into this promotion," MM said. "That's almost enough for a celebrity wedding."

"More than enough if the wedding is in the Bahamas or Canada," Sven volunteered.

Lily patted him on the bicep. "I love this guy."

"The *Times* also says that there have been almost a million hits of your promo video even though it's only been live for a week."

Sophia nodded. "It crashed the server, and our site almost went down too. The response has been amazing."

"And that's why you both look so happy," MM said sarcastically.

"We're just nervous," Ava told him. Usually she loved having their friends around but today, somehow, she wanted to be alone.

Ava never thought she would see Ohlfons as the answer to a

with messages in them sloshing endlessly behind her on the video screen, wondering how she was going to explain what had happened to the three hundred people now gaping at her.

Only she didn't have to worry about it. Because she and Sophia had been wearing microphones the whole time. Everyone there for the opening had heard their fight.

And within half an hour, another half a million people had listened to it on YouTube.

LonDOs

Check to see if your microphone is on

LonDON'Ts

See: Wikipedia.org, Ava London

See: Wikipedia.org, Sophia London

See: Wikipedia.org, London Calling

22

face-off

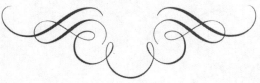

As she stalked from the stage Sophia felt furious, shaky, terrified—and free. She navigated around the cables attached to the generator and headed toward the first street she saw. She was just rounding the corner when she heard Lily shout, "Wait for me!" followed by Hunter commanding, "Stay right there, I'm going for the car."

She ran faster.

There aren't that many places where a woman with two-and-a-half-foot-tall hair in a watermarked silk gown and matching slippers with her face gently highlighted with glitter in the shape of fish scales could blend in, but the Santa Monica neighborhood of Los Angeles was one of them. She ran past a homeless man wearing a coat and hat both made of woven together pieces of newspaper, and a guy on a bike with a rainbow cape and a parrot on his arm passed her saying, "Looking good, sister."

"Sophia, hold up!" she heard, and glancing behind her she saw Lily standing behind a surfer kid on a bike, her hands on his shoulders and her feet on the pegs of his wheels as he pedaled furiously in Sophia's direction.

"Thanks, Marco," Lily said to the kid, who couldn't have been more than twelve, as she hopped off the bike.

"Any time, hot stuff," he told her with a wink and he rode away.

"I'm not going back," Sophia insisted, still running. "And I don't want to see Hunter."

Lily jogged along next to her. "Of course, that's fine. But you'll need these." She pressed Sophia's phone and her wallet into her hands. "Good luck!"

"Thank you," Sophia said, clutching them to her chest.

Lily pointed behind her. "There's a cab! Quick! Get it! I'll distract Hunter."

Sophia ran for it and got there just before the driver pulled into traffic. "Where can I take you?" he asked.

Sophia was about to say that she didn't know, but realized that wasn't true. "I'm going to see my friend Giovanni," she said.

"What's his address?"

"I don't know yet, but I'll find out." She got Giovanni's number by calling Mr. C. She dialed it. Before today she would have been nervous calling him but somehow having destroyed everything she'd built her life around made calling a guy seem easy. What was the worst thing that could happen?

Still, she was relieved when he answered. And impressed when the first thing he said was, "Tell me where you are and I will come pick you up."

"How do you know I need picking up?"

"*Stella*, do I need to again remind you I am psychic? Also, it stands on reason. You cannot stop thinking of my charms and require me to come and display them to you."

Sophia laughed. "Actually, I'd love to see your studio. Can you give me directions from— Where are we?"

"Culver City."

"Culver City?" Sophia repeated.

"Culver City? And who are you talking with? Already I am preparing to hear a story."

Giovanni gave her his address, and before long, the taxi pulled to a stop just as he was coming around the side of the building. Sophia was maneuvering her hair out of the car and he stood glued in place, taking in her gown and hair and makeup.

"So you were at a small luncheon with friends?" he asked finally. "Something casual?"

"Hiking actually." Sophia played along. "And then a picnic."

"Ah, of course. The silk slippers, they were the giveaway." Giovanni kissed her on both cheeks and led her through a small gate into a stone-tiled patio area. The walls were painted a rich cobalt blue and two of them were overgrown with bougainvillea which spilled fuchsia flowers all the way to the ground. There was a lemon tree with waxy green leaves in blossom in one corner, a handful of mismatched chairs painted bright colors, and a squeaky porch swing with cushions embroidered elaborately with fantastic animals. There were four doors, two of them with glass windows and one that said RECORDING STUDIO on it. A canopy of fairy lights stretched from one side to the other, giving the whole space a magical feeling.

"This is beautiful," Sophia said.

Giovanni stood with his hands on his hips and gazed around, as though trying to see it as she did. "It has some charms," he acknowledged. "The feel of unplanned, accidental. For you I would think that is troubling."

Sophia shrugged. "Not right now. Right now I think it's peaceful. Serene." She sat down at one end of the swing.

Giovanni sat down at the other, facing her. "I think perhaps you should tell me a bit about your day."

Sophia ran her finger over the dragon embroidered next to her on the seat cushion of the swing. She didn't know where to start. Telling a stranger that she'd escaped from her dream was fine, but with Giovanni—

"The other day I saw my reflection in a window and I didn't recognize myself."

"Perhaps he is not a very clean window."

Sophia shook her head. "Afterward I looked at videos of myself. Old ones. Recent ones. And it was the same, or almost. I felt like I didn't know who that girl was anymore. And that—" Her voice got thicker. Like it was being pulled out of a secret place inside of her. "If I didn't know myself, how could I know anything? How could I trust myself if I didn't even know who myself was?"

She cupped her hands around her elbows like she was cold, and closed her eyes. But the tears she was trying to hold back trickled out anyway. They had been waiting there, as she ran away, in the taxi, waiting until she was somewhere safe. Waiting, she realized, even longer than that: since her breakup with Clay, since her first fight with Ava, maybe even since that day, so many years earlier, when she'd tried to fly. Hovering there, the loss of control they signaled always a warning not to take risks, not to venture too far, not to try something she might not be good at. Now, as though the restraining gates had been lifted from a reservoir, she couldn't hold them back.

Giovanni slid toward her, put an arm around her, and pulled her head onto his shoulder as she wept. Not in wracking sobs but silently, face pressed against his chest, as rivers of tears streamed down her cheeks, leaving glitter streaks on his shirt.

"I'm sorry," Sophia said many minutes later, pulling away slightly. "I've ruined your shirt."

Giovanni shook his head. "It is the opposite. *Stella*, do you not know that the tears of the mermaid, they are magic? From today this will be my lucky shirt. I know it."

Sophia gave him a sad, appreciative smile. "I must look horrible."

"Of course not. Dramatic," he said. "Like a woman who has had an experience."

He pulled his arm out from under her head and sat forward and only then did Sophia really realize how intimately together their bodies had been. He could have leaned over and kissed her but he didn't and she wasn't sure if she was relieved or disappointed.

"Close your eyes," he said. Like he was seeing into her thoughts, he said, "Do not be concerned, I am not proposing to kiss you."

"I wasn't—"

His finger rested on her lips. "*Shhh*. Close your eyes."

She closed them, and felt the swing move as he got up. "Do not cheat," he admonished and she heard his footsteps cross the courtyard. A door opened and closed. She leaned her head back, picking up the faint note of a jasmine plant somewhere, the sound of a dog barking. Then the door opened and his footsteps crossed back to her.

The swing squeaked as he sat back down. She moved to open her eyes and he said, "No, keep closing the eyes, And now present your hands, please."

She held them out, and taking one in each of his, he pressed her fingers to her face. "This is you," he said.

She felt the planes of her eyes, her cheeks, her chin, her fingertips beneath his. She felt prickly and strange and curious about where this was going. Slipping back into her accustomed patterns when dealing with something that made her feel uneasy or unskilled, she applied herself to mastering the task as quickly as possible and then ending it. After a minute she dropped her hands. "Yes, okay, I understand that is—"

"*Tshup!*" he said, silencing her. She felt him spread something over the skirt of her dress then he took her hands and put something wet into them.

She frowned, trying to figure out— "Is this clay?"

"*Sí,*" Giovanni said. "Now you use that to duplicate what you felt with your fingers. A portrait of you. Eyes shut!" he added when she tried to open them.

"But that's ridiculous! How will I—"

"You are afraid," he said, his voice low, soothing. "Is okay. Do it anyway. There is no one here but you and a waiter."

Her hands stopped moving. "I'm so sorry about—"

"Yes," Giovanni agreed. "You will be sorry if you do not start making a face."

She picked up the ball of clay. "Can I feel my face again?" she asked. "Or is there a better way to do this?"

"You can do it however you want. You are in the charge. Whatever you do will be right."

A voice in her head started to protest, saying this was stupid, what kind of childish game was this, whatever she made probably wouldn't be any good. She would make a mistake and get it wrong and Giovanni would think she was stupid. This was pointless, she should just thank him and leave—

"The only way you can go wrong," he said, in that unnerving way he had of seeming to read her mind, "is not to try."

She took a deep breath and let her fingers dig into the clay. She didn't know how long she worked on it. It was soothing, sort of entrancing. Finally, after what could have been two minutes or two hours had passed, she held it out and said, "I'm finished."

"Look at it."

She opened her eyes and stared down at the little head in her hands. It didn't look anything like her, and yet she immediately recognized it as herself. More than the face in the mirror. Somehow she'd captured something of herself, an expression, an air.

Giovanni, who had been studying it too, said, "Stubborn. That is the face."

"I'm not stubborn," she objected, then laughed at the lie. She said, "But it's missing something," and tilting it in her palm, used her nail to put a scar on the chin.

"Yes, now is perfect," Giovanni said.

"No," Sophia corrected. "It's better. It's imperfect. I don't want to have to hide from things. I'm tired of being perfect."

"You alone expected that of yourself."

Sophia shook her head and said, a little softly, "Ava did."

"You believe this? Really?" Giovanni was incredulous.

But Sophia was too busy looking at the sculpture in her hand to respond. Because as soon as she'd said Ava's name, she realized that the sculpture wasn't her face, it was Ava's. Or maybe both of theirs, combined.

That was why she stopped recognizing herself. It wasn't because of Clay, because of the breakup. It was because Ava was missing. Sophia always thought she was responsible for protecting Ava, but with astonishing clarity she now saw that she had also been using Ava for her own protection.

To avoid ever having to chose for herself because she was always choosing for someone else.

No wonder Ava felt babied. Sophia had acted like she didn't trust her when really that had just been to cover up the fact that it was herself Sophia was afraid to trust. Herself she'd been afraid to look at too closely.

When she gazed at the window, the face looking back seemed strange because Sophia no longer knew who she was. It was because, for the very first time, she was seeing who she had always been.

"I—I have to find my sister," she said, getting up full of purpose.

Giovanni bowed and held out his arm. "My chariot awaits."

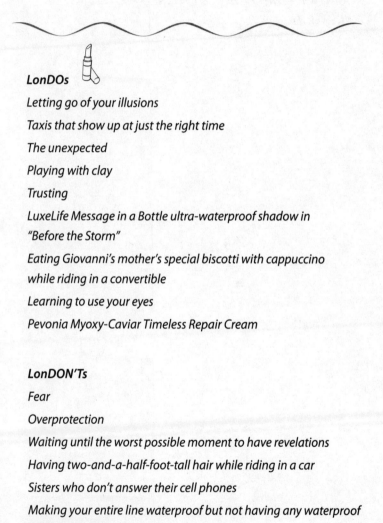

LonDOs

Letting go of your illusions

Taxis that show up at just the right time

The unexpected

Playing with clay

Trusting

LuxeLife Message in a Bottle ultra-waterproof shadow in "Before the Storm"

Eating Giovanni's mother's special biscotti with cappuccino while riding in a convertible

Learning to use your eyes

Pevonia Myoxy-Caviar Timeless Repair Cream

LonDON'Ts

Fear

Overprotection

Waiting until the worst possible moment to have revelations

Having two-and-a-half-foot-tall hair while riding in a car

Sisters who don't answer their cell phones

Making your entire line waterproof but not having any waterproof makeup remover at home

Sisters who are still not answering their cell phones

Trying to brush your hair after 4 cans of Aqua Net

Sisters who do not respond to calls or texts on their cell phones

Body glitter in your ears

Sisters who—WHY HAVE A CELL PHONE IF YOU WILL NOT ANSWER IT?

23

madscara

As soon as Sophia stormed off, Ava knew she'd made a mistake. Or more like a hundred.

She'd climbed off the bottle three steps behind Sophia and run after her, wanting to apologize, but by the time Ava clattered down the stairs from the stage Sophia had completely disappeared.

Ava ducked back into the trailer, but hearing footsteps approaching the front she'd grabbed her cell phone and gone out the back door turning left toward the mall at the end of the promenade. She couldn't think straight but she was certain of one thing: she had to get away. She absolutely couldn't face the thunderstorm of wrath that was about to be unleashed on her and Sophia.

It was all her fault. She was trembling, numb with shock and horror at what she'd done. What had possessed her? Why had she said all those things at that precise moment? Why hadn't she done it after? Or before?

Maybe that was the mistake, keeping it bottled up so long.

Maybe, she thought, you should sometimes read the hidden message.

That made her laugh for a second, and then start to cry. Not the regular kind of tears but the hard sobbing kind that feel like they could rattle your bones right out of you. Unable to see through her tears, she blundered over to the low wall outside the mall and sat down, burying her head in her skirt.

Someone tapped her on the shoulder. "You can't take your break here."

Ava sniffled and looked up from her skirt. "What?"

The man in front of her was dressed completely in silver, from his platform boots to his leggings to his double-breasted jacket, top hat, and sunglasses that dangled from his fingers which, like every other inch of exposed skin, were covered in silver makeup. Ava blinked at him. "I beg your pardon?"

"This is my patch?" he said, drawing a square with his finger. "I know a lot of you newbies think you can just muscle in, but don't try muscling in on Slade."

"I'm not muscling in on Slade," Ava said, trying to hold back her tears. "I was just lo-lo-looking for a place to sit."

"Right. Dressed like that." He bent down. "Look sweetheart, it looks like you're in a mood and I don't want to sound harsh, but this is my profession. Sure I work VIP celebrity parties and I have a human fountain outfit that the *LA Weekly* said was 'original' but basically this"—he waved an arm over his outfit like a magician—"is how I put food on my table. So as much as I'd like to take pity on you, I just can't afford to be softhearted. I fought for this primo spot and if I let you squat on it, then people will think Slade has gone soft and everyone will try."

Ava realized he thought she was trying to cut into his profits as a street performer. "This"—she pointed to her dress—"is from an event. Over there." She pointed behind her in the direction she'd come from. "There are tents and a wind machine."

Slade said, "Well that's nice, sweetheart. Why don't you just toddle back there." He put his arm under her elbow to help her up.

"*Nooo!*" Ava wailed, causing Slade to step back. "I can't." She leaned toward him. "They're going to come after me. I don't know what the punishment is for running away from them. What do you think? I signed something but I don't remember what it said. Do I have to give them money? Can they arrest me? Sophia always told me not to sign things before I read them, but I didn't listen! Now can they charge me with theft?" She went on, looking down at the expensive gown and shoes. "Whose clothes are these?"

Slade's expression had changed from skeptical to concerned. "Did you hit your head while you were getting away?"

"My sister and I—it was like a show? It was supposed to be the best day of our lives but I ruined it. I should have waited but I *had* to bring it up. Why?" Ava hit herself in the head. "I should have waited. But there we were on the bottle and I had to ask and then, just when the sailors came to pull us out, she—she left. And now she's gone. I should have read the message."

Ava was relieved when Slade said, "I understand perfectly," and sat down next to her. In an unnaturally cheery voice he said, "What you need to do is go back to the place you came from."

"I thought you understood. I can't. They'll—" Her eyes got huge with panic. "If they arrest me, who will watch Popcorn?"

Slade smiled encouragingly. "I'm sure there is someone you can call." He held out his hand. "Why don't you give me your phone and we'll find someone."

Ava started to shake her head when the mall sound system played the opening chords of "L.A. Sky" and she hesitated.

"*Aah,*" Slade said, reading her face. "You thought of someone."

Ava pulled Dalton's phone number up, then hesitated. "He won't come. Especially after what I did to Sophia."

"It can't hurt to call him," Slade said in that overly bright voice, the kind designed to keep a child or a crazy person from having a meltdown.

Ava said, "I don't think—" but Slade pulled the phone out of her hand. Using his regular voice, he said, "I'm doing this for your own good," and pushed call.

"Hello, is this Dalton Cute?" Slade asked, reading the name from Ava's contacts.

Ava dropped her head back into her lap and covered it with her arms.

"Oh, it's not. Sorry, but your first name is Dalton? Good. . . . Ava, is that her name? . . . Yeah this is her phone. . . . She needs someone to get her and bring her back to wherever she was. . . . I don't know, I thought you would. She kept saying she escaped. . . . Yes, escaped. . . . No, she didn't say from where, but it's got to be some kind of hospital. She thinks there are people after her—"

"There are!" Ava insisted.

"—who are going to punish her." Slade's voice dropped lower. "There may have been an incident, she's rambling on about sailors and needing someone to watch her popcorn. . . ." Slade nodded. "I agree. She also mentioned being 'on the big bottle,' which I assume means she was on some meds and is having withdrawals. . . . Yes, the big bottle. And she seems to have some amnesia too because she has no idea whose clothes she is wearing." Slade listened for a moment then started shaking his head. "Look, Mr. Cute, you've got to come get her. She needs professional help and lots of it. I can't watch her all the time and if she wanders off . . . You will? Excellent. Thank you."

"See?" Slade said, setting her phone down next to her when she still refused to look up. "Now that was easy. He'll be here in twenty minutes."

"I'm not crazy," Ava told him. "If you go to Third Street you'll see a tent and a wind machine and a stage with bottles with—"

"Of course I will," Slade answered in his "you are totally crazy" voice.

It was actually only seventeen minutes later when Dalton's gold Bronco idled next to the curb in front of Santa Monica Place. Dalton put on the hazard lights and ran toward the spot where Ava was still sitting, still crying.

Slade came over, breathless. "Are you Dalton Cute?"

Dalton hesitated then nodded. "I'm Dalton."

"Take care of her," Slade said. "And watch her head. I think maybe she hit it."

Dalton nodded and led Ava to his car. "*Did* you hit your head?" Ava shook her head and he said, "Yeah, I guess that would be pretty hard with that hairdo."

Ava didn't say anything and just sat crying quietly to herself.

"Do you—want anything?" Dalton asked, trying to distract her. "Ice cream? Candy?"

Ava shook her head again.

Dalton drove, glancing over at her from time to time as though he was afraid she was going to explode.

After fifteen minutes they pulled into a parking lot and stopped.

"Where are we?" Ava asked, speaking for the first time. She wiped her tears on the back of her arm.

Dalton reached behind his seat and handed her a beach towel. "We're at the happiest place in LA," he told her.

"Isn't that Disneyland?"

"This is better. Come on."

They crossed the parking lot and strolled up to a low wooden fence, behind which was the most beautifully manicured dog park Ava had ever seen. There were stadium-style benches around the edge and they went and sat on one, watching people and dogs playing.

"You were right," she said. "This is the happiest place in LA."

Dalton smiled. "Every now and then I get one right." Her

face changed, fell a little when he said that. "Do you want to talk about what happened? Or why you're dressed like a pirate bride?"

"They're related," Ava said.

"That's surprising. I assumed the costume and the call I got from an unknown street performer saying that I needed to come pick up an escapee lunatic were totally independent."

"I don't think I want to talk about it if that's okay. I think I just want to watch the dogs."

"Of course."

But less than thirty seconds had passed when she blurted, "I'm sorry. I should tell you that I don't think Sophia likes you."

He nodded. "Speaks well of her taste. I'm not sure I see how that's relevant though."

Ava smiled at his brave effort. Then she sighed and started to cry again. "I'm the worst person ever."

"Is that better or worse than being a Judgey McJudgeypants?"

"Worse. I said all these terrible things to Sophia and I didn't mean them."

Dalton leaned forward, arms on his thighs, hands dangling between them. "Why do you think you did it?"

Ava sighed. "Because I was lonely."

"You?" Dalton sat back, chuckling. "You've got people swarming all around you all the time."

"People are different from Sophia." Ava shook her head. "You know what it's like, you have a sister."

"That I do," Dalton said, something complicated in his tone.

"You understand how it is," Ava went on. "No one can replace her. But at the same time no one can hurt you like she can."

"Yes. And you'd do anything to protect her. If she'll let you."

Ava knew he was talking about his own sister, but his words made her think of Sophia. Of the way she always tried to protect her. Suddenly she saw it.

"She wasn't mad, she was *frightened*."

Dalton stared at her. "Are you talking to someone else?"

"Oh god. I owe her such a big apology. When we were in Italy, it wasn't that she was trying to get rid of me. She had been scared."

"I think we're at the part now where you should talk to her and not me."

"Yeah."

As he drove her home Dalton asked, "Why did your friend Slade call me Mr. Cute?"

"I have no idea," Ava told him, looking studiously at her fingernails.

Ava heard the sound of the TV through the front door and was both terrified of what she'd find inside and incredibly relieved that Sophia was there. She had taken off all her makeup and washed out her hair and was sitting in the living room watching a black-and-white movie on TV. The kitten was curled up in her lap and Sophia was stroking his soft little body. He was clearly enjoying himself, because Ava could hear him purring from halfway across the room.

Ava perched gingerly on the edge of the couch, trying to keep her dress contained. For a moment she thought about how all they used to fight over was who would get more couch square footage. Ava took a breath, trying to figure out where to begin.

"Don't even think about trying for one of the pillows," Sophia said without looking at her. "I am the mayor of this couch."

"I'm so sorry, Sophia," Ava blurted.

"You are?" Sophia asked.

"Yes—I was so focused on the fact that you disapproved of me and Liam that I didn't stop to think about why you disapproved.

And the reason is, you've *always* looked out for me because that's who you are, and I love that about you. With Liam, you were just trying to protect me from the same pain you went through. I'm grateful for that, and I'm sorry I wouldn't listen."

"I'm sorry, too," Sophia said, reaching out to squeeze Ava's hand. "I promise I was never trying to ignore you or leave you out. I was just trying to give you some space. I didn't realize that putting distance between us was the total wrong way to go— we're way too close for that to ever be an option."

And that was that. Now, suddenly, everything that had been so hard for weeks, the knot of tension, the pendulous weight of unspoken accusations and desires, just evaporated.

Ava looked at the screen and saw that the movie was *Roman Holiday*. "I was just thinking about Rome," she said. "About the trip we took there when we were little. When I got separated from everyone, since I wasn't even lost."

Sophia gave her a little smile. "I was thinking about how you've always been like that. Somehow, you always know where to go and what to do and it always turns out right. You're so brave, you just do things, leap before you look."

"That's because if I looked I might not leap," Ava told her. "You look and you *still* leap. That's true bravery."

"I was so worried about you that day," Sophia said, getting the distant look of memory in her eyes. "I was so scared something had happened, That I'd let go of your hand. When I saw your glove just lying in the street, I was sure you'd been run over by a car, or kidnapped, or both. Do you know how guilty I felt? What if something had happened? What if you'd been hurt or lost forever? How could I have explained that? Mom and Dad would have blamed me."

"But nothing bad happened." *To you,* a voice in Ava's head said. And then she had an epiphany—it was not just about her and nothing bad happening to her. It was about the effect what happened had on everyone else. Just because *she* was okay didn't mean everything was okay. "You finding that mitten was amazing. I wandered off, took a chance—and you were there, making sure it all turned out okay."

"It wasn't a mitten, it was a glove," Sophia said.

Ava shook her head. "No, it was a mitten, not a glove. And you didn't let go of my hand, I pulled away from you."

"That's not true, I completely let go. Besides, you were my responsibility."

And in that moment it wasn't clear if they were talking about all those years ago or now.

"We're responsible for one another. We have to trust each other," Ava said.

Sophia nodded. "I know that, now."

They sat side by side watching the movie together in contented silence, the kitten still purring away on Sophia's lap. As though she'd been working her way up to it, Ava blurted, "Why wouldn't you let me see your photos? I mean, I know I'm not an expert so my opinion doesn't count for anything but—"

Sophia looked at her in disbelief. "Did it occur to you I care what you think more than anyone else? That's why I didn't want to show you the pictures. I was afraid you wouldn't like them."

Ava's eyes filled with tears. "Of course I would. They're—Sophia, they're going to be amazing. Like you."

Sophia shook her head. "No they're not. And probably no one will buy them."

"We'd better hope someone buys them since neither of us seem to have a job anymore."

They both laughed, first small laughs which became a full-fledged giggle fit. It felt good. No, it felt great.

"It's glovely to have you back," Sophia said.

Ava raised her eyebrows. "Oh yeah? Well, I've sure been mitten you!"

As their laughter faded Sophia said, "There was a message from Corrina on the voice mail."

"Why did my heart sink a little bit when you said that?"

"I know—let the fallout begin. LuxeLife is having an executive meeting tomorrow to figure out if they're going to pull the collection. They think it's the most disastrous launch ever and Corrina says she's not sure if London Calling can ever recover."

Ava let Sophia's words settle in. "That's too bad." She looked at her sister. "But we're okay, aren't we?"

Sophia nodded. "We are. London Calling may not be but—"

"If we are, it is. I think that's what we lost sight of. London Calling is about us and what we care about."

"When did you get so wise?"

"I learned a lot from my older sister. She may not be able to decide on a name for her kitten but—"

Sophia's eyes lit up. "Phone," she said, holding out her hand. "I have an idea."

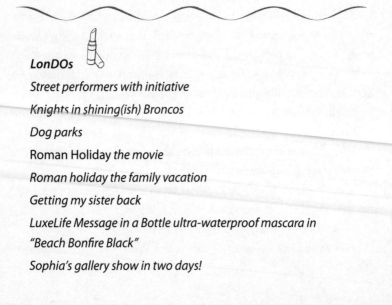

LonDOs

Street performers with initiative

Knights in shining(ish) Broncos

Dog parks

Roman Holiday *the movie*

Roman holiday the family vacation

Getting my sister back

LuxeLife Message in a Bottle ultra-waterproof mascara in "Beach Bonfire Black"

Sophia's gallery show in two days!

LonDON'Ts

Using adjectives with people's names in your phone's stored numbers

Kittens named Phone

Believing everything you remember

24

tongue in chic

"It really is pretty amazing," Lily said, leaning across Sophia's computer to get a better look. "I mean, you were completely sobbing, Little L, and your mascara and eyeliner stayed right where you put them."

Ava sighed. "We took our waterproofing very seriously for Message in a Bottle."

"Check this out," MM said, spinning his computer around to face the rest of the table. It was open to eBay where Message in a Bottle products were already selling for four and five times their original price. "You managed to attain cult-brand status."

"And without ever even having a brand," Ava marveled.

"But this isn't going to last," Sophia reminded them, bringing them back to the reason they were all sitting at Toast that morning. "That's why we have to take advantage of it now."

"I think it's a great idea," Liam announced, pulling Ava's hand up so he could kiss it before going on. "Sponsoring a charity event will refocus the conversation and put you back on top. If the event is a success, no one will remember the launch."

"That's not quite why we're doing it," Ava told him. "The idea is more to use all the press we're getting now to draw attention to the shelter and the fund-raiser for it."

"Whatever works," he said with a smile and the vague expression she used to think meant that he was enamored with what she'd just said but which she now thought meant he wasn't paying any attention at all.

"Ava spoke to Estelle at the shelter this morning and they need twenty thousand dollars to keep operating this year, so that's our bottom goal," Sophia said.

Lily, who had shown up at the meeting wearing a pin-striped suit, a Bluetooth earpiece, pearls, and carrying an iPad in a matching pin-striped case—"What?" she'd demanded when they asked why she was wearing a suit to brunch. "Is this or is this not a benefit committee? This is what you wear to a benefit committee"—said gravely now, "We can do better than that. It's for the animals."

"Our ideal goal would be a hundred and twenty thousand dollars," Sophia said. "That would keep them running and let them have a small endowment."

MM looked up over his laptop screen. "And we have how long to do this?"

Sophia took a deep breath. "Five days."

"I'll have Tana take over the PR," Liam volunteered. "She'll be happy to do it."

Ava picked Popcorn up from her lap and holding him in front of her face had him say, "Thank you, Uncle Liam."

Liam grinned and rubbed his head. "You're welcome, Poprock."

"Or Corn," Ava said, but Liam didn't seem to hear.

Hunter said, "I know you talked about doing it at the shelter or somewhere near there, but what about at my family's place on the beach? The shelter's small and not set up for it, but our place, you could have two or three times the number of guests."

"Are you serious?" Sophia asked.

Hunter nodded. "As a friend," he stressed. "I don't expect anything. I just—I care about you and want to see you happy."

"I'm speechless," Sophia said. "I don't know what to say."

"Say yes," MM urged her. "That house is made for a party like this." MM turned his computer so they could see his sketch of the entry of the Ralston house made over like a Roman temple. "And we call it a Beach Bacchanal."

Sophia looked around the table. "Okay then, yes. And thank you, Hunter."

"It's easy," he said. "You're also going to need a bank account. I'll have my guy handle it."

"He has a guy," Ava whispered to Sophia.

"I know. He has a lot of guys," Sophia whispered back.

Ava looked interested and whispered, "What other kinds?"

"You know the rest of us are still here and can understand what you're saying, right?" Liam whispered at them.

"Did someone say something?" Ava asked, leaning into Liam with a smile.

Lily tapped the headset on her phone and looked up from her iPad. "Okay I've got sponsors to cover the liquor, pass hors d'oeuvres, a DJ, and a bunch of doves to set free at the end. I've also nailed down two dinner packages, one surf lesson package, one dog massage package, and a weekend in a yurt so far for the auction items. What have you guys gotten?"

Everyone stared at her.

"When did you start working on this?" MM stammered.

Lily said, "When did we sit down?" When everyone kept staring she started playing with her pearls while explaining, "This is a contact sport for the women in my family. They will all be watching to see how well I do. My cousin Daffodil got sixty-eight auction items for her last benefit, including three involving private dinners with chefs, seven on boats or airplanes, and one with a clown. *A clown.* I intend to crush her." Lily put a piece of biscuit in her palm and squeezed, turning it to dust. "And I have a secret weapon."

"Oh? Really, what?" Sophia asked with some trepidation.

Lily's jaw was set, her eyes gazing over their heads with the kind of strategic look Ava and Sophia had seen in portraits of generals, or on the faces of women right before the doors at the Barneys Warehouse Sale opened. "Our benefit is going to go where no LA benefit has gone before. I'm going to get us a Dr. Janus nose job for the auction." She gave what could only be described as a cackle. "Eat your heart out, Daffodil."

"And I," Sven announced proudly, "will get a bouncy castle."

There was silence around the table.

"Where will you get that, sweetie?" MM asked.

"You do not worry," Sven said, patting him on the leg and beaming at everyone. "I am like Lily. I know men who know men."

"And that's my concern," MM told him.

"I'm not sure the doves are a good idea," Ava told Lily gently, as though she was worried she might insult her. "Since this is an animal rights kind of event."

But Lily took it well, nodding vigorously. "You're right. I should have thought of that. Besides, Daffodil had doves at her benefit." She paused, thinking, and then announced, "Got it!"

"What?" Ava leaned close.

Lily waved her back with one hand, thumbing through screens on her iPad with the other. "You'll see."

"No, really, what is it Lily?" Sophia asked, trying to keep her tone light.

Lily smiled again. "It will be a fun surprise."

Sophia's and Ava's eyes met, with twin looks of deep concern, and next to Sophia, Hunter mused, "Is it just me, or do the words 'fun surprise' sound different when Lily says them compared to anyone else?"

"It's not just you," Sophia assured him.

They went from Toast to Earl's Court, to enlist the help of the saleswoman who had tweeted about them when they won the Viewer's Choice Award, and then headed home. On their way Lily called to tell them she'd secured a private dinner for six at the Getty Villa and an afternoon of paintball as other auction prizes. "Dr. Janus is still being cagey on the nose job but I'm going to wear her down, don't worry."

Ava hung up the phone. "I don't think 'worry' means the same thing to Lily as it does to me."

"I'm not sure breathing means the same thing to Lily as it does to us," Sophia said. "But what she's doing is amazing."

They heard a strange noise when they were halfway up the stairs, like Popcorn was wrestling with something. When they got to the landing they froze. Their front door was wide open.

"Call nine-one-one," Sophia said to Ava.

"That won't be necessary," a voice said from inside their house. Lucille Rexford came toward them, pushed by Charles. "I just got tired of waiting outside so I picked the lock."

They didn't know which was more incredible, that Lucille Rexford was in their apartment or that she had picked their lock. Their shock at that erased, for a moment, the thought that Lucille Rexford had probably come to give them a piece of her mind, if not serve them papers in a lawsuit.

But now she was grinning over her shoulder and saying, "Charles bet me that it would take me six minutes. Underestimated me, didn't you, old man?"

"That I did. And I'm going to pay for it."

Lucille smiled at them now. "I used to be quite a lock picker in my day. Just relieved I haven't lost the touch."

"I'm sure everyone is," Sophia said. "If we'd known you were going to come over we would have arranged to be home."

"Frankly if I were you, I would have arranged not to be. Not with the shameful, disrespectful way you two acted yesterday," Lucille Rexford said, suddenly all business. "Come in here now and sit down. We have things to discuss."

"Is it too late to run?" Ava whispered to Sophia.

Sophia nodded.

Inside they discovered Cuddles, Popcorn, and the kitten curled into one ball together.

"Cuddles has been very anxious since yesterday," Lucille Rexford said. "He's been quite worried about the two of you. I told him you were fine but he—that's why we came. I felt if he saw for himself he'd be able to get back to sleep."

Ava glanced over at Cuddles who snored once, and snuggled up more tightly with the other two.

"He looks nearly catatonic," Ava agreed.

"Sit," Lucille Rexford ordered and Ava and Sophia both dropped onto the couch.

"You really made a hash of everything," she said, shaking her head.

"We're both—"

"Just so very—"

"Sorry," they said, so eager to get it out that they were finishing one another's sentences.

"Do you know why I wanted you for my company? It wasn't because you connect well with people, although you do. It was because you were sisters. Real sisters. Sisters who respected one another and saw one another's flaws and loved one another anyway. You were a team. Now look at you. You are an embarrassment to sisters everywhere."

"We were," Ava said. "But we aren't anymore. We worked it out."

"Which I'd say actually puts us in the credit to sisters every-where category," Sophia said. "Don't you?"

Ava nodded. Both girls looked at Lucille Rexford.

She gave a sharp nod. "Good. That is what Cuddles wanted to know." She paused. "I have heard that you are putting to-gether an event to raise money for the pet shelter."

"Pet Paradise. It's so old it—"

"I do not care for the sob stories of buildings. I wanted to say—" Her throat seemed to get clogged and she had to cough half a dozen times. "I wanted to say I'm proud of you. And that—apparently your products have inspired quite a following online. In fact, there's more demand for them now than we had forecasted if the launch had gone as planned. I was thinking LuxeLife could donate a percentage of the profits to your charity. But I wouldn't want anyone to know."

"That is incredibly generous—" Ava started to say but Miss Rexford interrupted her.

"You don't even know what I am going to offer. No one can be sure how much of the product we actually will sell, but given what we have seen I would say that twenty thousand dollars would be conservative. So, *ahem,* why don't I write you a check for that right now to get you started?"

Ava went over and put her arms around her. "Thank you."

Miss Rexford looked conspicuously uncomfortable. "That is really—that won't be necessary. Again."

"Of course not," Ava said.

Lucille looked at Sophia. "But if you must hug me too, I guess you must."

Sophia did.

Lucille adjusted her glasses and said, "Charles, we've dilly-dallied here long enough. We should be going."

"Of course, Miss Rexford," Charles said, grinning.

"Will you come to the event?" Sophia asked as they reached the landing.

Lucille looked shocked, or even, Sophia thought, frightened by the question. Her hand over her heart, she said, "Certainly not. Why would I do something like that?" Her voice was curt, designed to cut off any disagreement.

"But thank you for the invitation," Charles said.

Sophia and Ava had been sitting in their corners of the couch, each working on their computers for some time after Charles and Lucille had left, when Sophia said out of the blue, "Why do you think she's so determined to be lonely?"

Ava looked up from her computer. "Who?"

"Lucille Rexford."

"Maybe because she doesn't have a sister like you," Ava joked.

But Sophia had a serious look in her eye. "I'm going to help her. I have a gentleman to set her up with."

"And I'm going to help myself by pretending you didn't say that, forcing me now to imagine Lucille Rexford making out hot and heavy in the front seat of a car after a date."

Sophia gave Ava a bemused look. "That's not how all dates go."

"Can't hear you, busy pretending," Ava sang from a lotus position, her eyes closed, fingers on her knees, and low humming noises coming from her throat like she was meditating.

"I think when people do that, they tend to hum something spiritual, not the chorus to 'L.A. Sky,'" Sophia whispered in her ear.

"Still can't hear you," Ava hummed.

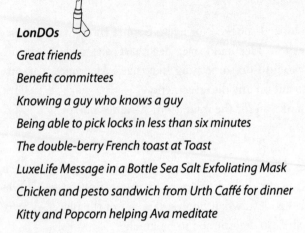

LonDOs

Great friends

Benefit committees

Knowing a guy who knows a guy

Being able to pick locks in less than six minutes

The double-berry French toast at Toast

LuxeLife Message in a Bottle Sea Salt Exfoliating Mask

Chicken and pesto sandwich from Urth Caffé for dinner

Kitty and Popcorn helping Ava meditate

LonDONT's

The second order of French toast at Toast

Fun surprises by Lily

Having a lock that can be picked in under six minutes

Not remembering people or pet's names

Not remembering that you are a dog and dogs don't eat sandwiches

People who do not take other people's meditation practice seriously

Getting out of the lotus position

25

fancy meeting you hair

Sophia stood at the desk against the back wall of the Max Houck Gallery practicing her signature, with Ava at her side. From the open door of the office behind them they could hear assistants leaving reminder messages for gallery VIPs about the opening that night and the soft tinkling of caterers setting out wineglasses filtered in from the next room. Otherwise they had the large white-walled, concrete-floored place to themselves.

Sophia was wearing skinny jeans, sky-skimming high heels, and a gold sequined top.

Ava watched Sophia sign her name with a looping S, and then again with a more reserved forward one. Ava was wearing a long gunmetal-gray silk sheath with a horse silk-screened on the front in silver and a black leather arm cuff studded with gems MM had made for her. No one seeing the sisters would have said they were bland. But the most important thing about them wasn't anything they were wearing. It was a new sense of maturity and confidence about them and between them, as though they'd been through an ordeal together and were stronger, more solid than they had been before.

And having more fun.

"That reminds me of when I was younger and I used to practice writing 'Mrs. Liam Carlson' all over my notebook," Ava said. "Swirly or not swirly? Heart over the I or no heart?"

Sophia jokingly dotted her name with a heart.

"I dare you," Ava said.

"No way," Sophia said, writing her name again, this time in a more severe, up and down architectural style. "How is Mrs. Liam Carlson looking these days?" When Ava didn't answer, Sophia glanced over at her. "Are things with Liam okay?"

Ava nodded slowly. "We have a lot in common."

"I'm betting well over five hundred things now."

Ava elbowed her. "That's not what I meant. But yeah, that too." She stopped. "Although I'm starting to worry I have attachment issues."

Sophia kept practicing, not quite happy yet. "Have you been reading the *Psychology Today* Web site again? Remember last time you did that, you diagnosed Popcorn with early onset dementia."

"He has many of the symptoms," Ava pointed out, enumerating them on her fingers. "He forgets whether or not he's eaten, he spends a lot of time revisiting places he's just been, and his attention wanders when you're talking to him. You could be in the middle of a sentence and *wham,* he's off sniffing your shoe. Just because those are also the symptoms of being a dog doesn't mean I wasn't right."

"Excellent point, your diagnostic skills are unchallenged. So tell me about your attachment disorder."

"Everything was great at the beginning. But all of a sudden

out of the blue my feelings for him were less intense and some-times—I can't believe I'm admitting this. You won't tell, will you?"

Sophia shook her head. "Of course not."

Ava lowered her voice anyway. "Sometimes I even think he's a little boring. But nothing changed. He didn't change. So I think it must be because of my Fear of Attachment."

"I can see that. Of course. And does your Fear of Attachment like you back?" Sophia asked Ava, keeping her voice casual.

"No, he—" Ava caught herself. "Ha ha. It's a psychosis, not a person."

"Sure he is." Sophia raised her eyebrows at Ava's exasperated expression. "It sounds like you have to choose one or the other. To stay with Liam and see if setting aside the attraction you feel for your Fear of Attachment makes your feelings come back. Or to break things off with Liam and spend some time getting to know your Fear of Attachment better." She held up the paper full of signatures. "What do you think?"

Ava pointed to one in the middle that was fancy but not swirly. "This one, definitely."

Sophia examined it. "I guess. Maybe I should do a few more."

"Or you are nervous and you're using this as a way to put off why we're here but now it's time for you to show me your photographs," Ava said.

Sophia nodded. "Or maybe that." She sighed. "Okay. I think I'm ready. Close your eyes. No peeking."

Sophia had called Max and asked if they could come a little early so she could give Ava a special viewing of her pieces before the show. He'd said of course and mentioned that it would be a good time to sign them too.

Sophia's mouth went dry and her stomach felt hollow as she led Ava over to the two walls of the gallery that held her pieces.

She couldn't believe how nervous she was about showing her sister her photos. Having strangers see them felt easy, a piece of cake, compared to this.

The wall above them had the words PICTURE PERFECT on it, the title she'd chosen for the collection.

"Okay," Sophia said, standing off from Ava a little with the hesitant expression of a child who thinks they might get slapped. "Open your eyes."

Ava's jaw dropped.

Sophia's five photos were big, ranging in size from three feet by four feet to a massive one that was eight feet by ten. Their subjects were the paparazzi waiting outside of LA's restaurants and clubs. One of them was a portrait of two of the paparazzi sharing a light, the scattered cigarette butts around their feet showing how long they'd been waiting there. In another six photographers lounged against a fence, necks hung with cameras sporting long lenses that made them look like baby elephants, phones in their hands. The third was captured at the moment they spotted someone coming out of a restaurant, catching them all in action as they moved into position, like runners taking off from a mark at a race. The remaining two showed them already in position, crouched or leaning forward or climbing on something, a horde of lenses directed at the same target like heat-seeking missiles on an enemy base. None of the photos showed the celebrities, making the photographers the subject. She used the map coordinates of the places they were shot as the titles rather than easier-to-understand locations to give them an archaeological feeling, pinpointing each one to a specific quadrant of the Los Angeles fame map.

"They're stunning," Ava said, close to tears. "Smart and funny and beautiful." She turned to Sophia. "I—I don't know what to say." Regaining her composure she added, "Except that for sure we're having you shoot the next London Calling campaign."

Sophia laughed. "If there ever is one."

They stood side by side looking at them, both smiling. "Do you really think they're okay?" Sophia asked shyly.

Ava hugged her. "You know they are. You don't need me to tell you. But I think they're amazing. And everyone else will too."

"I'm so glad you came," Ava said to Dalton and Kiss as she accidentally ran into them near the bathroom at Sophia's show.

"It was hard to catch up with you," Kiss said. "We kept seeing you but then you'd disappear."

"The crowd," Ava told her, gesturing to the packed space.

It was true that the opening of the photography show at the Max Houck Gallery was completely 3S—"I've seen Aunt Meryl, Aunt Barbra, and Aunt Demi already, and it's only six twenty-five," Lily had announced an hour earlier—but that wasn't the real reason it had been so hard for Dalton and his sister to catch up with Ava.

"Dalton said you were avoiding us." Kiss laughed.

Ava laughed too. "Of course not."

She studiously avoided Dalton's eyes because he was right. She was avoiding them. She'd seen them walk in and had been about to go to them when they made a direct line for Sophia. Dalton had smiled at her and introduced her to Kiss and even though Ava hadn't been able to see his expression, she was sure it had been filled with unrequited longing and—

She felt bad for him. That was all. It was sad to watch him pine for Sophia. So she had ducked around a partition, spent several minutes talking to the caterers about the virtues of still versus sparkling water, given herself a tour of the office, and finally ended up on the corner of the exhibition space near the bathrooms.

Where Dalton and Kiss cornered her.

She smiled at them now and said, "I should probably get back out there."

"She should probably get back out there," Dalton told Kiss.

Kiss patted him on the shoulder of his jacket and turned to Ava. "Dalton has something to tell you."

"I don't need—" Ava called to her but she was talking to her back. She looked at Dalton. For someone who was in the throes of unrequited love, he looked really good. He was wearing a faded blackish T-shirt with dark jeans and a gray blazer that, with his glasses, made him look like a cool, young professor.

"Um. Hi," Ava managed to say finally.

Dalton raised his hand in a short wave. "Hi." He cleared his throat. "This is awkward."

"It is. What did Kiss mean about you having something to say to me?"

"What?" Dalton asked. His eyes had strayed to something behind Ava's back. "I don't know, you know how sisters are. Speaking of which—"

Ava turned to see Sophia coming directly toward them. "Have you seen my phone?" she asked. "I can't find it."

Ava shook her head. "Are you sure you brought it?"

"No. I assumed I did but—" Sophia shrugged. "I guess it's not important. I should focus on who is here, not who isn't anyway." She smiled at Dalton. "Your sister is great."

"Yeah," he said. "She is."

"Sophia, come meet Roberto," Max Houck called. Dalton's eyes followed her as she turned and went, giving them a little wave.

"She looks really beautiful, doesn't she?" Ava said.

Dalton made an uncomfortable face that broke her heart a little. "Yes. She really does."

Ava shifted the subject. "Did you see her work? I—I know I'm her sister but I have to admit I was blown away."

"It was great," Dalton agreed. "You must be really proud."

"I am," Ava nodded. Kept nodding.

The silence between them stretched until Ava said, "I was going to call you today. We're doing a benefit for Pet Paradise. It was Sophia's idea. I wanted to see if your band would play."

He frowned. "What do you mean? What kind of benefit for Pet Paradise?"

"A fund-raiser. We figured that we have so much notoriety right now we might as well use it for something good. It's going to be next week. I know that's quick, but Hunter is letting us use his beach house and he got us checks with puppies on them and Lily has arranged all kinds of things and Sven, that's MM's boyfriend, is getting a bouncy castle although—"

"Sounds like a real carnival," Dalton said dryly. "I can't help wonder who it's going to help more, the shelter or the London sisters."

Ava was stunned by the coldness in his tone. "It might help us a little but what we really care about is the shelter. We've already raised five thousand dollars online and we have a private benefactor offering a lot more. We're serious about this."

"I'm sure you are," he said sarcastically. "The more money you raise, the more good press you get."

"We're saving the shelter."

"And there's your other tagline."

Ava was speechless. Almost. "I—I thought you'd think it was a good idea."

"What? That you're leveraging your fancy friends to help restore your reputation as just regular nice girls who care about cute furry animals?"

"That we are going to raise enough money to keep a roof over all those animals' heads and maybe even expand the shelter. You're the one who told me it was going to close if the phone-a-thon didn't work. Well, this is better."

"Better for someone," Dalton agreed. His attention had been divided between her and something behind her for the past few minutes, but now it shifted completely and his expression became grim.

"I have to go," he said and stalked off without even looking back at Ava.

She felt chilled and raw. Frozen. She stood staring at the space he'd just left. She could still smell him, beachy and fresh like the boardwalk air back home. Could still feel the sting of his words.

Why did she care so much what he thought of her—of the benefit, she asked herself. He was just one guy, and a rude one at that. Stomping away in the middle of a conversation just because . . .

Fairly sure what she would see but unable to stop herself, Ava turned around and looked behind her. The crowds were thick but through them it was impossible to miss Sophia laughing and smiling, with Hunter's arm around her waist. As if to confirm that was the reason for his abrupt departure, Ava made out Dalton practically dragging Kiss out of the gallery as though he couldn't stand to look at Sophia when he couldn't have her.

Ava watched him go, wishing she inspired that level of passion in someone. Not in *someone,* she admitted to herself. In—

"Why are you standing over here in the corner when you could be outshining everyone in the middle of the room," Liam asked, coming over and giving her a fast kiss on the cheek.

"I was just taking it in," she said, smiling up at him. "Where have you been?"

"I had a script I had to get back to my agent about." He looked around cautiously. "*Young Santa.* A funny Christmas action movie. Pure fluff. Still very hush-hush."

Ava nodded. "Sounds highly entertaining."

"There are some great snowmobile chase scenes." He cracked his knuckles in expectation, mind not at the gallery but seeing broad expanses of snowy wilderness, with him carving a path through it. "Would really help me plump my action chops." His eyes refocused on the present and he smiled down at her. "This is a great party. What do you say we give these photographers something real to take pictures of?" he said as he gave her a long slow kiss on the lips.

It was nice, she had to admit. Very nice. As they pulled away she was thinking that maybe she could put her Fear of Attraction aside. Since he, er, it wasn't interested in her at all.

And then Liam said, "How's Poptart?" and Ava knew she had to break up with him.

"He's fine," she smiled. "Are you free for dinner after this? I'd love to just have a chance to talk to you."

Liam got a strange, cagey expression on his face. "Unfortunately, I'm not," he told her. "That script I was mentioning? I need to make notes on it for a meeting early tomorrow." He looked at his watch. "I should probably leave now."

"Maybe we can hang out tomorrow then," Ava said.

"Maybe," he told her. He gave her another kiss, this one the short kind he did when no one was watching, then chucked her under the chin and headed for the door.

"'. . . evocative portraits of modern celebrity culture and the machine that propels it forward,'" MM repeated with a slight French accent. "That's what Claude LeBoufe said about your photos, princess. And he's major."

Sophia smiled and hugged herself, feeling slightly shell-shocked. The evening had been wonderful and exciting and strange all at once. Most people had said nice things about her photos—especially when she was standing there—but there was one critic who had been ruthless.

"This whole Who's Watching the Watcher thing has been

done to death," she'd told her companion, well within Sophia's hearing. "These have no sophistication. No taste. Flat, boring. I'd rather watch one of the girl's videos than look at this."

The critique caught Sophia off guard and she'd found herself in need of air, lots of it. She pushed her way out the back door and was standing in the far corner of the parking lot, taking deep breaths and trying not to cry, when a slightly accented voice from the shadows said, "Sophia? *Stella*, is that you?"

Before Sophia could answer, Giovanni was next to her. Without thinking, she pushed her face into his shoulder and felt his arms come up around her, holding her gently but protectively. He smelled clean, not like cologne but like soap and laundry detergent and fresh air. They didn't talk, just stood that way, until her breathing steadied and she pulled away.

Sophia shook her head ruefully and said, "How is it that you always see me at my worst?"

"I would say the opposite, *stella*," he told her, offering her another of his handkerchiefs. "I always see you at your bravest. Which is the best."

"I'm not sure the way I treated you after the champagne tasting was my best," Sophia said, fingering the hem of the handkerchief.

"Why?" Giovanni sounded genuinely surprised. "Because you made an opinion? Because you disagree with me? Perhaps this is hard on the ego, yes, a little, but also it makes me admire you more. It is, how do you say, the privilege to see you passionate."

Sophia found she was having trouble breathing again, but in a whole new way. She swallowed hard. "You were right, though," she told him finally. "The *LA Times* critic hated my work." She began to twist the ring on her finger, her eyes down.

"Ah," she heard Giovanni say. "I do not think you understood what I meant that night. Your work, *stella*, it is wonderful. It is only that you yourself are more wonderful. So—" He took her hand in his, stilling her fingers and making her look at him. "What I see is a beginning most impressive. And the more you become comfortable to show of yourself, the more outstanding your pictures they will become. You understand?"

Sophia felt like she could get lost in his eyes. "I think I do," she said, her throat dry, her voice low and husky. "But—I'm afraid."

"Of course. That is natural. But you will not let it stop you to do what you want." He held up a finger to her lips. "And do not say you don't know what you want. You will, when it is time."

They stood with his finger against her lips, his face smiling down at her, just inches apart. Sophia's heart was pounding in her ears, her eyes locked on his.

"Sophia, are you out here?" Hunter's voice called from the back door of the gallery.

Giovanni's finger slipped from her lips. He dipped his head toward her ear to whisper, "You must go." And then he turned and disappeared into the shadows between the parked cars.

"What are you doing out here?" Hunter said as she walked toward him into the puddle of light around the back door. He frowned. "Are you okay? You look—upset."

"I'm fine." Sophia realized she was biting her lip where Giovanni's finger had been. She gave Hunter a smile. "It's just—" She seized on the real reason she was outside, even though it felt thin now. "I overheard the *LA Times* critic savaging my work and I needed a little time alone."

Hunter's frown became more resolute. "I'll go talk to her."

Sophia put a hand on his arm to stop him. "No. It's—it's good for me. I want to learn. This is just the beginning."

Hunter's expression stayed fierce. His eyes went from her to where her hand was still on his arm then back to her face. "That's—a good attitude. But I think your work is great just how it is."

"Thank you." She tilted her head to one side, examining him. He'd been the perfect date all night and the perfect gentleman. He was funny and charming and handsome and made her laugh and supported her and looked at her the way she wanted to be looked at. She knew she could count on him to do anything for her, be there for her. He didn't question her. He didn't want her to be anything more than she was right at that moment.

She put her hand against his chest and looked up at him. "Would you be interested in taking a starving artist to dinner after the show?"

"I would be very interested in doing that," Hunter said. "Although I'm not sure you count as a starving artist." He gestured with his chin toward her two walls. "All of your photos sold tonight."

Sophia's face brightened, and she immediately felt like she needed to find Ava.

The rest of the night was a blur. She hugged Ava good-bye and Hunter took her to dinner but either the rush of adrenaline or the excitement of the past few days, or both, combined to make her fall asleep at the table after the first course. Hunter was nice about it, and drove her home with her head on his shoulder. She was having a delightful dream that started at a beach but had suddenly switched to a carnival, with a lot of flashing colored lights, when Hunter's voice, serious and urgent, cut in.

"Sophia, wake up," he said, shaking her hard.

Her eyes snapped open. The street outside her building was a parking lot of black-and-white police cars and emergency vehicles.

"I think—" Hunter's voice cracked. "I'm afraid something happened to Ava."

LonDOs

Sophia's photos

Sophia's show

Sophia's show selling out!

Maple bacon hors d'oeuvres

Caramel popcorn ball hors d'oeuvres

Swedish meatball hors d'oeuvres

Gallery shows

Facing Fear of Attachment

LonDON'Ts

Forgetting your phone at home—ever

26

house rules

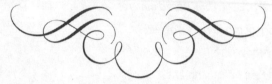

"Are you Sophia London?" a uniformed officer asked, shining a light into the car.

Sophia blinked against it. "I am."

"Come with me, please."

"What's going on? Where's my sister? Is she okay?"

"Just come this way."

Sophia tried to run ahead of the officers but they held her back. "What's going on? WHERE IS MY SISTER?"

"Calm down, ma'am," the officer said. "What's important is that you stay—"

"Sophia!" Ava called, running down the stairs toward her. "I'm so sorry, I tried to call Hunter's phone but I must have the wrong number and—"

Sophia grabbed her and held her. "Are you okay?"

"I am. I'm fine. And so are Popcorn and the kitten. But someone broke into our apartment while we were at the gallery."

Sophia looked at her. And started to laugh.

"Ma'am?" the police officer said. He looked at Ava. "Is she okay?"

"Probably," Ava said, taking Sophia aside. "Are you?"

"I'm better than okay," Sophia said, wiping her eyes. "I—I thought something had happened to you. A robbery is nothing. After the week we've had we can handle this in our sleep."

Ava smiled. "It's funny, that's kind of how I felt. I was more worried about the police freaking you out than anything else. Actually, that's not true—I was pretty upset when I couldn't find your kitten. Popcorn was unfazed but it took me twenty minutes to find your friend. He was curled up in the back of the closet. I'm not sure if the robbers scared him or if he just thought it was a good sleeping spot. But either way, you really need to come up with a name for him. You try calling a partially deaf, nameless cat and see how well it works."

"Thanks for handling it, Ava. I would have lost my mind if I was the one who came home and couldn't find him." As if sensing that he was being talked about, Glamourpuss/Starshine/Lightning came trotting out. Sophia scooped him up in her arms. "So what did they take anyway?"

"I can't tell yet. Things were tossed out of drawers and the pillows were pulled off the couch so the house is a mess. They don't seem to have moved much beyond the living room. Our closet was practically untouched. The police are in there now taking photographs but when they're done we can go in and look more closely."

"What about the video equipment? Computers?"

"All there," Ava said. "How was dinner?"

"I only made it through the first course," Sophia said, rushing to add, "—not because of my date. Because I was exhausted. Poor Hunter." She looked for him and saw him off to one side talking to the police. "I was lousy company."

"Watching you two tonight I had the impression that you might be getting ready to end your boytox."

Sophia nodded at her. "I had that impression too."

A male police officer whose tag said ELLINGTON waved them over and ushered them back into their apartment. His skin was the color of uncooked pizza dough, his eyes were like gray pebbles, and dark brown cropped hair showed beneath the sides of his uniform cap.

The cushions had been put back onto the couch and he motioned for them to sit down then consulted his notebook. "I have here that you were at a gallery show from about four P.M. until nine P.M. Is that correct?"

They nodded.

"But according to the Internet, the show didn't begin until five thirty."

"We went over early," Sophia explained. "Why?"

"Did anyone know you would be there early?"

"Probably," Ava shrugged. "Do you think the robbery happened early?"

"We're still just asking questions, miss," he said condescendingly. "It's how we do our job."

Ava found herself not liking Officer Ellington and that feeling only increased over the next hour as his questions got more and more specific—and specifically keyed in one direction. Finally he said, "There have been a lot of break-ins that look like this one in Hollywood in the past few months."

"There have?" Ava said. "Do you think it's the same person?"

She felt him watching her closely as she spoke, as though assessing whether she was lying. But about what?

"Surely you've read about them," Officer Ellington said.

"My sister and I have been trying to launch a business," Sophia told him. "We don't have time to read the thousands of e-mails we get every day, let alone the local news."

"Sure. Right," he said, sounding unconvinced. "Well, if you had been keeping up you'd know that in ten of the thirteen cases we were able to prove that there was no robbery; the women had staged it themselves for the attention."

"You're not suggesting we did that, are you?"

He pointed around the apartment. "You have thousands of dollars' worth of computer equipment here untouched. Thousands of dollars' worth of purses and shoes and makeup. Probably some jewelry. We don't know what's missing yet but I have to ask myself, what kind of thief walks away from all of this?"

"But why would we do this?"

"For the publicity. You said that you're working on launching a business. Well . . ." He leaned toward them. "Frankly, if that is why you did it, you couldn't do better than to admit it right now. I'm pretty sure no one will press charges. What do you say?"

Sophia smiled at him, a smile Ava almost never saw. It was her most dangerous smile. "You think we should confess to having faked a robbery, on the basis that you're pretty sure we won't get arrested? But either way it's good publicity?"

"There are a lot of bloggers and tweeters who follow the police scanner."

Sophia stood and Ava stood with her. "Please leave," Sophia said, pointing at the door.

"You're making a mistake. I see how you want to brazen it out, keep the charade going, but it's clear what's going on here. By your own admission, nothing is missing. You find something missing, really missing, something that will prove you were robbed, you call us."

He flipped a card onto the coffee table.

"We'll be in touch," Sophia assured him.

"I doubt it," he replied.

Sophia and Ava spent the next four hours putting things away and checking for anything that was missing. They managed to find Sophia's phone knocked under the coffee table, but as far as they could tell, there was nothing missing.

"Maybe they were interrupted," Ava suggested with a yawn.

"Or maybe they didn't like our style," Sophia offered. "Bed?"

"Bed," Ava agreed.

The man in the dark jacket and the baseball cap was on their landing, going through their mail when Ava got back from taking Popcorn for a walk. She'd slept late and been awakened by Popcorn breathing hot bad puppy breath in her face. Needing to take him out she'd opted for dark glasses over eye makeup, so she was feeling a bit ninja-like.

"Freeze!" Ava commanded in her scariest voice. "Or my dog will attack you."

Instead of growling, Popcorn bolted over and started leaping on the guy like he was an old friend.

"Do I have to keep freezing or can I pet him?" Dalton asked.

"What were you doing?" Ava demanded, looking from him to the mail he was still holding in his hand. "What are you doing here?"

"I was looking for an envelope to write a note to you on," he said, apparently avoiding her eyes. "I remembered my pen"—he held up a Bic—"but not paper."

"Why did you want to leave a note?" Then, like it just registered, she said, "A note to me?"

He nodded.

Everything told her that he liked Sophia, he'd told her that more or less, but Ava still wanted to spend time with him. "Does it have to be a note or can you tell me in person?"

"I can tell you but—" He looked around on the landing.

"No, you have to come in," Ava insisted, her heart racing.

"Popcorn, he wants you to," she added, not wanting to seem too eager.

They had a long-standing No Boys in Bedrooms rule but Sophia's door was still closed and she really didn't want to wake her. And it wasn't like there wasn't a desk and a chair and lots of places to sit and talk in her room that weren't on the bed.

Plus, Popcorn would be there, she reasoned.

Ava showed Dalton into her room and shut the door. Without waiting for an invitation he went and sat on the edge of her bed and, not to be rude, she went and sat on the edge a little away from him, with Popcorn between them. She didn't make him feel like he'd picked the wrong place. That was just being a good hostess.

Popcorn pushed his head under Dalton's hand and settled into his lap. Dalton smiled down at him, then looked around Ava's room, and finally let his eyes settle on her. Looking distinctly uncomfortable he said, "Ava, I'm not who you think I am. I've been to jail. I'm working at Pet Paradise as part of my community service. I'm not someone you can date. That's what I went to Sophia's opening to tell you but I didn't get around to it."

Ava frowned, taking that in. "You went to Sophia's opening to tell me I couldn't date you?"

He shook his head. "Not that part. The other part. About how I'm a bad guy. I assumed you'd figure out the last bit on your own."

But Ava was still stuck on something else. "So you're saying you're not in love with Sophia?"

Now it was Dalton's turn to look confused. "Sophia? Your sister? No."

"But you invited her to the party and got her a Nerds Rope," Ava blurted.

"Because she's your sister," Dalton said. "And the idea of making her happy seemed to make you happy."

"Last night you said she looked beautiful and you liked her pictures."

"She did and I do," Dalton said, still frowning.

"Why did you go to jail?"

"That doesn't matter. The point is, I'm not suitable for you as a boyfriend." He patted Popcorn then lifted him off his lap like he was getting ready to go.

"Sure. I can see that." Ava ran her pinkie over the flower pattern of her comforter.

"Good," Dalton said with a nod, leaning toward her.

"Good," Ava agreed with a nod, leaning toward him.

Her gaze went from his lips, up his nose, to his eyes, where they stayed. "Ava," he breathed.

"Dalton," she whispered. Just as his lips teased over hers. Just once, just like that.

Ava's heart stopped. Her knees tingled. They leaned their foreheads together and he brought his thumb up and brushed it across her lips.

Ava felt like her entire body was made of Pop Rocks.

"Ava, I can't, we can't do this—"

"I know. I'm going to make it right. I'll break up with Liam right now."

"It's not that, sweetheart," he said, cupping her face in his hand. "There are things you don't understand."

"Tell me."

"I can't." He swallowed.

"Then kiss me again," she whispered. "Please."

He did.

Sometime later his phone buzzed and he said, "That's my sister. I have to go pick her up."

Ava linked her fingers through his. "Will you come to the benefit? As my date?"

He shook his head. "I wish I could but I have—history with the Ralstons."

"What you said about Hunter. Being spoiled?"

"He and I used to be friends. But it's not that. He dated my sister. It didn't end well. That's why I wanted to warn your sister." He reached up to smooth the frown line that had appeared between Ava's brows away. "And don't ask me to say more because I won't."

"You know me too well."

"Not as well as I hope to," he said, standing up. He looked down at her and shook his head, an expression of wonder on his face. "I—I didn't think this could ever happen."

"Me neither," Ava said, standing with him.

"I have to go," he told her.

"I know," she said.

But for a moment they just stood there, fingertips and noses touching, feeling the nearness of one another. Then Ava pulled his hand up and kissed him on the palm, folding his fingers over it. "That's one for the road," she said.

Motioning for him to stay behind her she opened her door and peered out. With any luck Sophia would be in her room or the kitchen and Dalton could get out without her massive violation of the No Boys in—

Sophia was in the living room when Ava looked out. Ava said, "Hey," trying for a casual tone.

Sophia said, "You won't believe this but we're up to thirty-eight thousand dollars for the shelter and that—" She stopped and stared at Ava. "You're in love. That's the Ava-in-love look."

Ava turned scarlet and put her finger to her lips.

Sophia gave her a questioning look and realizing that she was busted one way or another, or at this point possibly both ways, Ava looked over her shoulder and said to her door, "You can come out now."

Sophia put on a stern frown. "You know this is a massive

violation of one of our house rules," she said, practically choking as she tried not to laugh. "There's a hefty fine for it."

"Which is?" Dalton and Ava asked at the same time.

"He's going to have to cook us dinner sometime soon," Sophia said.

Dalton nodded contritely. "I'll accept the judgment of this court," he told Sophia. Then he turned to Ava and said, "I really have to go."

She nodded and walked him to the door. After less time than Sophia would have imagined, Ava was back grinning from ear to ear.

"It looks like you've decided to embrace your Fear of Attachment," Sophia noted.

"It seemed like something I should get comfortable with," Ava agreed.

"And?"

"And . . . Sophia, he's wonderful."

A few hours later when they were both working Sophia said, "By the way, how many things do you two have in common?"

Ava looked up, thought about it, then shrugged. "I really don't know."

Sophia smiled.

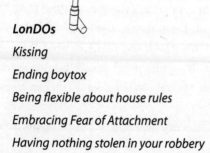

LonDOs

Kissing

Ending boytox

Being flexible about house rules

Embracing Fear of Attachment

Having nothing stolen in your robbery

Having raised almost $40,000 for Pet Paradise Beach Bacchanal still three days away

LonDON'Ts
Police who see having nothing stolen as a bad thing (see: Officer Ellington)
Popcorn's breath
Opting for dark glasses over eye makeup when taking your dog out

27

the laws of fame

The two girls on the beach in their flowing gowns could have been mistaken for water nymphs, if water nymphs wore gold-edged togas. They stood barefoot side by side, one blond, one brunette, hair fluttering around their faces with their toes curled into the cooling sand.

Sophia and Ava stood watching as the last rays of the sun painted the wind-sculpted surface of the Pacific Ocean orange and blue and pink.

Sophia said, "Five months ago, would you ever have imagined—"

"No way," Ava answered.

Behind them the Ralstons' house was filled with enough members of the photocracy to have the Beach Bacchanal officially dubbed a royal event. And a huge success. They'd raised over a hundred thousand dollars and the shelter was going to survive.

The London sisters were thrilled and humbled. But that wasn't why they had come out to the beach to celebrate.

Ava pulled out two of the gold-leaf-covered white chocolate lollipops that Lily's "little chocolate guy in Silver Lake" had made and handed one to Sophia.

"To us," Ava said.

They clicked lollipops, each taking a bite and letting the rich dark chocolate center explode on their tongue.

"Did you see Lucille Rexford?" Sophia asked Ava as she licked chocolate from a finger. "I couldn't believe she came."

Ava nodded. "I still haven't figured her out yet."

"Think we ever will?" Sophia asked, but was interrupted by the sound of a commotion that filtered across the sand toward them. Ava turned and shaded her eyes with her hand to get a better glimpse of the Ralstons' patio. "What do you think is going on up there?"

"Maybe it's whatever Lily got instead of doves," Sophia suggested. "Knowing her it could be alligators."

Ava squinted. "Or two men and they're coming down here. Probably reporters."

She and Sophia linked pinkies and turned to face the men crossing the beach toward them. As they got closer they looked less like reporters and more like—

"Sophia and Ava London?" the man in the suit jacket and chinos asked, as though their picture hadn't been on a dozen magazine covers and there was anyone else on the beach.

They nodded.

"You're under arrest. Please come with me."

"What are you talking about? There must be a mistake."

"Not if you're Ava and Sophia London," the cop said humorlessly.

Ava looked at Sophia and whispered, "Let's run for it."

Sophia shook her head. "Whatever this is—"

"—we're better off facing it," Ava finished.

"Probably."

They each took one last glimpse over their shoulders at the sea, then turned and followed the police.

What happened next had the surreal quality of a dream, or something that happened to someone else. Ava and Sophia were booked and fingerprinted and had their photos taken. They were separated and shown to interrogation rooms. They were each questioned about the three checks from their checkbook written for a total of $110,000 to CASH that had emptied the Pet Paradise benefit bank account the day before.

All three of which came from the end of the checkbook that Hunter had given them.

All three of which had been signed by Sophia London.

"Those can't be real," Ava and Sophia protested in their separate interrogation rooms.

Only later did they find out about the anonymous call that had been placed right as they were being escorted into the squad car. The call that got them freed.

The voice on the tape of the call the police played for them was scratchy and unrecognizable but the words were clear. All too clear.

"The London girls are innocent. It's Dalton Portland you're looking for, man P-O-R-T-L-A-N-D. He's your man."

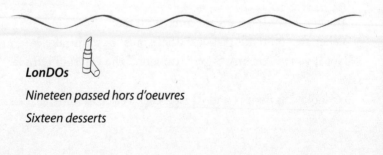

LonDOs

Nineteen passed hors d'oeuvres

Sixteen desserts

Lily's chocolate guy in Silver Lake

Bronzer from Blush.com

Getting out of jail after only two hours

Sophia ending her boytox

(*But with who?*)

(*You'll see*)

Large double-pepperoni pizza with cheese crust

LonDON'Ts

Getting arrested

In a toga

Getting released after only two hours because the guy you like was arrested in your place

Kittens who can't tell the difference between a table and a pizza

epilogue

friend or faux?

On a deserted beach near Zuma, he lit a bonfire. He stood, watching it sputter and smoke, hands in his pockets for a long time before trying to relight it.

From behind him he heard a woman's voice saying, "What are you burning? It smells foul." Peering into the flames she saw a large photograph of paparazzi gaping at the terrace of the Ivy curling at the sides as the fire licked it, the last three letters of the photographer's signature still visible.

"I hear they found the practice signatures in his hand when they went to arrest him. Nice work," the guy said.

She shook her head. "It was almost too easy the way they never lock the door of that trailer." Then she gestured at the curling photograph. "I wish you hadn't done that. I liked it."

"It's trash, babe. Besides, we don't want to leave any evidence behind."

She shook her head, sending blond hair flying left and right. "Always thinking. How much did we get?"

"A little over a hundred thousand dollars. And it's totally un-traceable."

"Not bad for an afternoon of work."

He draped his arm around her shoulders and together they watched the photo burn as the setting sun blazed a trail across the ocean.

Find out what happens next!
Don't miss the second London sisters novel,
coming Summer 2013.